HIDDEN

LISA SELL

For Mum, my original council estate mother .
Thank you for showing me how to never give up.

PRESENT

When I was fourteen, I killed a girl. It was 1987. The Great Storm raged through and I left a victim in its wake.

A faded memory of smashed glasses on a bloodstained track is clear again.

Her mother wants to go back there. Doreen is demanding answers. No one except me knows why Kelly died.

It will remain that way.

PRESENT

Doreen's e-mail resurrects the past. I couldn't face reading it straight away. Now I must.

Dear Jen,

I hope you don't mind me using this name. I always called you Jennifer, not realising until recently you don't like it.

Learning how to e-mail has changed my life. Thank God for spell check and a grammar app. You're so clever. I don't want to look stupid. I went to Adult Education to learn how to use computers and get my English GCSEs. I'm a bit smarter and back in touch with people from the Rembrandt Estate.

Graham died seven years ago, from lung cancer. Chain-smoking got him in the end. You'll understand why I don't miss my husband.

Do you remember my daughter, Kelly? Decades have passed. People move on. Of course, I'll never forget her and I need to know how she died.

Ellen Woods is still a good friend and has offered to help me. I'm sure you remember her, seeing as she lived on your road and you were good friends with Claire. Because Ellen worked for the local newspaper, she could be useful. Claire gave me your e-mail address. She's definitely her mother's daughter in becoming a reporter too.

Ever since the coroner's open verdict, I've not had peace. I won't accept it might have been suicide. Kelly had so much to live for, despite what people said. Graham was hard on us. I let Kelly down by not protecting her well enough but she was stronger than she appeared.

The police say to leave it alone. I expect they don't want to deal with shortcuts the coppers before them took. The coroner was too quick in leaving it open-ended. No one listened to me. I've always believed Kelly died in a horrible way. It probably sounds odd to need details but I do.

It's because you were friends, and walked back from school with Kelly that day, that I'm reaching out. Please help to find out why my girl ended up on the track.

There isn't long. Cancer's got me. I must know what happened to my daughter before I die. You might be the key to finding out.

With love from Doreen.

When I left the Rembrandt Estate, I thought I'd left my crime behind. I fight memories by manipulating stationery into sharp lines on my desk. Pencils cut deep with a sharpener. The rough action of slicing layers replaces the grating fear.

Nicole peers over from her office, offering another concerned smile. Gold lettering on the glass door detailing her counselling credentials shields me from full scrutiny. She is my boss and a friend. Losing her respect cannot happen, and Doreen's plea won't affect my role in the Headway Practice. When my degree ends, I'll be a counsellor too. The title upon *my* door is in sight.

I can help others but not Doreen. She may think she needs the truth but it won't give her comfort. Living with the knowledge I killed her daughter is unbearable. I should know. It's better for her to remain in ignorance.

I delete the e-mail.

THE REMBRANDT ESTATE, 1980S

In the late seventies, the local council had extra cash in the coffers. They decided to build an estate on the outskirts of the Oxfordshire town of Troddington. With the announcement, Troddington's population envisioned an elite area. As the years passed, the truth dawned that the Rembrandt Estate had become a dumping ground for undesirables, the financially challenged, and those trying to catch a break.

The first set of residents in the early 1980s rejoiced at being housed on a swish estate. Respectable families ploughed their hopes into three-bedroomed houses after living in cramped conditions. People sinking in the depths of the extensive council housing list envied those who floated to the top and onto the Rembrandt Estate.

The council bowed to pressure and shortened the waiting list, making hasty decisions. People were shunted into a false piece of heaven, far from the delicate eyes of Troddington's inhabitants.

Naming it the Rembrandt Estate was a masterstroke, with its suggestion of beauty and status. Realistically, the artist would have wept over residences left to decay and deteriorate. Glossy front doors, virgin-white window ledges, and scarlet brick walls became victims of careless minds.

Each road followed a similar pattern of bricked-up units, attached into terraces. The layout suggested uniformity. The roads, however, were distinct.

It was an estate truth that losers lived on Pollock Road. In sounding like *pillock*, it lagged behind. Sally Ponting lorded over her patch. Knowing a cheap imitation of a leader when they saw one, the neighbours ignored her.

Similar to their namesake's paintings, the residents of Picasso Way couldn't distinguish between their backsides and elbows. Where would the money come from? Why couldn't they progress? Children played "Dodge the Doo-Doo" on pavements riddled with dog mess. Bonus points were given if you discovered the lesser-spotted white crap.

Monet Drive divided the educated from the ignorant. Those who listened in French lessons teased neighbours who pronounced it *Monett*. There was an unspoken rule to leave the road name out of conversations to avoid being called a patronising git.

The more learned residents of Degas Drive had a similar problem. After a punch-up, resulting from a woman mocking her neighbour bellowing on the phone, 'It's Degas, rhymes with Vegas,' no one dared speak the name of the drive.

Turner Road became a magnet for criminals and wasters. The first road upon entering the estate set a low tone for the rest. Regular fights took place, among used condoms and litter spewed from overfilled dustbins.

Munch Drive was unfortunately named. Dope smoking munchies came to mind. The mispronunciation stuck. The drive's residents became poor cousins to the adjoining Renoir Road. They tried to maintain their exteriors and hide the tat. Some households accomplished it. Others scorned the effort required, content to be taken as found.

Renoir Road was the penthouse suite of the estate. A better class of people lived there. So they thought. Under Patricia Taylor's rule, driveways and gardens were immaculate. She demanded the removal of broken appliances from gardens and monitored the appearance of her road. Flower baskets lined front doors and razor-straight lawns stood to attention. When Patricia appeared, the neighbours hid, exhausted by her impossible standards. As Patricia's daughter, Jen, could relate.

The Rembrandt Estate made young Jen feel conflicted. She enjoyed belonging to a whole, faulty parts included. They were a solid community. The ignorance of the misguidedly patriotic residents was an irritation though. They voiced their annoyance at the estate being named after "those bleeding foreigners". The homage to the decidedly English J. M. W. Turner eluded them. Demands were made for road names to be changed to those of English painters. If anyone dared to ask for examples, the answer was, 'Blowed if I know, but the council should.'

The Rembrandt Estate and its residents were certainly unique.

14TH SEPTEMBER 1987

'You're doing it. It's final.' Patricia always won.

Jen looked across the kitchen counter to her dad, as if seeking defence. Mike busied himself with preparing breakfast. The wrath of Patricia in the Taylor household was always strong.

'It won't kill you to walk to school with Kelly. Do as your mum tells you.' Mike held a slice of toast, deciding to eat it on the way to work. A storm he wanted no part of brewed in his house. He placed a goodbye kiss on Patricia's cheek. The loving gesture left Mike feeling cold. His wife was a perpetual ice queen.

Patricia resumed command. 'Even your precious father says you have to. Hurry up, Jennifer. We mustn't keep Kelly waiting.' Patricia gave the directive to the mirror hanging on the kitchen door. All performances were assessed. Today's score: Dominant Mother 1, Pathetic Daughter 0.

The moment her mum came downstairs, Jen lost. Patricia didn't do family. Morning routines were too domesticated for her liking. Emerging before 10am was a rare occurrence. An early appointment at the hairdresser was to blame. Nothing stood in the way of Patricia getting her highlights done.

Although only fourteen, Jen began her mothering role in the mornings: preparing Mike's sandwiches and checking her younger sister, Mandy, wasn't consuming her body weight in Rolos.

Chewing a mouthful of cereal, Jen considered why she didn't want to spend time with Kelly Pratt. She refused to join in with the kids who called her "Smelly Kelly", but still, Jen couldn't like her. Kelly often carried a rancid odour of cat pee and chip fat. The stench was sometimes so pungent, Jen had to breathe through her mouth.

Not wanting to be around Kelly wasn't about losing credibility. Jen didn't care if others mocked her, and she already knew the consequences of judgement. Troddington looked down upon the council estate that blighted the town's reputation. She ignored the sneers when people discovered where she lived. They didn't see the estate's camaraderie and its ethos of belonging. For Jen, it housed some of the best individuals a girl could know. She had Claire Woods, also from Renoir Road, for female companionship. More than this, there was Johnny Rose, from Turner Road.

Going to school with Kelly would end walking with Johnny. He was her best friend and a crush she'd harboured for years, never to be declared. Their lives had become entwined when their families moved to the estate seven years earlier.

Johnny wouldn't object to Kelly's company. For a member of the Rose family, criticism was a regular occurrence. The problem was, he left earlier than Doreen stated Kelly must leave. Like Jen, Johnny parented within his household. Early every weekday, he took his brother, Benny, to the childminder, even though their mum didn't work. Johnny's other brothers, Anthony and Ian, were too lazy and selfish to help. Johnny didn't mind spending time with Benny. He adored the child.

The arrangement for Jen to accompany Kelly was confusing. Patricia and Doreen didn't move in the same social circles. Patricia often made snide comments about "that disgusting Pratt family". She detested the estate and regularly phoned the council, demanding a new home. The Pratts were one of her many reasons for leaving. They were one of the poorest families on the Rembrandt Estate. Doreen and Kelly wore jumble sales' offerings because of Graham's tight hold upon his wallet. His girls made do so he could make happy in the pub.

The Pratts' frugal world was far removed from Patricia's. She focused on social climbing in a mission to swap the crassness of a council estate for a cul-de-sac idyll. In the interim, she maintained the appearance of helping those less fortunate and seeking their adoration. Jen walking to school with Kelly became part of her manifesto.

The rebellious sound of her shoes scuffing against the kerb invigorated Jen. Patricia wouldn't abide an expensive pair of Clarks being ruined. Wearing them was a trade-off for Jen's choice of uniform trousers. For once, her dad mediated.

Jen decided to make the best of a bad situation. Kelly couldn't help what she'd been born into, any more than Jen. Maybe Kelly also lay in bed at night, planning a future that involved leaving her parents behind. Jen was certain Kelly's dreams didn't include being Johnny's wife. Her tummy somersaulted at the deliciousness of the idea. Thoughts of marrying Johnny at Gretna Green and riding off into the sunset on a Lambretta consumed her. The daydream shattered as she crashed into a pillar of knitwear and costume jewellery.

Sally Ponting made a show of using a wall for balance. 'Watch where you're going, Jennifer.'

Sally brushed away the invisible taint from her 1950s style twinset. She had one for every occasion, in every imaginable colour. The sleeve lengths changed with the seasons. A coiffured helmet head of hairspray topped each outfit.

'Sorry, Mrs Ponting.' Jen played nice. It would make life easier after Sally reported the incident to Patricia. In her mind, Jen apologised to "Picky Ponting", an estate nickname. In reality, being rude to one of Patricia's catty crew wasn't wise.

Sally looked towards the Pratts' house. 'I see Patricia has arranged for you to walk with Kelly. I assume that's where you're going?'

'Yes.' Jen always lost her words around Patricia's cronies.

'Kelly's often bullied. I'm so glad your mother sorted this out. She's such a wonderful giving woman.'

Jen gave a saccharine smile. Sally wouldn't sing Patricia's praises if she'd overheard her bitching the previous day about how Sally belonged with the other rough elements on Pollock Road. Fluffing her hair, Sally moved along.

Jen headed for the Pratts' house. Although only around a corner, the leap from Renoir Road to Pollock Road was pronounced. Jen noted pristine pavements morphing into an obstacle course of neglect. Kicking a crumpled can of shandy channelled her anger at Patricia, who wouldn't be seen dead there.

A realisation hit Jen. *This* was how she could turn it around *and* be a winner. She wasn't a snob, like Patricia, and never would be.

She knocked on the Pratts' door, deciding to walk to school with Kelly willingly. They might even become friends. Stranger things had happened.

5

PRESENT

K ay is a tornado brandishing a can of polish. She continues cleaning, viewing me as part of the furniture. The disapproving look for staying late again doesn't go unnoticed. I'm thankful for the tinny music from her headphones, distracting her from giving another lecture on how I work too hard.

My office is a second home. A coffee machine, toaster, and kettle are added comforts. Returning to a silent cottage isn't always worth the drive. Sometimes I need to be where others have been. Staying behind where activity and conversation have taken place satisfies my introverted nature.

Doreen's e-mail has invaded my sanctuary. It's odd how she thinks I was Kelly's friend. She must know the decision to walk to school together wasn't mine. Friends aren't in the habit of killing each other either. Not that Doreen knows about it, and never will.

She has Ellen and Claire's help. She doesn't need me. Claire won't get away lightly for giving Doreen my e-mail address. I shouldn't have joined Facebook or accepted Claire's friend request. Always focused on getting counselling business, Nicole sold social media as a useful networking tool. I couldn't explain why I needed to hide.

The opportunity to find my sister and my old best friend, Johnny, convinced me to sign up. Mandy isn't on there. Johnny ignored my friend request and messages. Scant details on a profile are all I have left of him.

When his picture changed to a wedding photo, the new millennium lost its shine and I gave up trying to contact him. Of course someone married Johnny. He was quite a catch, even as a boy: floppy fringe, ridiculously tall, and with a kind heart.

His wife's heavy make-up and guarded posture made me question his choice. My jealousy was surprising. I told myself to get over it. Johnny doesn't care about me. Not telling me his family was moving, a few months after Kelly died, confirms it.

I'm no longer a girl obsessed with Johnny Rose. A teenager's flighty dreams have no place in a grown-up world. I've worked hard to leave the past behind. Many mistakes were made along the way but I'm finally succeeding. Doreen will not jeopardise it.

'Fancy a bevvy?' I wish Nicole didn't creep around.

When I began working here, I changed my office layout. Facing the door was important. Regardless, Nicole's stealthy ninja skills allow her to enter rooms unseen and unheard.

'Not tonight, thanks,' I say. 'I've got the final assignments to complete.'

Studying after work is routine. I could do it at home but the television would go on and reality TV lures me in. Doodle manipulates my time too. He chews pens, sprawls on the laptop, and meows until he's stuffed with kitty treats.

'You're no fun.' Nicole sulks at the loss of a social partner.

I know she's joking. Nicole's encouragement convinced me to begin the counselling degree. She noted my compassion for our clients. Listening to her gripes about being married to an oncology consultant, who's hardly ever at home, was added to my skill set.

'Two assignments to research and write and I'm done.' I make it sound easy.

I had to study an extra year because of appalling previous qualifications. There are also the complications of a demanding full-time job and having enough baggage to make me a more suitable client than counsellor. Still, I'm almost there. Soon I'll be joining the Headway Practice as a counsellor rather than balancing the books, fixing printers, and keeping the clients rolling in.

Nicole understands how much this degree means. That's why I interpret the wave as she leaves as one of solidarity and not grumpiness. Two glasses of wine are always her limit anyway. Guilt makes her leave the pub in a panic. Her children need one parent to show their face before bedtime. Nicole will not, 'Allow my kids to think mountain girl, Heidi, is their new mummy.' I tried to explain the au pair is a Dane called Eve, but an irate Nicole is a hard woman to reason with.

I'm surrounded by reminders of mothers: Nicole, Doreen, and my own. Although labelling what I had as a *mother* is far too generous. When it came to Mandy and me, Patricia Taylor didn't have a maternal bone in her body.

6

13TH JULY 1985

Patricia had no patience for anyone who fell short of her exacting standards. Apart from her son, Liam, the Taylor family proved to be a disappointment. Liam pandered to her narcissistic needs and was seemingly obedient. Being attractive benefitted him. Visuals meant everything to Patricia. Her roots never showed, a hair was never out of place, and make-up enhanced every feature.

On the perfect appearance front, her daughters were a let down. They'd once been bright young hopes for moulding into Patricia's image. Both were pretty but oblivious. Jennifer and Amanda refused to bend to perfection's will. Jennifer was going through a phase of wearing shapeless second-hand clothing. To Patricia's horror, her daughter scoured charity shops, rooting out clothes people probably died in.

After Jen purchased a cardigan, a neighbour expressed her joy to Patricia that her cast-offs still had some wear in them. Patricia was humiliated by her offspring wearing the estate's rags. It was even more shameful to Patricia that Jennifer owned the garment of a woman rumoured to have an uncomfortably close relationship with her own son.

Amanda's shortcomings were Jennifer's fault. After all, she provided most of her sister's care. Under Jennifer's supervision, Amanda didn't embrace femininity either. Her penchant for wearing dungarees was an abomination. Amanda had such potential, with naturally white-blonde hair Patricia would kill for. It was wasted on her child.

Patricia didn't understand these girls who changed their names to Jen and Mandy. She'd tried to establish them with feminine names. Whenever they used the shortened versions, rage stirred within her. Patricia was convinced they did it to wind her up.

'For crying out loud, Jennifer. Move this stethoscope away from under my flaming feet.' Patricia kicked the offending item.

Jen grabbed the stethoscope, concerned for its fate. She took a seat alongside Mandy, who was blowing bubbles in the paddling pool.

Cushiony grass lessened the throb in Patricia's foot. She wondered, once again, why her daughter persisted in the foolish dream of becoming a doctor. Twelve-year-olds changed their minds every five minutes. Jennifer would too. Doctors didn't wear The Cure T-shirts and grubby clodhopper boots. Patricia cursed Mike for giving Jennifer money to buy her own clothes and allowing her to pursue an unobtainable future career. His belief in his daughters bordered on the ridiculous.

Patricia refused to have any dealings with the local GP who had recently visited Jen's school to talk about his job. While the other children numbed each other's arms with a blood pressure cuff, Jen was transfixed by the doctor's speech. She'd wanted to be a doctor since she was eight. It began when Liz Norman, from Picasso Way, gave her a toy doctor's case. Soon after, Patricia disposed of it. The gift confirmed Liz's continual interference in Jennifer's life. Dumping it kept Jennifer and Liz in their places. Patricia knew Jen put the rubbish out. It wasn't about the box being gone but rather that Patricia allowed no one to have aspirations above the station she allocated. Finding the precious item at the bottom of the bin,

Jen retrieved it. Losing it meant letting go of her ambition. Afterwards, the medical case lived in the safety of the Normans' flat. Unlike Patricia, Freddie and Liz enjoyed watching Jen pursue her hopes and dreams.

While Patricia found it admirable that Mike considered an ambulance driver a close friend, she was annoyed with Scott Reilly. He passed on a doctor's old stethoscope to Jen. It was a folly to allow the girl to harbour such notions, considering Jennifer would amount to little. She spent too much time listening to gloomy music, shutting herself away or gadding around with the odious Johnny Rose. Jennifer would inevitably become another council estate mother. Giving her practise in caring for Amanda was doing her a favour.

Liam would be the only one of Patricia's children to do great things. Her perfect creation couldn't fail. She beheld the immaculately presented fifteen-year-old boy emerging from the house. His sultry brown eyes and slick quiff emulated the brooding heroes from her romance novels. When girls sniffed around him, Patricia shooed them off. Her advice to Liam in the ways of dating was, "Don't bring them home and don't get them pregnant."

Patricia admired Liam's ripening biceps as he dragged the television into the garden. Putting the gym equipment on the catalogue account had been a smart move. Mike complained about the garage no longer housing his shoddy Fiesta. As usual, his complaints went unheard.

An extension lead dangled near the paddling pool. Patricia considered mentioning it. Jen raised from the lawn, poised to shield Mandy from danger. It required too much effort for Patricia to intervene. Instead, she pulled the sun lounger closer to the television and slathered baby oil on her legs.

'Does that man have to be on the telly?' Patricia spat venom at Bob Geldof. 'How dare a second-rate musician ruin my viewing? He could've brushed his hair before sitting next to Charles and Di. When's Duran Duran on, Liam?'

'Don't think they're playing.' From the other lounger, Liam lowered his Aviators to focus on squashing an ant with his thumb. Despite the heat, Jen shivered.

If Patricia couldn't lust over Simon Le Bon, no one was watching *Live Aid*. She lunged for the television set and snapped it off.

'But Mum…' Jen despaired at missing The Style Council. She wanted to compare notes with Johnny if Paul Weller still cut it, after his iconic years with The Jam.

Hopefully, Johnny was recording the concert, but the chances were slim. Rob Morgan, his mum's boyfriend, often pawned their electricals. Rob was always involved in dodgy schemes and took risks. He wasn't so reckless when it came to keeping his easily rankled partner happy though. The pawning ceased when *Dynasty* returned. Johnny's mum wouldn't miss salivating over Blake Carrington for anything.

Patricia's sour face rendered Jen mute. Mandy stopped splashing. At six years old, she was already accustomed to her mum's temper. Silence reigned in the Taylor garden. Patricia's dominance sliced through the summer's day. A shadow swept across the lawn and rested on Jen and Mandy. The Taylors separately idled the afternoon away.

'U2 are on later. Put the telly back on.' Liam's command broke the peace.

His stare honed in on Patricia. Did she see control there? She decided not. Not her subservient boy. Liam understood Mummy knew best.

'We must watch then, darling. I can't miss Bono. A man with a mullet really does it for me. Switch the television on, Jennifer.'

Nauseated by her mum's overt lust of a pop star, Jen welcomed the distraction. She complied. The weather obeyed Patricia too as the sun returned and rested upon her body. It bent to her desire to cultivate a tan to outdo Felicity Smith, frying in a hot pink bikini next door.

Jen sought shade by the shed, taking her stethoscope with her. She marvelled at Ultravox belting out *Vienna*. Midge Ure understood the trials of being the lesser recognised one, having a background role in the *Live Aid* partnership with Bob Geldof. Jen felt an affinity with Midge as he sang, wearing a heavy coat, on one of the hottest days of the year. She decided Midge Ure knew that, eventually, you can have your moment in the sun.

7

PRESENT

Doreen's mission continues with daily phone calls and a mountain of messages left for me at work. So far I've avoided her. Let's see which of us breaks first. The reception temp was instructed to ask who is calling. Simple, you'd think, but I've had a narrow escape involving slamming the phone down on Doreen. I don't want to do this, but she's infiltrating my life. How did she find out where I work? I expect Claire's to blame, again. She used to be a friend. Now she's more of an enemy.

My mind is full of paranoid questions. Is Doreen messing with my head? Did she see something that day? I fight the urge to answer her calls and detail what I've lost: not being a doctor because of poor exam results, no family bonds, close friends, or partner, and a lifetime of guilt. Wallowing in a pity party against a woman whose teenage daughter died is shallow though.

I spend most nights staring at the ceiling, replaying the day of Kelly's death. The line between truth and lies is blurred. It's like digging out a beloved childhood film as an adult, only to be disappointed. Except with this, I have no fond memories to begin with. There are no rose-tinted specs to brighten up the barbarity. A girl died. There was blood. I made the blood flow.

LISA SELL

I've not always been so introspective. Once, I was a party animal who sought thrills. To avoid probable death from excess, I had to choose sobriety. I've lost sight of it. Calling it medicinal, I'm drinking again. I must not open another bottle. Only months of rehab and sheer grit got me out of the pits of addiction.

I look around the call centre, noting how grubby it's become. Decoration is low on the list of financial priorities. Listening Ear getting a building in Oxford was a stroke of luck. We used to work from a tiny office in the middle of nowhere. Since the move, we're more accessible for seeing people face to face, as well as talking on the phone.

A beep signifies a call coming in. It's my turn to help someone.

'Hello, you're through to Listening Ear. I'm Jen, ready to listen.'

The line is quiet for a while. It always is. Callers often question if they can go through with it. I give the caller time to decide. I've been volunteering here for years. Human nature seldom changes.

'I need help.' Her voice scratches at the vocal cords to make sounds.

'You've made a brave step in phoning us today. You're safe. Can I ask your name, if that's okay?'

'Amy.'

It's probably not, but it doesn't matter.

'Hello, Amy. We'll take this slowly. If it gets too difficult to talk, silence is fine. This is about what *you* need. Would you like to talk?'

Silence.

The call centre is heaving. Each volunteer sits at a desk, poised to help. We're in this together; helping those feeling hopeless and listening when people need to be heard. I've memorised the current tag line. This is no mean feat considering it changes each month.

Amy exhales. 'I'm not sure if I can say.'

'If you need to hear a friendly voice, rather than speaking, it's okay. No pressure or judgement here.'

I'm lying. Since Kelly's death, I constantly judge myself. You're talking to a fraud, Amy. Don't trust me.

Her words tumble out. 'I did it. I did something awful. It's my fault.' The hatches of her fear burst open.

'Let's take this one step at a time.'

Perspiration tingles between my shoulder blades. People near me notice I'm not maintaining my usual calm exterior. We're closely seated to fit in the volunteers. An elbow nudges mine and nerves make me jump. Swivelling the chair away, I swipe my sleeve across my forehead. Amy's words are making my remorse pour out.

'Are you able to talk about what you did?' I ask, not sure I want to know the answer.

Coming here tonight was a mistake, but letting people down isn't in my nature. I could have called in sick for the first time in seventeen years, but Jen has to be on top of things. Jen is unravelling. I'm losing it.

Amy continues. 'I killed her and I deserve to be punished.'

I tear off the headset and dart for the toilets, rushing past looks of concern and bemusement.

...

After emptying most of my stomach, I sit on the floor of the cubicle, gripping the lino. I hold on, trying to stop everything falling away.

'Jen, are you okay?' The manager, Hilary, stands outside.

Between me and this door lies either sharing my criminal act and watching my life come tumbling down, or devising a lie to keep it together.

'I'm fine. Be out in a sec.'

I wipe my face with toilet paper. The items in my bag, which I grabbed in the rush, offer little by way of repairs. For once, I wish I was more girly. Having cosmetics would've helped. I make do with a tissue-spit wash and lip balm instead.

There's no movement outside. Maybe Hilary has gone. I'm not ready to give a detailed explanation, although it feels like I've been

LISA SELL

found out anyway. Amy's words were my own. She made my confession.

I inch the cubicle door open. Hilary leans against a sink.

'How can you still look so pretty after being sick?' Hilary asks.

I don't reply. My ego isn't boosted when someone says I'm attractive. It's not about false modesty. Searching for beauty is damaging. I dealt with a mother who gave more love to her reflection. I refuse to be like her, even though we have the same nose and cheekbones. DNA should be able to be replaced. Inheriting Dad's brown hair and eyes isn't reassuring. He ceased to be a part of me when I left.

Hilary offers a mint. 'Are you okay?'

Her head tilts to one side as if to say, "I am giving you a listening ear." It's her thing. Hilary eats, sleeps and breathes this place. She confided at an after-work social that she's never had a partner. I spent the first part of the evening trying to keep her off the commiseration sherry. The rest of the night, I held back her hair as she lost most of a bottle of Croft Original. If my current situation weren't so dire, I'd joke about our role reversal.

How do you tell your boss you killed someone and fear going to prison? How do you share that, with every shift, you've considered you should be on the other end of the line?

'I must've eaten something that was off.'

At least she won't think I'm pregnant. Not spinster Jen.

'You need to go home. I'll drive you.'

'I'm okay, thanks. Tentlebury is out of your way. I'll take it easy.'

Hilary gives my arm a reassuring squeeze. 'Don't come back until you're ready. Make sure you've dealt with things first. I can get cover.' She knows it's more than food poisoning and I'm hiding something. Of course she does. She's a renowned psychologist and a brilliant reader of people.

Still, I must keep up the pretence. 'It'll be over soon.' If only.

Hilary turns around, ready to leave, then faces me again. 'I picked up the call from Amy. She was in a state, thinking she'd killed her daughter. The child was playing in the front garden and Amy got distracted by a text. Her daughter ran into the road and was hit by a van. Today's the second anniversary of her death. I told her we sometimes carry guilt that's not ours. People can hold onto events they mistakenly believe are their fault.' Veiled advice given, she returns to others who need her support.

...

I realise, as I sit in my car, I have to face the past too. It's time to take charge. Unlike Amy, I won't receive absolution. Doreen will have my "help". She won't stop phoning until I agree. I'll pretend to help when really I'll steer her away from the truth.

I fish a ball of paper from the bottom of my bag and smooth it flat. Somehow, I knew I'd need the phone number the reception temp passed on. I prepare to hurtle into the past while trying to protect my present.

The call connects.

8

16TH JULY 1983

Patricia trailed her fingers around the telephone dial, careful not to snag a nail. Perspiration dared to spot upon her forehead. She dabbed the offensive bodily fluid with a kitchen towel.

'Felicity, darling,' she said, 'is it still 1pm for the soirée?'

In response to the piercing voice emitting from the receiver, Patricia scrunched her nose. Jen pinged marbles across the floor.

'Yes, dear, I *know* you sent an invitation,' Patricia garbled around applying lipstick, 'but you have a habit of running somewhat late.'

The shrillness became a screech.

'Of course, Felicity. We will see you anon.' Patricia replaced the receiver. 'Bloody harridan.'

'What's a *harridan*?' Jen dared to ask.

Patricia startled. Her daughter's existence often eluded her. 'What you'll probably grow up to be. Stop denting my units with those marbles.' She lifted Jen and deposited her on Mike's lap. 'Yours, I believe.' Patricia left.

Jen poked her dad's chin. She squealed as he pretended to bite her finger.

'I'm trying to watch the television. Shut up.' Liam increased the volume to a roar.

Mike turned off the set and placed Jen back on his knee. 'Get changed, son. We're leaving soon.'

'Don't call me *son*. I'm not going to the Smiths'. They're pompous morons.'

Mike considered how to reprimand a child for speaking the truth. He wondered why the Taylors were attending the Smiths' barbecue considering Patricia constantly bitched about Felicity. The answer was there. They were going *because* of Patricia. After salivating over a mammoth barbecue in an episode of *Dallas*, Felicity had purchased one. A select few were invited to coo over it. Desperate not to be outdone, Patricia needed to see the barbecue to know what to order for the Taylors' garden. A tape measure sat in her pocket, ready for a crafty measuring of the Smiths' contraption.

Patricia re-entered the room, putting in her earrings. 'Haven't you told Liam to get changed yet? You're useless, Michael.'

Mike didn't reply. It would only lead to an argument and Patricia's outbursts were always scathing. Being forced to wear a garish Hawaiian shirt was humiliating enough. The Magnum fetish was bordering on ridiculous. Mike thought he was a decent-looking bloke without intervention, although the emerging beer belly required exercise.

Patricia led Liam upstairs to change. He dragged behind, kicking each step.

Mandy climbed onto Mike's other knee. He wished it could always be this way; just his two girls and him. Liam was hard work. Patricia was, well, Patricia. Deciding her dad's shirt wasn't bright enough, Mandy coloured in a flower on the breast pocket with a felt tip. Mike didn't protest. Fun rarely happened in their house. Jen widened her eyes then grinned at Mike's naughtiness. She grabbed a pen and joined in.

...

'You're late. It's hardly a long trek from next door.' Felicity seethed at the Taylors standing outside her front door. 'You could've gone straight to the garden.'

'Felicity, dear, I *never* enter an abode from around the back.' Patricia led her clan through the Smiths' house.

Mike prayed for beer. Liam hoped for rain. Jen reminded herself of the rules of good behaviour. Mandy chewed a crayon.

Like boxers in a ring, the Pontings huddled in one corner and the Smiths took the other. The Pontings' attendance was unexpected, due to a recent spate of discord between Felicity and Henry Ponting. Jen couldn't keep up with estate politics.

Felicity sashayed across the lawn, lowering a grey sweatshirt from her shoulder. She was working the *Flashdance* look despite leg warmers increasing her chances of heat stroke. Patricia enjoyed observing the sweat patch forming on Felicity's back. Fashion was supposed to work for you, not against you.

The wobbly heated air from the barbecue transfixed Jen. Bricks from the walls altered from rigid lines to dancing waves. She revelled in the magic and swayed to the music.

The track changed to *Cruel Summer*. Mandy sang along for a while, stopping to ask, 'What does *cruel* mean?'

Jen pointed to Patricia. Mandy nodded her understanding.

'Go away, this is a private party,' Felicity addressed Kelly, revolted by her clashing outfit of stripes and spots.

Kelly slipped from balancing on the edge of the kerb outside the Smiths' gate. 'I'm only walking past.'

'Weirdo,' Liam said. He stuck out his tongue and then continued reading *Frankenstein*. If he had to endure the charade, he would make his own entertainment.

Kelly wiped her runny nose on her sleeve and moved on. The party continued as if she'd never appeared.

Jen carried Mandy to the cool of the Smiths' dining room. The tapestry lining on the chair made her legs itch. She regarded the scene in the garden. Why these adults insisted upon spending time together when most of them hated each other was puzzling. Jen didn't play with kids she didn't like.

Patricia sneered. Felicity's fretful trampoline eyebrows bounced. Mercedes and Porsche Smith tried to catch Liam's attention. He kicked a ball to Sylvia and Virginia Ponting. An outsider would call it *playing*. Fortified by cans of bitter, Mike ignored the situation forming around him.

Jen tired of the oppressive heat, the pretensions, and snobbery. She cast a longing look at the youngsters in the park. Johnny waved his gangly arm, catching it within the chains of the swing. His younger brother, Benny, whooped with glee, demanding Johnny push him higher. *There* was where Jen and Mandy should be.

A wail disrupted the barbecue's conversations and latent bitching. Sylvia's mouth stretched wider to let out her fury. For a four-year-old, she boasted a magnificent set of lungs.

Sally ran to her child, soothing away the hurt. 'What happened, sweetie?'

'Hit me with ball.' Sylvia pointed a podgy finger at Porsche, who was sitting next to Liam.

Porsche gasped. 'I did not.' Her eyes pleaded with Liam to intervene. He raised his novel and continued reading.

Felicity placed a territorial arm around her eldest. Porsche was Felicity's reflection, with a sweatshirt falling off the opposite shoulder. Patricia lay back, sipped her cocktail, and enjoyed the drama.

Henry joined the fray, grabbing Sylvia from Sally. 'What the hell is a teenager doing attacking a four-year-old?'

Porsche cried. Mercedes lined up with her mum and sister. Her outfit of shorts and a vest top showed she'd missed the *Flashdance* memo.

'Porsche didn't touch the little shit,' Mercedes said.

'Charming language, Mercedes Smith,' Henry replied.

When Jen related the event to Johnny, her imagination conjured a western. Within the hush, a tumbleweed drifted across the garden. The music stopped. Felicity placed a hand on her hip, the other ready to shoot. Henry gave Sylvia back to Sally and prepared to draw.

'It is *Smythe!*' A puce Felicity looked set to combust.

'It is *Smith!*' Henry threw his arms into the air, possibly calling for divine intervention to smite Felicity.

'Get out of my house and take your shabby family with you,' Felicity said.

'Says the woman who named her daughters after cars?'

'Says the pretentious prick who named his after characters in books?'

Loyal to her husband but petrified of Felicity, Sally mumbled, 'They're named after authors.' She picked at the hem of her purple twinset.

The kids in the park couldn't believe their luck as they applauded and heckled the free show. Johnny mouthed, 'Can I help?' to Jen who was creeping alongside the Smiths' shed, seeking an escape. She shook her head and held Mandy close as the Pontings drilled past.

'That's the riff-raff taken care of.' Patricia clapped. 'Let's get this party properly started.' She entered the dining room and dropped the needle on a record.

Tears for Fears declared it's a *Mad World*.

Yes, yes it is, Jen thought, hoping she wouldn't always be part of it.

...

Kelly returned, continuing to walk tightrope on the kerb, her face serious with concentration. Way past its time for a cut, her fringe fell into her eyes. As she slipped, she noticed Jen and Mandy inching towards the gate.

'Are you okay?' Kelly asked, aware the girls' movements were unusually cautious.

'Shh.' Jen hoped she would take the hint. Kelly's big mouth could get her into trouble.

Jen was silent as they crept out of the garden. What could Kelly Pratt do to make it better? She didn't understand Jen's life at all.

9

PRESENT

I haven't been to Aylesbury since I was a child, when a trip there was a day out. A group of estate kids caught the bus to spend our pocket money in a town with better shops than in Troddington.

Mandy always rushed to get a seat at the front of the top deck. From there she could watch as the "dragon bus" ate cars. She had a theory that when the bus pulled up behind vehicles, they disappeared into its mouth. Bus rides were an adventure.

On approach to the gyratory, I recall its legend. Drivers who'd passed their tests reinforced the myth of how the gyratory system defeated learners. I realise this is the first time I've driven on it. Deggsy, a ropey ex-boyfriend, taught me to drive around the busy streets of Oxford. At least he was good for something.

Whitworth Road sounds elegant. Driving along it, the reality begs to differ. Doreen has swapped the dereliction of Pollock Road for its cousin. Crude graffiti daubs walls. The sign is cracked, with letters missing. Holes and leeching moss riddle fencing panels.

I curse myself for judging this area. My beginnings were similar. Living in a middle-class Oxfordshire village doesn't alter my roots.

Sometimes I wonder if I'm becoming like my mum. Earthier, "normal" Jen rails against it.

Doreen's front door is peeling blue paint, revealing a base white layer. At least it's not coated in dog crap. When she lived on the estate, Doreen scrubbed the mess spiteful kids smeared there. She never complained. Her Marigolds were snapped on and she cleaned. It wasn't right she had to do that.

I take a breath and push away indignation. My anger has never done me any favours. When I joined the Headway Practice as Practice Manager, Nicole offered counselling, as she does for every employee. Keen to make a good impression, I accepted. She uprooted my hidden anger and encouraged directing it positively. I couldn't tell her where the fury originated. She was fobbed off with sob stories of being bullied as a child. I didn't add how the bullies were my mum and, more harmfully, me.

No longer meek Jennifer, I bang my fist upon the door. I'd suggested a coffee shop, but Doreen insisted on meeting in her home. I figured she wanted the advantage of being on her territory. Standing in front of me, it's obvious Doreen has other reasons.

People age and change. We can usually see hints of who they once were. I look at individuals on social media and spot dimples that can't be erased, teeth never straightened or the sharpness of blue eyes that never dim. Doreen is a stranger.

Loose skin hangs from her jaw, indicating a previously nourished woman. Doreen was slim but now she's verging upon skeletal. Her eyes have shrunk into dark circles and her wispy hair is a symptom of the ravages of chemotherapy. I came here to control her. My resolve weakens. She extends clawed hands for a hug but I can't reciprocate. Better she thinks I'm repressed than to know my fear of embracing death.

'Come in, Jennifer.' The birth name, as always, jars.

I follow along a narrow hallway, frozen in the seventies. Swirls of brown and orange whirring across the carpet and wallpaper make me giddy. Doreen unwittingly leads her daughter's killer into her home. My heart hammers out guilt with each step.

I sit at the table. Doreen is of the old school. Important matters take place in the kitchen where the tea and biscuits are. When I was a child, women chatted for hours in their kitchens; feeding on juicy gossip and salacious stories.

Doreen rummages around a high cupboard, picking up a teapot. The effort of lifting makes her wince. I take the teapot and am rewarded with a smile. I don't want tea. I don't want to be here.

'You were always such a kind girl, Jennifer.'

'It's Jen.'

'Of course.' She measures tea leaves. 'I keep forgetting how you young 'uns shorten your names. Can't say I'm a fan of it, but each to their own. I'm glad Kelly never shortened it to "Kel".'

"Kel" rhymes with *tell*. Something I will never do. It also rhymes with *smell*. Poor girl never stood a chance. Smelly Kelly, from "Pillock" Road, who was a Pratt, had the naming odds stacked against her.

Doreen completes the ceremony of making tea. I add a splash of milk and three sugars. Normally I have one. The sweetness will cushion any shocks to come. In true Jen style, I'm prepared.

'Thank you for speaking to me, at last,' she says.

I'll let her earlier harassment go but I need to be firm. As much as I can be with a woman who's a shade more than a corpse.

'I'm not sure how I can help. Wasn't it sorted out back then? Everyone said she'd killed herself.' I wince at my bluntness.

Doreen doubles over and splays her hands across the laminated table. The squares resemble graph paper. She's on a downward curve.

'What can I do?' I ask.

'Grab those pills please.' She points to a collection of boxes by the sink.

Doreen has more medication than Boots. Not knowing which

ones to bring, I drop the lot in front of her. With barely a glimpse at the labels, she opens a box and swallows a few tablets.

'The cancer came back.' Her shoulders droop. 'I thought they'd got it. Even had my boobs lopped off. The blighter worked its way through and set up home in my spine.'

I was prepared to be firm but how can I when she's dying in front of me? I have to get out of this. Shame will trip me up and my mouth will blab the truth.

Rubbing her shoulder is an ineffectual form of comfort. I don't want to be here, touching the mother of the girl I killed.

'The tablets will kick in soon.' She tries to straighten.

I never appreciated how strong Doreen was. I admire her resolution to fight this illness, if not her determination to find out what happened to Kelly.

'Kelly wouldn't have chosen suicide,' Doreen says.

'Why?' It's all I have. The tough persona isn't working.

'She hated violence because of what Graham did to us. She wouldn't inflict more harm upon herself.' Doreen takes a sharp breath. 'I did some digging around back then. One of the PCs said Kelly's head injury seemed odd. It didn't appear to be from the train. They couldn't say for certain though. I need *proper* answers. I won't rest until I find out who murdered my daughter.'

'Murder?'

Doreen leans over the table. The squares shrink.

'I'm convinced Kelly was murdered and you know something about it.'

The cup slips from my grasp and smashes against the stone tiles.

10

8TH APRIL 1986

'I know.'

'Know what?'

'I know where you live. Freddy is coming to cut you up. Sleep well, Smelly Kelly.'

A chorus of jeers followed the threat. Kelly placed the receiver back in its cradle and prepared to move on. She accepted constant ridicule; such was the lot of the Pratt family. The Freddy Krueger impression was new though. Maybe Freddie Norman, from Picasso Way, received a similar call if the idiots were on a roll that afternoon.

'Who was on the phone?' Graham's voice boomed across the house.

He'd been sleeping off a hangover, coupled with fatigue from working as a bin man. Kelly cursed the caller for awakening the slumbering ogre. She'd have to explain. For Graham, answers were given in person and he always expected answers.

Kelly tiptoed from the hallway and into the lounge, trying to avoid standing on the carpet's circles. If she missed them, maybe Graham wouldn't be too harsh. She knew it was foolish for a thirteen-year-old to rely on made-up superstitions for survival but it was worth a try.

'Just a double-glazing salesman,' she said from the doorway, safe from his lair. Saying it was a prank call would only rile him.

'Bastards, ruining my kip. I hope you told them where to go.'

Graham heaved himself from the faded corduroy sofa and sparked a cigarette. He gave a throaty cough and scratched his groin, inadvertently shifting his Y-fronts to give a less than pleasant view.

Kelly looked away at a framed photograph of her parents' wedding day. When did the handsome man with the natty suit become this thing? Back then, Graham had been well preserved, considering he was nearly twice Doreen's age. Kelly couldn't reconcile the man who posed in the photo with the aged husk, trying to ease his crotch rot. Brylcreem slicked his steel grey hair, appearing greasy rather than styled. His wolfish sideburns gave him a sinister edge. Sweat stains yellowed a white vest no amount of hot washes could remove.

Kelly resolved she'd never marry a man who treated her how Graham behaved towards Doreen. She wondered if every male eventually became manipulative. Her mum may not have been clever but she had common sense. Had Graham deceived her when they'd met? Kelly hoped not all men began as charming, only to become beasts. She had little evidence to draw upon, beyond Graham. There was only the one of her dreams. Surely he wouldn't hurt her? She thought about him often. No, he'd never turn into a nightmare. An explosion in her head halted the fantasy.

'Listen to me when I'm talking to you.'

Cigarette ash spilled, blackening the front of Kelly's blouse. Graham unfortunately still had a good aim, even at a distance. A stone ashtray landed at her feet. Kelly had taken her eyes off the threat, when usually she made sure she was prepared. She rubbed underneath her fringe and removed her glasses, relieved not to be bleeding. Blood made a mess. Graham despised mess. She resisted soothing the pain. Graham detested weakness too.

'Get that tidied up.' The cracking of his knuckles made Kelly flinch.

Ash marked her tights as she knelt. Cigarette butts merged with the rug's circular pattern. Kelly filed the dream about her beau away. It wasn't the time for fantasising. In the future it would become a reality and Graham a figment of the past. She needed one male in her life and it wasn't the slob that had been snoring on the sofa.

One day, Kelly decided, she would be free to be with the only one who mattered.

PRESENT

I've cleared away my broken teacup from Doreen's kitchen floor. It delayed the conversation while I made a show of retrieving every piece. The time for stalling is over. Questions must be asked.

'Why do you think I can help with what happened to Kelly?' The edginess of my voice betrays attempts at confidence.

Doreen tilts her head back. The meds are working. 'You walked to school together. I'm sure you'll remember something important. Maybe someone who was mean to her?'

It would be easier to sift out those who'd been civil to Kelly. 'You know Kelly wasn't liked by many people?'

I wait for tears or an outburst. Neither comes.

'I'm not stupid. I know what most people on the estate thought of us. As soon as Graham died, I asked for a transfer. He saw it as a matter of honour to stick it out where we weren't wanted. As soon as he passed, I went to the council offices, played up the widow and bereaved mother thing, and demanded to be housed elsewhere.'

Doreen isn't as dumb as we decided she was. We cast her as the estate's cautionary tale of a feeble woman who allowed a man to beat her, and her daughter to be bullied. We knew nothing of her life. Underestimating Doreen could be dangerous. I need to watch her more carefully.

'Kelly was called names, spat on, and hit. I dealt with the aftermath.' Doreen's volume rises.

Rather than being afraid, for the first time, I admire Doreen Pratt. *This* is how anger is channelled positively; by protecting your own. I consider sharing with Nicole what I've learned, seeing as we discuss anger so often in our mentoring sessions, but she doesn't know about this and never will.

'Someone might have taken it too far.' Doreen twiddles a ring that threatens to fall off her finger. 'Their hatred of Kelly could have made them kill her. I don't want to think it but it could've happened. It's hard, knowing the child you doted on was rejected and used as a target.'

The striped wallpaper pulls inwards, trapping me within the room. The air is thick. Against the fugue of Doreen's last meal, I catch breaths. This isn't the time to falter. I have to stick with the plan.

'I'll help you.' Knowing I'm a rubbish liar, I look away. Mum saw through it in an instant. Doreen is smarter than I gave her credit for.

'That's great, Jen.' She envelopes me within her bony frame.

Who is this woman? Her drive to want to solve what happened to Kelly is disturbing. The past is not a good place to return to. Why can't she let it go? Shame gnaws at me. I caused this. If I confess, she can stop searching, but I have too much to lose.

'Claire and Ellen are on the team too, as I said in my e-mail. Ellen's been such a supportive friend, even after I left the estate. Claire's worried you're annoyed with her for passing on your details. Go easy on her. She was helping, like you are too now.'

After spending hours duping a sick woman, sipping tea, and being force-fed pink wafers, I leave Doreen's exhausted. There's no going back. I'm equipped with Ellen Woods' address and instructions to follow the breadcrumbs to her home for the next instalment of "The Kelly Chronicles". This is no cosy murder mystery though. This is death in its violent glory.

7TH AUGUST 1986

'George Michael doesn't love boys.' Mandy's wailing travelled from the park.

Darting from their house across the road, Jen came to the rescue. 'What the hell's going on?'

Mandy grabbed Jen's legs, smearing chocolate onto her sister's trousers. Jen didn't mind. The washing was one of her many chores. She encouraged Mandy not to fear getting dirty when playing. Her sister would never have to stick to Patricia's rule of remaining spotless. As much as she hated doing the laundry, Jen liked finding grass stains on Mandy's jeans or holes in her jumpers. They signified her freedom to be a child, something Jen never had.

Claire joined them, shoving misbehaving shoulder pads back into place. A teenager wearing an oversized purple velour jacket on narrow shoulders wasn't a successful combination. Jen grinned at her friend playing a martyr to fashion.

'You must be sweating your arse off.' Jen tried to remain serious. 'If you're not, your mum will definitely kick your backside for raiding her wardrobe again.'

· · ·

Claire squared her shoulders. At least someone noticed the outfit. Style was lost on the other kids.

'Mum won't find out. She's working, as usual. I'll return it before she gets home. The reporter image suits me. I'm Mum's prodigy.'

Claire thrived on learning new words, except she didn't always use them correctly. Her favourite part of the day involved joining Ellen after dinner to seek complex words from the thesaurus.

'It's *progeny*, you wally,' Jen said.

Claire looked down at her mum's slingbacks. She wanted to be a reporter, like Ellen, except Claire focused on the nationals, not the *Troddington Echo*.

Holding back an apology for questioning Claire's word skills, Jen decided Claire needed to realise life was tough. Parents didn't always love their children unconditionally and nurture them into rosy futures. Jen felt conflicted for thinking it. Claire was daft but with a generous heart. Ellen had the positive attributes Patricia lacked. Jen offered a strawberry lace to make peace. Claire's frantic chewing signified her forgiveness.

Jen addressed a pitiful Mandy. 'What's upset you? I'm trying to watch *EastEnders*. If I can hear you inside, Mum can too.' She tried to avoid speaking publicly about Patricia's dominance but Jen needed Mandy to learn the lessons for a quiet life sooner than she had.

'Claire said George Michael loves boys, not girls.' The statement shattered Mandy's seven-year-old world.

Claire screwed up her face at the snitching Mandy. 'It's best you find out. I'm doing you a favour. Imagine how stupid you'll look if you tried it on with him in the future.'

Mandy blushed at the discovery of her fantasy. Ever since she'd first heard *Bad Boys* on the radio, George Michael had captured her heart. Andrew Ridgeley was too quiet. When she grew up, George would meet her, fall in love, and become her husband.

Jen pierced Claire with a look that made wonky shoulder pads the least of her worries. 'All kinds of inappropriate going on here. She's only little, for goodness' sake.'

Claire kicked the swing in a show of fake defiance. Seated on the swing, Mandy took it as a double blow and began to cry again. Claire was the breaker of dreams and possibly limbs.

'When did Mandy become so needy?' Claire asked.

Jen pulled her aside. 'Please tell her George Michael isn't gay.'

'What's *gay*?' an innocent voice enquired.

'We'll talk later, bat ears.'

Mandy shrugged. Claire was given "the look" again. Jen had perfected it after being on the receiving end from Patricia for years.

Claire stopped Mandy mid-swing. 'Okay, brat. George Michael likes girls, not boys, and one day he'll marry you.'

Jen took charge. 'Go and get ready for bed. I'll be there in a minute.' She lifted Mandy from the swing and gave her a pat on the backside to move her along.

Mandy's delight that George could still be hers spread across her face. She skipped towards the house, stopping to talk to children sitting on the pavement and swapping football stickers. Mandy explained to them how George Michael was king even if Wham! was over. *One thing at a time*, she thought. She couldn't handle dealing with two disappointments in the same day. George was free from the band and had more time to find her. Life was sweet.

'Get indoors!' Jen shouted.

Satisfied Mandy was inside, Jen knew she should follow. First, she needed to sort out Claire. 'Stop teasing her. You know how delicate she can be.'

Claire sat on the swing. 'I'm toughening her up. It's a hard world out there.'

'So much wisdom for a thirteen-year-old.' Jen kicked Claire. The steel caps of her boots made an impression on Claire's shins.

'Ouch. You've got dirt on the bottoms. Mum will lose it if she sees this.'

'The outfit isn't working for you, is it.'

'I'd better clean them before Mum gets back.'

Claire jumped off mid-swing and performed a gymnastic landing. Jen admired the unfamiliar show of grace.

'Oh, and Claire,' Jen raised her voice as her friend walked away, 'George Michael? Totally gay.'

13

PRESENT

'Hello, twonk.'

'Hello, wazzock.'

Despite my annoyance with Claire for sharing my contact details with Doreen, I can't resist falling into our old routine. On Ellen's doorstep, Claire draws me into a stifling hug. I swallow the lump in my throat. Open emotion is weakness. She's not my kooky friend Claire, anymore. She's someone I need to deceive.

Claire doesn't overshare on Facebook. I've never seen any pictures on there. For the first time in decades, I'm seeing her. If you took a fourteen-year-old girl, stretched her out, and stuck on boobs, it would result in adult Claire. She's hardly changed.

The difference between my tallness and her short height remains. She hated being small and loathed her jug ears even more. For most of the eighties, Claire sleeked her hair with gel to cover her ears. Age has brought confidence if the high ponytail is any indication.

Her jumper with its fancy appliqués and soft cashmere is probably a designer label. It jars against the casualness of utility trousers and a bare face. Claire has always been a mass of contradictions.

She frowns. 'You're making me look like a munchkin, being so tall. Stop gawping and come in.'

Ellen has upgraded from Renoir Road. Houses aren't cheap in this chocolate-box village. Being a reporter must've been lucrative. The Rembrandt Estate is a slum in comparison.

'You're wondering how Mum could afford this.' Claire used to know me well. It freaks me out she still might. How does it bode for keeping things from her?

'No.' I try to convey I'm a mystery to her.

Deciding this posh abode merits it, I remove my trainers and follow her into the lounge. It's a display of neutrals and good taste.

'My parents got it for a song in the nineties,' Claire says. 'This house and the one they bought next door were a wreck. It gave Dad a project until he took off with another woman.'

'I'm sorry.'

Alex was her hero. I envied their relationship. He used to raise her onto his shoulders. She looked how she must have felt; like royalty.

'Don't worry. It happened ages ago. Dad never could keep it in his pants. I'm astounded Mum stayed with him so long, but she struggled with breaking up the family. Much as I love Dad, I told her leave. He's living in Birmingham and on wife number three. I go there a fair bit. Birmingham's got great clothes shops.' Claire sighs, probably at the thought of future shopping trips. The clothes obsession hasn't waned.

Photos of various people adorn every wall. Knick-knacks are assembled into groups, according to the countries Ellen has visited. The arms of chairs and backs of seats are worn, a sign of the regular company of guests. This is a home, not a house. It's what I've always wanted. I walk towards the mantelpiece, needing a distraction. Claire's staring is unrelenting.

'You've been busy, unless you kidnapped some beautiful people off the street.' I hold up the photo of her with a toothpaste advert smiling man and a teenage girl who's undeniably Claire's daughter.

I know Claire's married with a child, but small talk makes the situation less awkward.

'Cheeky cow. That's Seb, the husband, and my daughter, Matilda; we call her "Matty". Mum made us do a portrait session. I took the mickey the whole time. My two scrub up well though.' Love oozes from her. It's nauseating in other parents. With Claire, I find it endearing.

This is the girl who would never marry or have kids because, apparently, feminists don't. She read it in a seventies textbook from the library. I said I wasn't sure it worked that way. She advised I was setting back the cause with my "concessions to patriarchy". It was the first time she'd used a complicated set of words in the right context, if not with wisdom.

I take a seat, jolting upwards when she dives next to me. The closeness is stifling. We're not those girls who huddled up anymore. Claire's never respected boundaries. I shift along until the lowered wooden edge digs into my hip.

'Mum will be here in a sec,' Claire says. 'She's waiting for the plumber, next door.'

'Does she still own that too?'

'Yes. We live there: Seb, Matty and I. Mum's playing good landlord. Toilet keeps getting bunged up and there's crap everywhere.' This is Claire; always straight-talking and never one to use the plethora of words she spent most of her childhood digesting.

'So, you became a reporter too?'

Claire smooths her hands over her ears. My mean streak rejoices in them still being a hindrance. I'd rather not be the only one here with issues.

'I'm freelance and have had some blinding stories in the odd newspaper. Got a website too, where I report on local news. There are loads of followers but I've not hit the big time yet. *The Guardian* will soon be knocking down my door.'

Her self-belief was always admirable. There's no doubt she'll keep chasing her aspirations. I'm a little jealous I had to give up on mine. Doctors need decent qualifications. They also save lives rather than take them. Still, I'm proud of what I've achieved. Becoming a counsellor isn't a poor second.

'Cooee.' The owner of the exuberant voice used to share pear drops with me. She made dinners that warmed my stomach and soul. I remember a wide and caring smile. The past collides with the present when Ellen enters the lounge.

'Jen, it's so wonderful to see you.'

I forgot the bear hug is a family thing. A flowery scent tickles my nostrils. As I come up for air, I'm greeted by a welcoming face. Time has been kind to her. There are more wrinkles and her hair is shorter, but she's still the same Ellen.

She always dressed in a distinguished way. The trouser suit she's wearing has a sharp houndstooth pattern. Her motto was: it's best to dress up rather than down. If you begin smart, you can take it down a few notches, but it's harder to scrub up if your baseline is unkempt. I wonder what she makes of my tatty jeans.

Ellen takes a seat. 'I said you'd grow up to be a stunner, like your mother. Isn't she a looker, Claire?'

Claire seems to be cringing at how mums can fixate upon their daughters' looks. I stretch my hoodie out of shape, wanting to hide under it.

'Did you make Jen a cuppa, love?'

'We got chatting.' Well-trained, Claire gets up.

'I see you're wearing my jumper again,' Ellen says. Claire's pilfering habits haven't disappeared. The girl is playing dress-up again.

'Laundry day tomorrow,' Claire offers. 'I'll get Jen a brew.'

'I'm fine. Doreen's already plied me with tea.' I don't want to be here any longer than I have to.

'Poor woman. She's been through so much.' Ellen speaks in the quiet respectful tone reserved for talking about the dying or dead. 'The least we can do is to help her find out what happened to Kelly. You're a good girl for joining us, Jen.' Ellen pats my thigh and draws in so close our knees touch. Don't these two value personal space?

If she really knew me, Ellen would realise I'm far from good. I stopped being a good girl in 1987. I've been trying to redress the balance since. What is *good* anyway? I help people, donate to charity, and floss my teeth. Does it mean I'm good? Can you ever be good if you've done something incredibly bad?

Claire still has the talent of talking and hardly taking a breath. I catch the tail end of her spiel. 'Because she's fourteen too.'

'Sorry, what did you say?' I've failed to follow the conversation.

'Matty, my daughter. She's the same age Kelly was when she died. It makes me feel old. When Doreen spoke to Mum a few months ago about this Kelly stuff, I thought of Matty. If my child died, I'd want to know how it happened. I'm bewildered at how long it's taken Doreen to start the process. In my opinion–'

'Opinions are like bum holes,' Ellen says.

'Everyone's got one but we don't need to hear them,' Claire finishes.

We explode into laughter. Ellen used to be extremely proper. Her daughter's potty mouth was a continual embarrassment. The quip is surreal.

'Apologies, Jen.' Ellen covers her face. 'I've been spending too much time with Matty.'

'Like mother, like daughter?' I question Claire. She slides down the sofa to affect shame while giving a devilish grin.

'This has plagued Doreen for decades.' Ellen's seriousness ends our comedy act. 'I visit her often. She's never stopped talking about how Kelly didn't kill herself. When Graham died, Doreen tried to investigate it but didn't get far.' Ellen practically spits Graham's name. 'Now there's not long left, she wants to find out the truth.'

Ellen dabs at her eyes. It's been a long time since I've seen someone use a handkerchief. Mums used to carry them. Not mine though. She never cried. Johnny always had one to mop up my tears.

'I'm not sure I can offer anything useful,' I say.

I await a reply of, 'You had nothing to do with this. Have a cuppa and a chocolate biscuit before you go and let's never meet again.' Of course, it doesn't happen.

'I'm sure you know stuff.' Claire's stare could cut Teflon.

'You *must* know something,' Ellen adds.

'Wow, you two really are reporters.' I try to sound calm, against feeling like I'm stuck in an inquisition.

'Not me anymore,' Ellen says. 'I retired a while ago but like to keep involved.'

Lucky me for joining these roving reporters. I have so much they can uncover.

Claire grips my hand. Her rings dent my fingers. I swallow the gasp, remembering "Crusher Claire" and her wrestling obsession. The memory is unsettling. No way do I want to get on her wrong side.

Claire eases the hold. 'I saw both of you coming back from school, after they told us it was shut. Remember the tree that fell on it?'

'That storm was something else,' Ellen says. 'I get so annoyed every time we have a fart of wind, pardon my French, and someone likens it to the Great Storm.'

'Anyway,' Claire interrupts Ellen's reminiscing, 'I was sent to school too, even though I told Mum it wouldn't be open. I think she knew and wanted me out of her way for a bit.' She gives Ellen an affectionate wink.

I recall Mum sending Dad up on the roof to replace tiles. She summoned me from bed too, to hold a swaying ladder while we ducked the storm's carnage. Mum declared it was character building even though she didn't help. No one asked for Liam's assistance.

Claire breaks into the memory. 'I stopped off at the corner shop for sweets and saw you and Kelly. I shouted but you didn't answer.'

'We had to get back so I could check Mandy was with Liz Norman.'

Liz spared me a chore by taking Mandy to and from school in her van. I didn't go with them as I enjoyed being alone with Johnny until I had to walk with Kelly.

'At what point did you leave Kelly?' Claire asks.

'Why do you ask?'

Breathe, Jen, breathe.

'I'm wondering when you left as I spoke to Kelly on the railway track. She was upset and covered in blood.'

My pulse beats in my ears. A flash of memory attacks my mind; a scarlet pool forming around a body.

If Claire saw her alive, when did Kelly actually die?

I thought it was instant.

14

16TH OCTOBER 1987

Compared to other parts of the country, Oxfordshire came off lightly from the storm. Items strewn across the estate and debris from battered houses still ignited Claire's reporter instinct.

She regarded Mr Avery's Cortina, caved in by half a wall and keeping her away from her investigation. Claire helped to move each brick, hoping for early release from the mind-numbing task. She often assisted others, especially where gossip could be gleaned. However, shifting bricks from one pile to another took up valuable time she could spend interviewing the estate's residents for her radio show. Mr Avery was a dull man who gave one-word answers. Noticing Claire's waning enthusiasm, he sent her away with a handful of Murray Mints for her efforts.

Claire carefully selected the interviewees for her radio project. Each week she recorded *Into the Woods Radio* on cassette. Family and friends were "encouraged" to listen. They always did. A sulky Claire was most persuasive.

Tanya Madd, from Monet Drive, was a poor interview choice but so far the day had offered slim pickings. Most people stayed inside, either afraid the storm would return or making the most of an unexpected day off.

Tanya sat on the park bench, smoking and swishing her pony-tail like an agitated mare. Her tracksuit radiated neon green with an orange trim. For the sake of professionalism, Claire willed her sarcastic nature to be silent.

When asked to give her opinion on the storm, Tanya appeared to welcome the opportunity. Eager to have something to report, Claire joined her and pressed the *record* button. Before Claire began her questions, Tanya opened her mouth and spat into the microphone. The only comment given, 'You're such a loser.'

Claire snatched the tape recorder away, shaking the mike. Never one to be defeated, she replied, 'I'm a loser? Still haven't got a job? Still lounging about on your fat arse?'

'Come here, you gobby bint.' Tanya had a generous rear but the truth wasn't one she cared to hear.

She hauled herself from the bench and flicked her cigarette at Claire. The situation became serious. Tanya never gave up on a smoke. Claire had learned the reporter's art of self-preservation when Ellen taught her how to spot an incoming punch. Confident of her advantage over Tanya's daily two packs of cigarettes level of fitness, Claire scarpered. She headed for the train track on the edge of the estate. Tanya was unlikely to make it that far.

Never knowing when to quit, Claire couldn't resist making jibes as she ran. She mocked Tanya's unmarried parents who "churned out babies like they were on a factory line". To Ellen's horror, Claire often repeated her mum's opinions.

Claire held on to the tape recorder, considering how to extract phlegm from the microphone. She feared touching it and contracting an STD. Tanya's sexual favours to the estate boys, in exchange for a toot of speed, were infamous. Rumours spread she'd offered herself to Troddington's main dealer to cut out the middle-men, or boys. The pusher turned her down. Tanya shook it off and continued to trade with the lads.

Safely out of Tanya's sights, Claire came to a halt. *Here* was a story.

'This is Claire Woods, reporting for *Into the Woods Radio*. I'm at the scene of the railway track on the edge of the Rembrandt Estate, a popular place for dog walkers and kids wanting to hang out. Devastation is all around. The view is one tantamount to an apocalypse.' She mentally high-fived her sophisticated vocabulary. 'This long-forgotten line has become even more of a wasteland. Trees are uprooted and lay across the banks, like bodies slashed at the feet. Fortunately, the track is clear and the sporadic trains that still pass through will not be disrupted in their daily business.'

She continued walking, scanning for officials. Everyone knew the railway track was off limits. It made it more desirable to the estate's children, and for adults using a shortcut into town. The maintenance men who appeared usually ignored trespassers. The more officious took names. Colleagues ribbed them mercilessly when they reported Richard Head or Drew Peacock for being on the line.

Claire was on a mission to find something worth reporting. Fallen trees were okay but she craved reporters' gold. She believed she'd struck it when a figure in the near distance emerged from the ground. *What the hell are they doing, lying on the track?* she thought. *Do they have a death wish?* This could be the story.

When Kelly Pratt came into view, Claire's notions of reporter stardom faded. Kelly was always picking herself up off the floor, often because someone put her there. Moving in closer, Claire realised this was more than a scuffle. Kelly's hands were covered in blood.

'Are you okay?' Claire berated herself for the amateur question. It would never elevate her to the level of the *BBC News* team.

Kelly looked up. Claire gasped. The blood saturating Kelly's shoulders became visible as she bent to pick up her glasses. Blood stained her back and a slick patch darkened her brown hair. Unable to tolerate the sight of blood, Claire swayed. Her parents always turned the television off when *Casualty* came on. Unfortunately, she couldn't switch off this particular view.

'Flipping hell, Kelly. What happened? We need to get an ambulance.'

Kelly touched the back of her head. She brought her hand forward to assess the damage. 'It's fine. It's not bleeding as much.' She slipped on her broken glasses.

Claire wanted to weep at the sight of the damaged girl. It was well known Kelly's life was dreadful. If Graham wasn't slapping Doreen around, his boot went into Kelly, who was already sporting bruises from the bullies.

Claire never heard Kelly complain, cry, or tell on anyone. It was difficult to comprehend and made Claire feel even more conflicted about Kelly. Sometimes she wanted to hold and soothe her, which was ridiculous. They were both fourteen, and beyond open displays of affection. Other times, Claire fought the urge to give Kelly a slap to make her fight back.

Claire didn't understand a victim's life. No one bullied her, not least because Ellen would hunt them down. Claire was brash, funny, and a fighter; attributes that made her popular.

She'd developed an interest in wrestling when her dad rooted out his Big Daddy match videos. The big splash move was a work in progress. She'd practised it on a kid at school when he called his sister retarded because of her speech impediment. Claire slipped and kicked him in the mouth.

Later, his mum appeared at the Woods' house, demanding compensation for the false teeth her son needed. He grinned, revealing gaps. The smile disappeared when Claire related how the boy hit his sister and called her names. The little bully not only lost teeth but also the feeling in his backside when he returned home and the slipper came out.

'I'm okay.' Kelly disrupted Claire's memories.

'You don't look it. What happened?' Claire focused on Kelly's face rather than the carnage.

Kelly removed her glasses. Claire noted deep brown eyes that had previously gone unnoticed. Kelly was almost attractive. Her clothes needed updating and her teeth a good scrape, but she had potential. Claire was annoyed with herself for evaluating a person's worth by their appearance. She wished she was more like Johnny and Jen, who had their own style and didn't care what anyone thought.

'I was talking to someone, got a little excited, and fell over,' Kelly said.

'Who?'

'No one you know.' Kelly cleaned glasses she'd never wear again.

'You can tell me. I'll sort them out.' Claire pulled herself up, exerting the full four feet and ten inches of her physical authority.

'No, you won't.' Kelly spoke to herself then addressed Claire. 'I'm going home to clean up in a bit. I want a few minutes on my own.'

Kelly's confident tone quietened Claire's niggling concerns. 'Make sure Doreen takes you to the doctor. Will you be okay?'

Kelly sat on the side of the track, tightening the strap on her shoe. 'Don't worry. Thank you though. You never know who your true friends are.'

Claire knew no reply would be sufficient. Kelly wasn't her friend and they both knew it. Claire walked away, waving a farewell.

Claire considered why she hadn't helped Kelly. She would never have left Jen alone in such a state. The guilt receded when Claire returned home. It disappeared when she played the radio show to Ellen, who heaped on praise.

...

A burden of remorse hit Claire the next day. The estate buzzed with the news Kelly had died on the track. For the first time, Claire Woods, reporter extraordinaire, didn't want to pursue the story.

PRESENT

Claire's shame at leaving Kelly on the railway track is noticeable. I hope mine isn't. Claire's account of that day makes me question many things. When did Kelly die? Was it before the train hit her? Did I strike a blow that brought a slow death?

Claire fiddles with her hair. I hate myself for saying nothing to ease her guilt.

'I should have stayed, or at least walked her home,' Claire says.

'You weren't to know, darling,' Ellen replies. 'I've said it many times. Doreen understands you did your best.'

Ellen cocoons her daughter within a voluminous cardigan. Liz's caring smile flashes into my mind. She was the mum I never had. I look away from Claire and Ellen to watch the hands of a carriage clock tick.

'Would you like a cup of tea, sweetheart?' Ellen asks Claire.

'Yes please.'

'Jen, why don't you come and help?' It's not a request. Suspicious of this ruse for us to be alone, I join her.

Ellen's kitchen is modern but homely. The scratches etched into the table signify many family meals held there. Personalised table mats have Ellen, Claire, Seb, and Matty's names on them. I consider the tragic scene of Doodle and me eating our dinners from named trays.

The kettle takes forever to boil. Ellen's staring rivals the pressure a *Countdown* contestant is under when working against the clock to come up with a satisfactory answer. Ellen hasn't asked anything yet, but it's coming.

'You have a beautiful house.' It's the best I have. Everyone likes to know they have good taste.

'Thank you. It's certainly a step up from Renoir Road.' She's paving the way to take us back. 'Do you ever think about the Rembrandt Estate?' Ellen finally begins.

'No. You remember I left when I was sixteen.'

'Yes, I do.'

She turns to get mugs from the shelf. Reaching up high with ease, I wonder where Claire got her short-arse genetics from. Alex is tall too.

'You were living with Freddie and Liz before, weren't you?'

'Yes.' Ellen knows I was. Why must we dance around?

I picture both their faces this time. Liz, with a halo of auburn wild curls bursting forth. Freddie is ruddy-faced, with mischief-making eyes. Whenever I consider them, they're always happy. It gives me peace. When I left, I expect they were far from happy.

'Lovely people, the Normans,' Ellen says. 'I never believed a word of those allegations against Freddie. Mud sticks though, particularly on a council estate.'

'What do you mean?'

'Didn't you know your brother alleged Freddie had been inappropriate with him?' She acts surprised.

She was angling to share this from the beginning. This is why we are in the kitchen, making tea no one wants. The Brit remedy for tragedies and traumas is tea. I prefer coffee.

She continues. 'I refused to put it in the paper. The editor threatened me with the sack but I soon made him see sense.' Tea splashes over the sides of the mugs as she whacks in sugar. I pity her past editor. 'It was a relief when nothing came of it.'

'What happened?'

'It wasn't long after Mandy had gone. I expect you don't know she left as soon as she could too. Patricia took Liam to Troddington police station. All and sundry were informed that Freddie needed locking up for touching her son. She said it happened years ago when Liam went to collect Mandy from the Normans' flat and she wasn't there.'

'Liam never picked Mandy up from anywhere. Anyway, Freddie wouldn't do something like that.' I didn't think I could be more ashamed of my family. I was wrong.

'Most of us didn't believe it either, but you know what those nasty bitches on the estate were like. Felicity Smith set up a campaign to get him removed, giving out leaflets labelling him a paedophile. As she was posting one through my letterbox, I opened the door and told her she could stick it where her husband feared to enter.'

Despite the seriousness of the situation, I can't help but laugh. Someone had to confront Felicity. The woman's poison dripped over the estate. If she didn't like you, she tried her best to push you out. She passed it off as a responsibility of her made-up Neighbourhood Watch coordinator role. We didn't even have Neighbourhood Watch. No one could so much as pass wind without everyone knowing. An official programme wasn't needed for us to keep an eye on each other.

'Felicity didn't succeed, did she.'

'No. Freddie and Liz had enough friends to make sure of it. Most figured it was bullshit.' Mortified at her swearing, Ellen slaps her wrist.

'Do you think Mum was behind it?' I already know the answer.

'I had a chat with Kevin Brown, an old contact. He was a PC at the time and was there when Patricia made the allegation. She took over, insisting Liam was traumatised, so she'd speak for him. Your brother was an adult and he hardly needed looking after.'

Mum was never far away from Liam.

Ellen continues. 'Weird thing is, Kev said Liam seemed bored. Whereas Patricia was hysterical and threatening all kinds of action against the police if they didn't cooperate.'

I can visualise her, decked out in a fake fur coat, hair tonged, and reeking of perfume. She's slapping her hands on the front desk and digging in manicured talons.

Ellen rummages around a cupboard, bringing out a packet of biscuits. She resumes the story. 'Poor Kev said he didn't know what was scarier: Patricia wailing like a banshee or Liam staring right through him.'

'What happened?'

'It was soon thrown out. No proof whatsoever. Your mother let it drop, having already done the damage. Freddie was gutted and Liz distraught. I'm glad neither you nor Mandy witnessed it.'

I haven't felt the embarrassment of being a Taylor for years. When I meet someone new, I never mention my family. It scares me how the sense of culpability has returned. I don't want to make apologies for my parents' and Liam's actions again. Those ties were severed.

'I'm sorry.' Old habits die hard.

'What have you got to apologise for, love?' Ellen offers a garibaldi. I shake my hand away from them. Squashed fly biscuits are rank.

'Your mother was a beast.'

Ellen's judgement is refreshing. Adults never said anything negative about Mum. They didn't seem to see what youngsters did. Mum's peers were either fooled or frightened.

'I'm sorry to speak ill of the dead, but she was a detestable woman.' Ellen flings the biscuits onto the counter.

Mum is dead.

16

1ST APRIL 1986

G ladys Greene, from Picasso Way, would have turned in her grave, if she was in it. She was close to getting there, this being the day of her funeral. Her son, Ray, agonised over the date. When the funeral director proposed first April, Ray requested another day. Superstitious Gladys wouldn't have tolerated a burial on April Fools' Day. Ray halted the process of looking for other dates and put himself first for once. He'd gone beyond devotion in caring for Gladys for years. If life could begin at sixty-four, this was his time.

Gladys had had a good innings. Living to ninety-two was a blessing and a curse. Ray adored his mother even though she unwittingly became his jailer. From childhood, he'd intended to leave home as soon as possible. The desire to make a fortune increased until his father died of a heart attack when Ray was seventeen. United in grief, Ray stayed to mourn, alongside Gladys. Then he stayed and stayed some more. Whenever Gladys moved house, he swore this time he'd go, and yet his possessions always made their way to the spare room.

Never a fan of making a fuss, Gladys prided herself on not bothering the doctor with her ailments. Ray wished she had. She endured a set of complications, resulting in her body shutting down. Gladys was from hardy stock that got on and did until she no longer could.

When Ray finally persuaded her to seek medical advice, it exposed the consequences of her pride. Poorly managed diabetes meant she couldn't walk unaided. Her eyesight diminished until the world disappeared. Gladys became housebound.

She begged her son to leave. Carers could have tended to her, but the reality was Ray had nowhere to go. Living with Gladys was all he knew and it gave him a purpose. Alone, he'd have to start again. He hadn't been ready to cut his mother's apron strings. Death severed the cord.

Ray stroked the glossy white coffin, recalling papery blanched hands touching surroundings to find their way. Gladys's stubbornness often resulted in Ray finding her lying on the floor. When he left the room, she asserted her independence. Each time she fell. Gladys hated being a burden.

The Rembrandt Estate grapevine shook with the news Gladys's coffin lay in the Greenes' living room. Children dared each other to sneak a peek. Heavy net curtains preserved Gladys's dignity. Undeterred, the youngsters created stories of her haunting the estate. Younger kids went home before dark. Their older siblings took them, relieved to have the excuse. Neurotic adults stated a dead body spread germs if left in your house. Others cracked inappropriate jokes to mask a fear of death.

Doreen understood Ray's need to have Gladys near. Doreen had enjoyed sitting with the old woman after she'd brought over a meal. Ray insisted he could cook. Gladys confided to Doreen how four days on the trot of baked beans on toast was wearing. Wanting to help, Doreen made extra dinner when it escaped Graham's notice. As soon as her husband left to do whatever he did of an evening, she took a plate of food round to Gladys. Having the Greenes' company made her believe she had the better end of the deal. When she began helping them, she didn't realise she'd receive empathy for the first time on the Rembrandt Estate. She didn't expect Ray would offer even more.

Marriage was sacrosanct for Doreen. From the moment she spoke them, her marriage vows remained unbroken. Hidden from sight, as Graham's chainsaw snoring increased in volume, Doreen sat in the darkness of the dining room. Loyalty wouldn't allow her to fantasise about another man when lying next to her spouse.

Ray wasn't particularly good looking and he hadn't turned her head. His plainness gave her security. She knew she was no oil painting herself and Graham often reminded her of the fact. It was Ray's kindness that proved irresistible.

Ray knew Doreen's ugly truths. He noticed the injuries and listened to her accounts. Until Graham's death, Ray was the only person she told of her husband's abusiveness. In contrast, Ray was a gentle soul. Unlike macho men who had something to prove, he didn't threaten violence in return. Instead, he offered Doreen a way out. Whenever he proposed escape, she refused.

That day was their turning point and not because of Gladys's burial. Doreen's answer had to be final. Ray was moving. Being a stationery salesman allowed him to relocate anywhere in England. The next day he was leaving for Northumberland. Moving as far north as possible felt right. The new start needed to be far away from Oxfordshire and its memories.

Doreen cut the sandwiches into triangles for the wake. The kitchen clock ticked, counting down her prospects. Kelly whistled a tune as she took sausage rolls from the oven. Doreen appreciated her daughter lightening the sombre mood. Kelly didn't know Ray and Doreen were not only mourning Gladys but also the death of their relationship.

Doreen could not leave.

Ray promised to make a home for her and Kelly. She believed Kelly would be happier, living with this man. She doted on him. He'd already become a father figure in helping with her homework, playing board games, and listening to her incessant chatter. Doreen regretted allowing their bond to form.

Doreen could not leave.

From the moment she met Graham, Doreen's chances of happiness evaporated. Kelly would grow up and move on into a future of freedom. Doreen had made her bed. Messy and tangled as it was, she had to lie in it. As a matter of ownership, Graham would never let her go. If she left, he wouldn't rest until he brought her home. Ray didn't deserve a life of looking over his shoulder. Doreen refused to be the anchor holding him back.

'We have to go,' Ray said, touching her cheek.

Doreen startled, relieved Kelly hadn't seen. Following Ray, Doreen took a breath and prayed for strength.

A gathering of the estate's residents stood outside: some to see a coffin for the first time, others to report on the funeral details, many to say goodbye to one of their own. Respectful parents removed boys' caps. Heads bowed. A hush descended. Gladys Greene left the Rembrandt Estate.

…

The next day, Ray Greene left too. Watching his car turn out of the estate, Doreen struggled to stay upright.

'We should have gone too,' Kelly said, holding her mum around the waist.

Doreen could not reply. Kelly knew more than Doreen realised. Shielding the girl had proved useless.

Just over a year later, Doreen tortured herself for allowing Ray to leave alone. If she and Kelly had left with him, her daughter would still be alive.

17

PRESENT

The humming of the fridge in Ellen's kitchen is the only sound. She shrouds herself within her cardigan. I have no words.

'Your mum died about five or six years ago,' Ellen says. 'I thought you knew. It was a heart attack. Doreen found out from one of the old dears who attends Aylesbury's community centre. She used to be Patricia's cleaner. Only woman I've ever known to have a cleaner for a council house. That was Patricia for you.'

How do I process this information? I spent most of my life wishing Mum would disappear. Grieving for her would be hypocritical. I didn't want her as a mother and she certainly didn't want me. Her biggest regret was not stopping at one child. She regularly told Mandy and me she'd only ever wanted Liam.

'Are you okay?' Ellen steps back to assess the damage. 'For once I'm sorry I was the one to break the news.'

I shrug. Better to hear it from her than to deal with Dad or Liam. Does Mandy know? I'm certain she would've taken it similarly. It's like when you read of a celebrity's death. It may be a shock but it's none of your business.

'I hate to speak ill of the dead, but Patricia was evil for what she did to you and Mandy.' Ellen slams down the mugs of tea.

I find my voice. 'What do you mean?' What does she know of my childhood?

'I saw the bruises when you played with Claire. I regret making myself believe your claims that you were clumsy.'

'I *was* clumsy.' Remembering how I wore long sleeves to hide the evidence, I rub my forearms. Some habits are ingrained.

'I knew how difficult Patricia could be,' Ellen says. 'Once, she grabbed Mandy so hard her arm almost wrenched out of the socket. I shouted over, pretending to want to speak to Patricia. She let go of Mandy and the poor girl dropped to the floor.'

I don't need to imagine it. This is one event, of many, I remember.

Ellen continues. 'I asked about putting an advert in the paper for her clear-up initiative. The face she pasted on, from previously being so spiteful, was chilling. She picked Mandy up, said, "Silly thing is always falling over," and carried on as if nothing happened. I should've done something.'

'Why didn't you?' I push the chair back and it hits the oven. 'Why didn't you help us? There were so many adults on the estate and not one of you intervened.' My younger self is screaming at the grown-up who didn't save me. 'We needed someone like you to speak for us. We were only children.'

Ellen's eyes dart left to right. 'I was afraid. Some residents didn't take kindly to me covering their misdemeanours in the paper.'

'What on earth has that got to do with this?'

'They smashed our windows, slashed my car tyres, and even put a burning copy of the newspaper through the letterbox. They could've done something to Claire. So I stayed out of estate business afterwards. I didn't report on anyone who lived there, calling it a conflict of interest. I stupidly ignored what Patricia was doing too. She was a formidable woman, I confess, I didn't want to cross.'

'You think I don't know what she was like?'

Anger tingles around my body. I'm scared I could hurt Ellen for allowing Mum to continue the abuse. Pushing my nails into my palms, I retreat. Ellen reaches for the sink behind her. She's petrified. I'm afraid of me too. When I'm in this strange place, I kill people.

Claire enters the room. 'What's going on?'

Ellen puts her arms around me. Claire joins in, sensing the need to diffuse the situation.

'I'm so very sorry.' Ellen repeats the apology as if it will magically erase the damage.

The word *sorry* penetrates the place in me seeking self-preservation. It's one I often used when faced with Mum's annoyance or for covering up the truth. I refuse to be that sorry person anymore.

'It wasn't as terrible as you think. I was accident prone. Mum got a little moody sometimes.' Removing myself from the huddle, I step towards the door.

'But Jen—'

'Leave it, Mum.' My childhood friend can still detect my emotions.

Ellen gets the message. 'Let's focus on finding out what happened to Kelly, shall we?' She scoops up the mugs and leans away from me as she passes. I resolve to work harder on controlling my anger.

I join them, knowing we'll be facing more complex matters than uncovering my mum's sadistic depths. As a family, I believed we'd done an acceptable job of hiding it.

My secrets are being discovered. Hopefully, this is where it ends.

18

12TH OCTOBER 1987

Alex Woods knew living under the roof of two reporters, at different stages of their vocations, was risky. When engaging in a secret life, you had to be extra careful under journalistic observation. This time he'd gone too far. The adage about not defecating on your own doorstep summed up the situation.

To date, Ellen had discovered two of his affairs. There were more but he wasn't foolish enough to question her investigative skills. Alex considered himself lucky she forgave those she knew about.

Being a postman had its perks. Getting plenty of fresh air and not being cooped up in an office were two. Having such a sociable job was another. Women were always on the other side of a door.

Alex despised his cheating alter ego. He tried to fight it but blamed being a textbook cheat on deceitful genes. His mum had left when he was five. The cliché of running away with the fair held true. His dad, fortified by whisky, shared stories of what a lying whore Alex's mother was. Instead of winning a goldfish at the fair, she bagged herself the bloke from the waltzers.

Alex found it easier to blame his unfaithfulness on his mum than to take responsibility for his actions. As soon as he was old enough to have a girlfriend, he decided having more than one at a time increased the odds of finding "The One". He was content loving and leaving them until Ellen came along.

When he heard her bawling out a man for trying it on, outside the chip shop, he knew he'd met the woman he would marry. Ellen was more than his equal. They married and had a child. Alex thought he had it cracked. For years he remained in a blissful bubble of family and faithfulness.

Then the itch ignited. It tingled under his skin at night and crackled by day. Other women existed. Alex noticed their allure beyond mothering and being a wife. Females were the kryptonite he needed to scratch away.

He didn't want to go for a drink when the woman asked as he handed over her parcels. He vowed to have one and then return home. Several pints later, he woke in an unfamiliar bed, to a familiar shame. He told Ellen he'd stayed at a mate's house. Her face contorted with duelling disbelief and flimsy trust.

The affairs began. Two discovered, threats to leave, and promises made. Promises were made to be broken.

...

Ellen stirred the casserole. A longing seized Alex as she lifted her hair, exposing the back of her neck. He'd never stopped loving her. Ellen had curves in all the right places and a sharp wit that confirmed he was punching way above his weight. She remained the only woman he'd ever want to spend the rest of his life with. Still, the damn itch distracted him.

There was the added complication of a fourteen-year-old daughter who was getting wise. Claire was the compass of the Woods' marriage. They'd planned their only child as such. Neither Ellen nor Alex could imagine sharing their parental love between several children. Alex considered the irony of how he could readily share his affections among many women. Claire was a different matter. He knew he would eventually let her down. She asked questions about where he went and what he did in the increasing absences. A postman works set hours. The pool of excuses ran shallow.

Alex watched Claire and Jen, lowering their heads over the books scattered across the kitchen table. Alex was pleased Claire had such a loyal friend. Jen was a great girl who, Alex couldn't fail to notice, was no longer a child. He shook the nastiness away. He would not be *that* man. Shame already gnawed inside when he considered how appalled his family would be with his latest indiscretion.

No, you certainly do not crap on your doorstep, but Alex was doing his business far too close to home. The thrill of hiding in alleyways on the estate, with his bit on the side, made his head and other parts throb. It had to stop. It was beyond wrong.

Ellen offered the spoon for him to sample the casserole. *Just a taste*, he thought. Alex's problem was that he never took a little. He had to have it all.

He regarded his innocent wife. 'It's perfect. Don't change a thing.'

Alex had to end the affair. He hoped she would be a good girl and not make a fuss. Otherwise, he'd have to silence her.

19

PRESENT

I turn on the light and shut the door on the world, within the safety of my cottage. The sofa is my target. Doodle knows my weary body won't make it to bed. A ginger ball of fluff lies across my feet, staking its sleeping claim. We tussle for the blanket. As usual, he wins.

It begins.

We're investigating Kelly's death. How did I get here when I'd removed myself from it as far as possible?

When I left Ellen's house, Claire's eager voice assaulted my ears. A new story is in her sights and she won't let go of it. I hope I'm clever enough to lead her in the wrong direction. Claire's lost none of her ditziness, but she's still shrewd.

Ellen's content to take a back seat in doing her part from home. Apparently, we "youngsters" can do the legwork. I'm aware I'm not young anymore. When I chat with my colleagues at Listening Ear, my middle age becomes obvious. Mentions of *Bagpuss* result in blank faces. The only reason they are aware The Clash existed is from the mass-produced reproduction tops they buy from the high street.

Johnny and I considered sixteen as the golden age. Exams over, we'd be able to leave home. Reaching our forties was never in our plans. Sixteen was always the goal. How could we foresee I'd ruin everything before we reached it?

Claire's going to network with other reporters, trawl newspaper archives, and call in favours with the police. I didn't ask why the police owe her. Ellen's finger on her lips signified I didn't want to know. Troddington no longer has a police station. The nearest is fifteen miles away. Ellen ranted about cutbacks. Claire's willing to go there, with daughter Matty tagging along. The instinct to gain justice within that family is strong. Matty wants to be a lawyer. The future criminal world should reconsider its options if she's as tenacious as her mum.

Claire and Ellen haven't given me much of a task yet. I explained how busy I am working at the counselling practice, studying, and doing voluntary work. The praise-seeking do-gooder image makes me cringe. I realise I was trying to convince Ellen I'm not the earthquake that had erupted in her kitchen.

Impressed by my busyness, Ellen directed me to record memories around the day of Kelly's death, in case anything useful comes to mind. I'll cobble together a believable fiction placing me nowhere near the railway track. Creativity is lacking tonight. They can wait for the lies. It shouldn't take long. Lying is second nature. In some ways, I am like my mum.

Mum is dead.

Convention says I should be upset. Instead, I'm numb. I was dead to her the moment I was born. When I was old enough to realise she'd never be affectionate, I mourned her. For me, Patricia Taylor died a long time ago.

I leave the lamp on and close my eyes. The darkness enhances disturbing pictures running through my head. The reel illuminates onto the canvas of my mind. Having a light on throughout the night sometimes keeps the twisted film of the past at bay.

Doodle stretches and settles. The clock above the fireplace ticks hypnotically. Maybe, for the first time since I was a child, I'll sleep through the night.

20

15TH OCTOBER 1987

'You're a liar,' Johnny said.

'Up yours. Where do you get off, calling me a liar?' Jen wouldn't allow anyone to question her honesty. She shoved Johnny off their wall at the top of the estate.

Milking a phantom injury, he lay on the ground. 'You've broken my arm.' He rubbed the limb and gave a wink. 'Do you know a doctor who can fix it?'

Jen forgave the insult. He believed in her ambition when most people scorned it. Council estate kids weren't supposed to have aspirations. Johnny understood the desire to follow a dream others didn't understand. Ever since his older brothers, Ian and Anthony, discovered Johnny wanted to be a vet, they'd begun the Dr Doolittle jibes. Dead mice and birds on his pillow followed.

'Fix that, vet boy.' Anthony would point and cackle at the deceased creature. Johnny rarely fought but where animals or his mum were concerned, he didn't hesitate. A tussle with his brother had taken place earlier. The squashed frog inside Johnny's boots took it too far.

Touching the bruise forming on his cheek, Johnny figured a grazed elbow from falling off a wall was a small concern, compared to Anthony, who came out of their spat with a few less brain cells, if he'd had any to begin with. Johnny chuckled at his choice of weapon. Whacking Anthony over the head with Benny's Optimus Prime was a smack of genius. The Transformers saved the day. Ever the accomplished villain, Anthony would seek revenge. Johnny resolved to sleep with one eye open and his boots under the bed.

Jen jumped off the wall and stamped her foot. 'I'm not lying. There *is* a storm coming. My dad spoke to a bloke who works in Budgens, whose brother's into weather stuff.'

'Meteorology,' Johnny said.

'Yeah, that. The bloke's brother says there's going to be one hell of a storm. Biggest one to happen in centuries.'

'It isn't even windy.' Johnny held out a finger to check. 'You know better than to listen to the rubbish Mike spouts after he's been to the pub. Was he drunk?'

'No.' The need to defend her dad when he never did the same for her was baffling. It was 5pm and he'd shared the information an hour earlier. Lager fumes penetrated his breath.

'Chill out, Wincey Willis. I believe you.'

Jen needed Johnny's belief. She couldn't imagine life without him. He was the only person she wanted to while hours away with: talking, sharing dreams, and forging a deeper connection.

Johnny stood and checked his jacket for tears. 'Hope school is shut tomorrow. I can't be doing with art and that moulding clay rubbish. We spend the lesson chucking it at each other. I get the whole day with you if we have a day off too.'

Jen spotted Johnny's "Mods Rule" badge, lying on the grass. It must have fallen off when she'd pushed him. She knelt as if to tie her laces and pocketed it. Stealing from Johnny was wrong but taking the item meant having him close, without the embarrassment of confessing.

. . .

Johnny decided never to tell her he'd seen her take the badge and the excitement he felt knowing she wanted something of his.

Jen also hoped school would be closed so she wouldn't have to walk with Kelly. Jen couldn't tolerate being around the needy girl for much longer. Kelly didn't take hints. When Jen put headphones on, Kelly still nattered. She seemed to hold her words in overnight and spewed them out in the morning. Jen heard Graham favoured a silent house. Kelly probably only got to talk at length once she was outside. Jen tussled with the guilt of not liking the girl. She tried to be nice, but truthfully she wished Kelly would go away.

'Penny for them?' Johnny poked her.

Jen stuck out her tongue, pretending to be disgusted at his touch, and shook her head. Her thoughts were worth little. An inner conflict raged that she, of all people, had unkind feelings about a fellow girl born into grim circumstances. Knowing she had friends and was strong, she ignored the discomfort. Jen Taylor would never be like the Kelly Pratts of this world.

'Wonder where he's going,' Johnny said, as Alex Woods gave them a half-hearted wave. They watched as he turned around into the estate, quickening his step.

'Claire says he goes out a lot. She asked me to help spy on him but we'll only get caught. It's weird how people on this estate always have secrets.'

Back on the wall, Jen held her Walkman aloft as a sign. Johnny sat beside her. Over time they'd perfected a routine of stretching a set of headphones to be joined by the music. Their heads touched. Jen wondered if thoughts worked like osmosis and hers would seep from her brain and into his. Nervous at the idea, she placed her hand between them to create a gap.

The song began. Johnny gasped. 'Spandau Ballet? Seriously?'

Jen ejected the tape. Mandy had used her Walkman again.

21

PRESENT

I've been at work for hours and achieved little. It's been a difficult week since I saw Doreen, Ellen, and Claire. I can't sleep. Every time I shut my eyes, a pained face appears. Last night, I gave up forcing sleep to come. I put on my gear and ran until I was exhausted.

Nicole was horrified when I mentioned going on night runs. In a mentoring session we discussed my coping strategies for balancing work and study. Running helps to conquer my body and mind. When I run, my head empties and my feet offer an escape. Sometimes I don't want to turn back. Nicole gave me a rollicking for running alone in the dark. I brushed it off, careful not to add that, if someone attacked me, Doreen and Kelly would have justice in my brutal death.

Passing my office, Nicole waves in acknowledgement. I can see she's concerned. I'm trying to keep up the illusion of being in control but jangled nerves and hitting the bottle aren't helping. This morning the wine fog descended and I didn't have the energy to iron a shirt. Getting caffeine down my neck was more important than being presentable. This isn't me. Tapping the keyboard mimics the composed and busy person I used to be. The screen spouts gibberish.

'Don't worry, love, I can see her.' I recognise the voice infiltrating my workplace. Claire stands behind the computer.

She looks more like the old Claire, in a flowery dress, battered denim jacket, and DMs. Ellen's wardrobe is safe, for once. The eclectic look suits Claire. Why she steals her mum's clothes when she's got her own style is baffling. I remember how Claire wasn't as confident as she wanted people to believe.

'How's it going, numpty?' She's determined to continue using the abusive terms of endearment from our childhood.

I don't answer in kind. 'What are you doing here?'

'Nice way to talk to your mate.' She creates shapes with paperclips across the desk. Damn her for looking so vulnerable.

'I wasn't expecting you and I've got a lot of work to do.' I snatch the tub of paperclips from her. She's disrupting my system.

'Get up late this morning?' Claire asks. 'Your hair could do with a brush. I always envied you being a brunette. My mousy mop was hideous.' She flicks her blonde streaks, waiting for a compliment, and then pouts when my hangover slows my reactions.

Alerted by Claire's booming voice, Nicole joins us. 'There's nothing that can't wait while you go to lunch.'

'The rotas have to be sorted for next week.' I shuffle papers to show my workload. Nicole raises an eyebrow. I am holding brochures, not rotas.

Claire sits on the corner of the desk. 'You need some time out. Doesn't she?'

Nicole extends a hand to Claire. 'Hi, I'm Nicole. Jen's boss, I suppose, although this place would fall to pieces without her. Go for a break, Jen. You look like you could do with it.'

Great. Nicole has noticed what a state I am, even after a quick whore's bath from the ladies' sinks and ingesting a packet of Polos. She's always polished, with her hair cut in a neat bob, and clothes so starched they could stand up alone.

'I'm Claire. Jen and I were besties.' She beams at the fact.

I warm to her. She used to be a ray of sunshine in an often-dark existence. I didn't realise she considered us such close friends. Johnny and I worried she felt excluded, although we tried to include her as much as possible.

'Lovely to meet you. Enjoy your lunch.' Nicole lifts me from the chair, adding a shove towards the door.

Claire whispers as Nicole leaves, 'She wears nice threads. Her jacket's definitely a designer label.'

Barely able to focus on what I'm wearing, let alone Nicole, I don't reply. Approaching the reception area, I glare at Temp Number Four of this month, for allowing Claire into the office. Temp Number Four responds with a glazed expression and continues swiping on her phone.

'Don't blame her for letting me in,' Claire says.

'I wasn't.'

'I know you. When people don't do things the way you want, you get stroppy. Just like your…' She colours. 'Never mind.'

I do her the favour of ignoring it. Focusing instead on why Claire has hunted me down. What does she know?

22

PRESENT

We head to the park around the corner. Claire leads me to a bench facing the playground. There's a chill in the air which I accept as a potential hangover cure.

'Sorry you didn't know your mum is dead,' Claire says. 'If it helps, Mike's alive.'

'Does he still live on the estate?'

'Mum said he does.'

'Right.' I'm not surprised Dad hasn't moved. That requires being proactive.

'Liam is–'

'I don't want to talk about him.' To emphasise the point, I kick the bench leg. Liam's nothing to me. As for Mandy, it hurts. I've tried to find her but never succeeded. 'Do you know where Mandy is?'

Claire shakes her head, and my hope vanishes. 'She went to Southampton University. After, I'm not sure. Do you want me to look into it?'

'No thanks.' I don't want Claire's pity and there's already too much going on. I will take her up on the offer in the future though. I'm determined to find my sister and make up for abandoning her.

Claire offers sandwiches wrapped in cling film. 'Cheese and pickle or tuna mayo?'

I have no appetite, not least because they appear to have been sat on. However, I need Claire to think everything is fine. 'Cheese and pickle please.'

'Good choice. There may be dog hairs in the others. Adie tried to eat them.' She shrugs.

'Only you would have a dog named Adie.' I imagine her in a domestic set-up with her handsome husband, smart daughter, and mischievous dog. As a child, she modelled her future career on the reporter Kate Adie which involved copying her voice. Claire stopped when Johnny questioned why she was talking like a robotic toff.

Claire takes a generous bite of her sandwich.

'Are you seriously eating that?' My delicate stomach rolls.

Claire used to eat almost everything in sight. While the rest of us obeyed the ten-second rule for dropped food, she figured if it was on the floor a little longer, an extra dusting off was enough.

'Once you've had kids, you don't blanch at hair, dirt, and the like,' she says. 'Besides, I'm starving and the dog had a bath yesterday.'

I poke her in the ribs to show my amusement. She swats my arm. We settle to take in the view. The park is well maintained. When I allow myself breaks, I come here. The open space helps me to think and relax. We watch women pushing toddlers on the swings. Claire and I used to swing alongside each other and share our secrets. Well, not *all* our secrets.

'Remember those swings and how blisteringly hot they were in the summer? What cockwomble decided to make them from tyres?' Claire says.

'Are you some kind of thought-stealing witch? I was just thinking about that.'

She chuckles. 'I avoided wearing shorts after burning my legs on them. When we got the plastic liner out and coated it with water and washing-up liquid, I took a few runs on it to relieve my scorched arse.'

Although I'm wary of her being here, I can't help but laugh. I've missed having banter with someone familiar. Claire is a reminder that not everything from the past is ruined.

I bring us back to business. 'Why are you here?'

She becomes interested in her sandwich. 'I was passing through.'

'Claire Woods.' I adopt my best authoritarian voice.

'It's Dalton, nowadays.'

'Claire Dalton, then. I can tell when you're lying. Your ears turn red.'

She covers them. 'Flaming things. I spent my childhood plastering my hair to them and they sprung through. My twenties were full of hideous hairstyles as cover-ups. I then considered pinning them, but it's too expensive. Now they're roaming free.'

'They're still the best lie detectors in the world.'

She clasps the sides of her head. 'Damn my grampy and his jug-ear genes.'

I elbow her as a distraction from the trauma. She nudges back. Our playfulness reignites past joy, long forgotten. Someone's coming off this bench and I'm determined it won't be me. I aim to give her another push when a sharp competitive elbow forces me onto the grass.

Claire pulls me up. 'I may be small but I'm powerful.'

Playtime is over. 'You're not passing through, are you. Headington is miles from Harplington.'

'Rumbled.' She brushes crumbs from her lap and produces two cartons of Ribena. 'Want one?'

'No thanks.'

'Turns out Matty's too old for Ribena. She threw a diva strop this morning, saying I'm infantilising her. Since when did fourteen-year-olds use such fancy language?' Claire's forgotten her fourteen-year-old self, who's coming back to haunt her through her offspring.

'Doreen's worried.' Claire's tone becomes serious. 'You never answer her calls. I'm here to check you're okay. We realised you might not be comfortable thinking about the past.'

There's a reason Doreen hasn't been able to contact me. I've screened my mobile and asked that none of her calls are put through at work. At least Temp Number Four got that right.

'I'm fine. I've been busy.'

'Me too.' Claire's jiggling makes the bench creak. 'Nice workplace, by the way. Love the fancy artwork and the cream leather suite. You've done well for yourself, Jenny Wren.'

The endearment Johnny and Liz Norman used catches me unaware. 'Thanks. I'm getting there.'

'I thought I'd give you a run-down of what Mum and I have covered so far. How did you get on with writing your memories?'

'Done,' I lie. 'I'll e-mail it later.'

'Thanks. Did you know Doreen is Graham's third wife?'

'No.' I didn't take an interest in the Pratts, beyond listening to Kelly's chatter.

'Doreen told me,' Claire says. 'She was being cagey about the previous wives but I could tell it wasn't good. It was hard for her, talking about that scumbag.'

'She's had so much to deal with.' I hide the sandwiches in my bag, hoping Claire won't notice.

Claire continues. 'I got in touch with Kev Brown. He used to be a copper. Do you remember him?'

'Yes.' I blanch at the name of the man who dealt with Mum and Liam's attempt to ruin Freddie's life.

'Kev still keeps up to date. He's in his seventies but they have a lot of respect for him at the police station. He often pops over there for a gossip.'

I let Claire continue without interruption. It's easier to let her keep talking. The sooner she's finished, the quicker I can return to work and normality.

Claire has the news scoop look in her eyes. 'Kev dug up reports on Graham. Get this, Graham killed his first wife.'

23

21ST JULY 1984

Graham sneered at the balloons outside the Reaston/Dean house, on Pollock Road. After living together for years, Pete and Shirley were getting married. Graham didn't see the point. On his third marriage, he was expert enough to warn others not to bother. Women were ineffective as wives. They began docile and sweet, luring you in. Before the ink dried on the marriage certificate, they made demands and underwent personality transplants. Graham considered advising Pete to duck out of it. "Living in sin" even sounded more exciting.

After the previous two wives, who couldn't keep their mouths shut or their legs open enough, Graham thought Doreen had promise. He liked them young. Catching them when they began formulating ideas, he'd sweep in to show the correct way. Doreen bucked the trend. The cunning minx got pregnant at sixteen. Children never featured in Graham's plans. Doreen's militant parents demanded he married her. The wedding was a rushed affair which he left Doreen to arrange. Buying a new suit was Graham's only concession. Doreen's cousin was a bridesmaid and blatantly had a thing for him. He dressed to impress the bridesmaid, not the bride.

The investment paid off behind the village hall holding the wedding reception.

Doreen's unhappiness was her own doing. If she hadn't got pregnant, neither of them would be miserable. Kelly, the stone around his neck, walked alongside him. He could have tried to love her if she'd been better looking or outgoing. Instead, he fathered in his unique way. Kelly had an advantage over Doreen in knowing that, from the beginning, Graham ruled. It took Doreen too long to learn. She expected romance and intimacy. On their wedding night, when she dared to call him *Gray*, she learned the true nature of their relationship via his fists.

Graham pushed his daughter towards the soon-to-be Reastons' house and left.

Kelly couldn't believe he'd accompanied her as far as the few houses along their road. Doreen pleaded with him to do so, aware Kelly might be bullied. Kelly wondered how to gain acceptance when even your mum didn't consider you passable in a bridesmaid's dress. If Kelly had asked, Doreen would have told her it was *because* she looked so different that Doreen feared the estate kids' reactions.

As she'd placed flowers within Kelly's freshly washed hair, Doreen was overcome with pride. Kelly was radiant. Even the leaping pink poodles embroidered on her ivory dress couldn't detract from the transformation. Being Graham's wife had made Doreen a realist. She knew Kelly wasn't a conventional beauty, but was convinced her daughter would emerge to show everyone her attributes; inside and out. Shirley asking Kelly to be a bridesmaid was a kindness Doreen didn't know she could ever repay.

Eleven-year-old Kelly was excited to wear full make-up for the first time. Doreen applied light touches Graham wouldn't notice and demand the removal of the "whore's mask". Doreen's cosmetics bag hid in her underwear drawer, appearing only when having "girls' time" with Kelly. Feeling rebellious, Doreen coloured in her own sallow face. Graham refused to attend the reception she was helping set up in the back room of a pub. The Pratt girls were free to shine.

Waiting for someone to answer the door, Kelly braced herself for an insult, as Charlie Pullen cycled towards her. The Pullen boys, from Turner Road, made a sport out of mocking her. Whenever Charlie or Glen were nearby, Kelly's insides tightened and she willed herself to disappear from their line of sight.

Charlie skidded to a halt. Kelly waited for the dig. He jerked his head back to assess her.

'You look sort of okay,' he said, and then pedalled away.

Kelly would take that. It was preferable to being called a heffalump, his latest barb. She couldn't swear to it, but Charlie seemed to like what he saw.

...

As she held Mandy aloft, Claire wobbled. Claire had complained the five-year-old would be a hindrance, forgetting that wherever Jen went, her sister often tagged along. Claire's issues with Mandy's presence soon disappeared. Mandy's stealthy skills were a bonus as she reached the tops of rose bushes and ripped off petals.

The girls were making a wedding present for Shirley. She was one of Claire's most favourite people. Pete and Shirley ran a poodle-grooming parlour from their house. While the neighbours complained about the dogs' noise, Claire loved being surrounded by canines. Because of her dad's allergies they couldn't have a pet.

Perfume for the bride was a perfect choice. The concoction of petals and water was a favourite, although earlier attempts proved its short shelf life. Claire figured it would be okay for Shirley to dab on for her special day. When first hearing Kelly was a bridesmaid instead of her, Claire sulked. After Shirley explained why Kelly needed this moment, Claire got over it and focused on an amazing gift instead.

Before they began, Jen stipulated not to touch Patricia's prized roses. If she discovered they were for Shirley, their lives wouldn't be worth living. Patricia vocalised her thoughts on Pete and Shirley getting wed and how being unmarried for so long was an abomination. She conveniently forgot her own hidden pregnancy when she married Mike. Unknown to her and the rest of the estate, Shirley kept her baby a secret too. Six months later, Matilda was born. She would be adored by Claire and the inspiration for naming her own daughter.

'Don't squash them,' Claire said, watching Mandy drop petals into the carrier bag. They'd managed quite a haul. Renoir Road and Monet Drive provided a bounty because the residents tended their gardens. The girls made a mistake in trying other less civilised roads first. Mandy disrupted the venture by grasping a patch of stinging nettles. Dock leaves rubbed on her palm and a lesson in differentiating between weeds and flowers avoided further errors.

...

Holding their creation, Claire decided they had the best wedding present ever. She'd emptied the last of Ellen's Opium bottle down the sink to hold the new scent. Her mum only used it for special occasions and wouldn't notice straight away. Jen wrote Shirley's name on a label in fancy handwriting and Mandy drew a border of flowers. They looked more like raindrops but Claire figured Shirley was too kind to mention it.

Kelly answered Pete and Shirley's door. Claire wouldn't have said Kelly was beautiful but rather that she shone. The confidence of wearing cosmetics, accessories, and a tailored dress changed her.

'Flipping heck,' Claire said. 'You look nice.'

Kelly blushed from neck to hairline. A stranger to receiving compliments, she didn't reply.

'Can you give this to Shirley please?' Claire handed over the bottle. 'Make sure she knows it's from Jen, Mandy, and me.'

'I will.' Kelly fanned her face.

...

A procession of poodles, meringue dresses, and foil balloons burst forth from the Dean/Reaston house. A gathering awaited the bride, curious if the rumour of a poodle-themed wedding was true. Shirley lingered in the doorway, awaiting instruction from the photographer. Six apricot poodles snapped at each other, weary of being tethered to ribbon leads. Kelly ducked behind Shirley's princess dress, wary of the onlookers' judgements.

The bridesmaids followed Shirley to the limousine. Her adult sisters stood either side of Kelly, creating a spectacle of ivory satin and pink poodles. A real poodle cocked its leg and urinated on Kelly's silk shoe. She'd been waiting for her moment of glory to end. This was it. Kids sitting on the pavement guffawed. More polite company pretended not to notice.

'She looks lovely,' Johnny said.

Jen appraised the scene. 'If you like poufy wedding dresses.'

'Not Shirley. Kelly.'

Jen had to agree. Pee-stained shoe aside, Kelly Pratt had turned into a swan, albeit one that shook its foot a lot.

The photographer rolled his eyes. 'The youngest bridesmaid, can you stop hopping please?'

Always ready to obey, Kelly stood still. Urine seeped through her tights and pooled in the bottom of her shoe. Still, she did not move.

'How do they do weddings in your country, Dino?' Ernie Bowers, from Pollock Road, asked.

Dino, from Degas Drive, sighed. 'Exactly the same, seeing as *this* is my country.'

'I thought you're Spanish.'

'I'm half Spanish. How many times do I have to tell you I was born here?'

'Oh, okay.' Ernie moved on. Porsche Smith lingered nearby. When she was around, no one else existed. Ernie affected the sexy smile he'd seen his dad give his mum on Saturday nights. Porsche nudged her sister, Mercedes, remarking on how the boy appeared to be having a stroke.

People gasped as the bridesmaids and Shirley's dad wedged the bride into the waiting car, hoping she'd fit. Dads remarked upon the "sweet motor". Mums prayed Shirley's dress wouldn't rip. Tightly packed, the bridal party left for the registry office; a source of conversation for those divided about the lack of a church wedding. *Everyone* held an opinion on the Rembrandt Estate.

'I'll give Pete two months before he kills Shirley,' said "Porky" Pullen, getting into the party spirit with a can of bitter.

His spouse, Annette, put on her sunglasses, incensed at being shown up again in public. 'Killing his wife, indeed. Who ever heard such a thing?'

24

PRESENT

'Graham killed his wife?' I wonder if I've heard Claire correctly. My hangover is still in force and I was focused on getting back to work until she dropped the bombshell.

Claire leaps to her feet, demanding full attention. 'Graham hit his two previous wives too. He lived with both, consecutively, in Troddington, so was known to the local police. Kev said they barred him from his house after the second wife's legs were broken. Nasty bastard ran over them in his car. You've gone pale.'

A few bottles of wine the night before will do that to you.

'I'm fine. Carry on.'

'Graham said he didn't see her standing behind the car. After totalling her legs, he drove off and left her there.' Claire's face reddens.

I wish I could say Graham's level of evil is unique, but I've lived with it. My mind flits to Mum moving a stepladder away when I was in the loft. I was looking for my missing medical textbooks, desperate not to lose the route to escape. When I came back down, the ladder disappeared and I fell. My arm cracked on impact with the floor. Mum's only response was to command I never go into her loft without permission again. I screamed in agony. She stepped over me and left. Dad took me to the doctor, explaining how the resulting fracture was from accidentally knocking the ladder away. We knew Graham's type of nastiness and covered it up in our own house.

'Wow,' is all I can manage, in response to Claire's telling of Graham's violence.

'I don't think Doreen knows he killed the first wife.'

I pat the bench, inviting Claire to sit. The constant pacing is making me giddy. 'Are you sure he killed her?'

Claire gives a heavy sigh as she takes a seat. 'Yes, Jen. Their house blew up.'

'How did it happen?'

'Gas explosion. Graham played the grieving widower but Kev and the other coppers never bought it. Graham told them he'd gone to the corner shop to get dog food, heard the bang, and ran home.'

'I don't see how it makes him guilty.'

Unable to settle, Claire stands again. 'Graham and his wife didn't have a dog. The neighbours swore to it.'

She gives me a moment to process the information, but Claire can't be silent for long. 'The cooker's hobs were on. It was early morning, and his wife died in bed. She wasn't making breakfast. Someone else must have turned on the gas. A man on their road also found a box of matches discarded in his front garden.'

'Was Graham arrested?'

'Nope.' The word darts from Claire's lips. 'He worked the police a charm. A few pints down the pub, a duff investigation in the days when forensics were virtually non-existent, and Graham got off scot-free.'

'It makes you wonder what he put Doreen through.'

'Kelly too.'

This new prospect of Kelly's dad as a villain could be to my advantage. 'We need to investigate Graham more.'

'I'm on it. I wouldn't be surprised if he had something to do with Kelly's death.' Claire's taken the bait. Graham was hardly a saint. I try to convince myself it's not as devious as pointing the finger at a living person. My conscience doesn't like me very much.

My phone rings. When I see who the caller is, I end the call. It rings again. I'm not quick enough to move it from Claire's sight.

'You'd better get that,' she says.

How do I explain why I don't want to answer? I swipe to accept.

'I know what you did, Jennifer. Be at my house tomorrow, at eleven. No excuses or I'll go to the police.'

The call ends.

I make hurried apologies to Claire about needing to return to work immediately. The disbelief on her face is clear but I don't give her a chance to protest. I seek shelter around the back of the toilets and slump against the wall.

It has come to pass.

Doreen knows I killed her daughter.

25

23RD JUNE 1984

'She's murdering it.'

'Be nice, Claire,' Liz said.

Natalie Baker, from Renoir Road, gave her interpretation of *London's Burning*, in Freddie and Liz's flat. After spending the earlier part of the school year as a target for her recorder teacher's baton, she had to nail the tune.

'Why is she playing anyway?' Claire's volume was always set to maximum. 'It's *Star Wars* night, not amateur evening.'

Liz noticed Natalie's bottom lip tremble and hoped a situation wasn't forming. The determined girl came to the Normans' flat every day, desperate to play well. The Bakers' ears were saved by the intervention. Liz decided, as her teeth tingled at the screeching, Natalie was tone deaf. Freddie clapped vigorously. His guests joined in weak applause.

'Thank the gods of good taste that's over,' Claire said.

'Don't be nasty.' Freddie's bushy eyebrows furrowed. 'Just because you're Darth Vader, doesn't mean you have to be cruel.'

Claire always behaved around the Normans. They were kind to her and she'd never cause problems for them. 'Bloody brilliant outfit, Natalie.'

. . .

Natalie blushed under green face paint and squinted to see Claire through her sunglasses. Her attempt at dressing up as Greedo was more successful than her recorder playing. She'd been looking forward to this event for weeks. An invitation to one of the Normans' themed evenings was an honour. The events were so popular, Freddie and Liz invited groups of children in rotation, their flat being too small to entertain the hordes.

Stars and planets floated from the ceiling. The *Star Wars* soundtrack whirled on the record player. A spread of space cupcakes, honeycomb moon rocks, and fizzy rocket fuel for the Millennium Falcon, soon disappeared.

Each partygoer chose a character. Mandy desperately wanted to be Luke Skywalker, but Patricia wouldn't allow her daughter to dress as a male. Surely there were pretty girls in the film? Jen being the main woman, with a nifty hairstyle, was a coup. They reached a "compromise". Mandy left dressed as a "pretty girl". A quick change into a white bathrobe and grabbing the lightsaber she'd made at the Normans' kept her happy. The cardboard tube, covered in foil, struck Claire's legs.

'Watch where you're swinging that thing!' she shouted.

Mandy chuckled. The fight was on.

'Call that a lightsaber?' Claire brandished Alex's replica weapon. Her dad was a *Star Wars* geek, with a cupboard stuffed full of memorabilia. He insisted on buying Claire an authentic Darth Vader costume. No child of Alex Woods would be half-arse joining The Dark Side.

Claire's weapon whooshed and its light strobed towards Mandy. Her makeshift version bent on interception.

Johnny gave Mandy a hug. 'Don't worry. I can mend it. Besides, you win by slaying Darth Vader.'

'I thought tonight is based on *New Hope*,' Johnny's older brother,

Ian Rose, said. 'Darth Vader doesn't die in the first film. It's about the details, thicko.'

Jen stuck a misbehaving hairgrip into her left bun. 'If details are so important, then you should've made an effort. What are you supposed to be?'

Ian tightened the bandages across his shirt. 'A stormtrooper, of course.'

Johnny stood by Jen's side. 'I said I'd help you with an outfit, Ian.'

Johnny's sibling did nothing he could make others do. Ian not only resembled a weasel with his beady eyes, elongated head, and thin frame, but adopted their wily ways too.

'Get a load of Han Solo rescuing his Leia. So touching.' Ian bared yellowed teeth, from a gobstopper-sucking habit. Johnny wished gobstoppers were literal.

Jen had enjoyed playing the other half of a well-known love story with Johnny. She hid her upset as he edged away in response to Ian's comment.

Johnny cursed himself for putting embarrassment above his secret infatuation with Jen. At eleven, he was hardly a smooth romantic, and anyway, they'd always be just friends.

Liz joined Ian on the sofa. Her more accomplished stormtrooper outfit, purchased from a fancy dress shop, cast him in her shade.

'When's your mum due?' she asked the Rose boys.

Their heavily pregnant mother begged them to go to the *Star Wars* night. Swollen ankles made kicking Ian and their other brother, Anthony, up the backside for their mouthiness, a challenge.

'Any day soon.' Johnny's glee spread across his face. He hoped it would be a girl this time and not obnoxious, like his siblings. Being the child of the objectionable Rob Morgan didn't offer the best odds though. Rob decided it was definitely a boy and they would call him Benny. Rob usually got his way.

'She's outside, alone again,' Freddie said, his fluffy arm holding the cord on the kitchen blind.

Freddie's natural hairiness meant he could only ever be Chewbacca. Claire was disappointed he hadn't styled his own body hair, but had to admit the costume, made from a shaggy rug, was incredible.

Liz joined him in watching Kelly, sitting under the park tree. 'I invited her but she said she'd never seen the film.'

'That doesn't matter.' Freddie wiped fluff from his tongue.

'She said they couldn't afford an outfit. I told Doreen I'd take care of it, but you know how proud she is.'

Overhearing their conversation, Jen looked at her own dress. Liz had worked on it for days. Styling her hair had taken an hour. Jen felt a pang of remorse at wearing what might have been Kelly's costume.

'I'll keep an eye out for her,' Liz said to Jen, noting the frown. 'Maybe she'll come in when everyone's watching the film.'

The music changed to Madness, singing of *House of Fun*. Al Priest, from Picasso Way, loved to get a party started. His version of Obi-Wan Kenobi bust some moves, holding R2-D2 and C-3PO aloft. His three-year-old twins made for adorable droids. Liz inhaled the warmth of her home, filled with friends and happiness.

The house of fun toppled upon Anthony Rose's arrival. Liz always gave him a chance but had to admit he was hard work. At fifteen, he demanded the rights of an adult while resembling and behaving like a child thug. The flabbiness of his baby face contrasted with the skinhead cut.

Freddie took the cans of lager from Anthony. 'It's not that kind of party, Ant.'

Anthony scowled. 'You better give those back before I leave.'

'I wouldn't steal from you.'

'Unlike her.' Anthony pointed at Carrie Waite, who also lived on Turner Road. 'Nail down your belongings, everyone.'

Carrie launched her equally generous frame at him.

'No fighting.' Freddie stood between them.

'She is a tea leaf though,' Claire said, her breathing authentically laboured by the claustrophobic helmet. 'They caught her in the Co-op last week, nicking steaks.'

The Waites shoplifted to order. Their booty kept the unscrupulous in luxuries they couldn't afford or were too stingy to buy. Carrie was an established member of the family trade at ten years old, although she needed extra training in not eating the goods she pilfered.

'Get stuffed!' Carrie yelled. 'I have every right to be here and I haven't taken anything. See?' She unzipped her tracksuit jacket and turned out her pockets.

'Couldn't be bothered to dress up though, could you.' Claire never gave up on a fight.

'Neither has he.' Carrie pointed at Anthony, who had grown bored with the argument and was ready to start another.

The others circled around the Priests, enjoying the performance. The twins swayed on uncertain legs. Liz took photos of the duo, cooing at their cuteness.

'Nice one, Al!' Anthony shouted above the music. 'Your lot always dance good.'

Al stood still. 'What do you mean?'

'Black people, innit? You've all got rhythm.'

The Priests were the only black residents on the estate and Troddington was a mainly white town. Along with the Hernandez family, who had Spanish roots, the Priests challenged racism and tried to inform the residents of misconceptions. Al always did so with good grace. The union with his white wife, Marie, also drew ignorant comments.

'Go look up the word *stereotype*, Anthony. Get yourself educated, boy.' Al continued dancing.

Knowing when he was beat, Anthony headed for the door. 'Carrie, do you want to see what's worth swiping from the dairy?' He grabbed the six-pack from the counter, cradling it like a newborn. Carrie joined him; both united in a mission and their earlier row a distant memory.

Checking everyone was settled, Freddie left.

...

Kelly recognised the tune coming from the Normans' flat as from the cantina scene of the film. She jiggled her book on her knees in time with the jaunty beat. When Liz invited her and offered to make an outfit, Kelly was ecstatic. She loved *Star Wars*. Doreen refused. If Graham discovered they'd accepted charity, there would be consequences.

Kelly drew her costume on a bookmark. She would have been the feisty and beautiful Princess Leia. Seeing Jen going to the party, dressed as the character, deflated Kelly's ego. Jen wore the clothes she wanted to wear and lived the life Kelly wanted to live.

26

23TH JUNE 1984

S ounds of happiness trickled from the Normans' kitchen window, reminding Kelly she'd always be on the outside. Her resentment towards Graham increased. Without him, Doreen and Kelly might have integrated into the estate. She ground her knuckles into the tree bark, sucking in air as blood seeped. The physical pain dulled the ache in her throat and chest. She hid her wound as a furry form loomed.

'Why don't you join us?' Freddie stepped closer.

Kelly recoiled. Men sometimes scared her, even more so when dressed as wookies.

'I'm fine.' She raised the book in front of her face.

'That's impressive, reading *Wuthering Heights* at your age.' Freddie removed the mask to reveal his usual grin. 'No one will hurt you when I'm around, I promise.'

'I might come later.'

They both knew it was a lie. Cautious of applying pressure, Freddie returned home.

...

Liz fixated on Kelly. Ominous clouds descended over the park. Liz opened the window further, seeking fresh air against the cloying mugginess. The plastic costume made sweat pool in the strangest of places. With this distraction, no wonder stormtroopers missed their targets.

Lightning crackled. Thunder became its companion. The twins cowered under Al's cloak. Ian fronted it out, hiding his fear of thunder. Liz knew of his phobia and how Ian threatened to break limbs if it became known. Mandy huddled between Johnny and Jen. Claire brandished the lightsaber, announcing the storm was a vehicle of her wrath. Still smarting from Claire's earlier criticism of her recorder playing, Natalie told Claire to stop talking over the film.

Liz ran to Kelly, unable to bear her being exposed to the elements. 'Come in. It's dangerous to sit under a tree in a thunderstorm.'

Kelly's face was wet. 'It's safer than going home.' She shielded the novel under her blouse.

Liz knew a child's defiance when she saw it. Jen taught her well. She admired it to a degree, but was frustrated at Kelly not listening to reason. Liz sped back inside. She stalled dialling the Pratts' number when she spotted a figure rushing across the park, covered by a golf umbrella. Doreen temporarily rescued her daughter. They ran from one danger to another.

In that moment, Liz hated the world. The merriment in her flat brought no comfort. She despised men like Graham, who had children they didn't want. Liz's attempts at getting the police involved when she saw Kelly's bruises never came to anything. He was a convincing man who manipulated his wife and daughter to say the right things. Liz watched Freddie, surrounded by youngsters. *There* was a man who would have been a wonderful father.

She allowed the tears to fall, knowing the mask concealed the hurt. An arm snaked around her waist and she stroked the fur.

Husband and wife united in grief at multiple miscarriages and the final diagnosis they would never have children.

They turned together to look at the youngsters in their lounge. *Here* was their family.

27

PRESENT

The certificates on Nicole's wall don't do her justice. She's more than a set of qualifications. Empathy oozes from her and she can read a person within minutes of meeting them. I like our mentoring sessions. Her room is always inviting. The calming yellows and creams are an informed choice for creating a peaceful environment. I move to Nicole's chair to avoid the lowering sun hitting my eyes. On the desk, sunflowers spring from a vase.

I'm reminded of when Mandy and I competed with a group of estate kids to grow the tallest sunflower. We entered the *Blue Peter* competition, certain our green fingers would make the Rembrandt Estate famous. Our sunflower towered over everyone else's. Perhaps we gloated too much about how the *Blue Peter* badge would be ours. One morning, we found our sunflower chopped into pieces and scattered over the lawn. No one confessed. We didn't expect any less on an estate where "no grassing" was a hallowed rule.

Mandy cried for days, mourning her flower friend, Sunny. She lost more than a bloom. She'd nurtured and shared her troubles with Sunny. Liam sang floral-themed songs, accompanied by snipping actions. He hated others having fun. He hated Mandy and me, full stop. I never understood why. It's not as if we were rivals for our parents' attention.

When Nicole enters, I move to the other seat and refrain from making a joke about stealing her chair and status. Her expression suggests a sense of humour might be missing.

'They got the stationery order wrong again,' she says. 'I figured you could do without the hassle. You looked upset when you returned from lunch.'

'I had a headache. It's passed.'

'It seems to be more than that. I'm worried about you.' Caring Nicole switches from Dictator Nicole.

'I'm fine. Getting the assignments done is stressful. You know how it is.'

'I do. Sometimes though, I'd love to go back to that time when I was a student and childfree. Mothers shouldn't say such things, should they?'

'Don't you like being a mum?' What was intended as a question becomes more of an outburst.

'Of course I do.' She breaks eye contact. Nicole's rarely flustered, and it's unsettling I made it happen. 'I wouldn't give up my children for anything. The past can seem rosier sometimes though, don't you think?'

'Maybe.' Not always. Not much at all.

'Talking of the past, it was nice meeting Claire. You need more friends. Are you seeing her again soon?'

'I have to.' My reply is harsher than intended.

'Why do you *have* to?'

I note the counsellor's tool of repeating what's been said. To satisfy her curiosity, I decide to share the bare minimum. If I don't offload some of the recent events I'll mentally combust.

'When Claire and I were fourteen, a girl on the council estate where we lived died. Her mum wants our help to find out what happened. It looked like suicide or an accident but she's convinced it's something else.' It's good to tell someone, even if it's only the headlines.

'That's the most you've shared about your past in the seven years I've known you. So, you lived on a council estate?'

Pride kicks in. 'It doesn't make me a bad person. I'm fed up of people thinking those from council estates are scrounging scum.'

'Calm down, class warrior. I was taken aback because you've not said *anything* about your background. I only know you lived in Troddington because of your CV, listing the local schools.'

My attempt at making her believe I'm okay is failing. Anger wins again.

'Sorry, it's a sore subject,' I say. 'Anyway, Claire's on my case. Her mum and Doreen, that's Kelly's mum, the girl who died, are pushing me to help. It's getting too much.'

My nails embed into my palm and the scar flares. I've tried to break the habit but the pain is a distraction. Each time the heat of the scar pulses, I'm transported.

The wound is from cutting my palm on a broken glass while washing up. I cried for help. Mum continued chatting on the phone. Her only involvement was an instruction to bleach the bloodstains from the sink. I patched myself up as best as a seven-year-old could. The sink sparkled. My palm was permanently marked.

Once again, my mind has drifted. 'What did you say?'

'Why do you have to be involved?' Nicole relaxes into the chair and peers over her glasses. I am the naughty student being reprimanded by the head.

'I used to walk to school with Kelly. Doreen thinks I might know how she landed up on the railway track. I've said I don't, but Doreen's dying and I feel guilty. I mean, I feel sad for her.' Nicole's counsellor radar better be switched off. 'The coroner's open verdict hasn't helped Doreen to have closure.' We both wince at the therapy cliché. We have a list of "Wanky Words" in this practice. I should've added *journey* and *ownership* for good measure.

'Poor woman,' Nicole says. 'I can't imagine dealing with your child being dead, even years later.'

Is that a tear she's wiping away? She gives a pointed look, defying me to expose her weakness. Out of respect, I let it go.

'Doreen needs peace before she dies. That's why I've got to help. If it means helping her come to terms with Kelly's death, in the gentlest way possible, then it's what we'll do.'

'You're a good person for doing this.'

No, I'm not. If you knew what I am, Nicole, you'd boot me out.

She assumes a prayer position, inviting the confession of my sins. 'You need to balance it with work and study. Are you drinking again?'

'Yes.' There's no use lying. You can't fool a woman who's fluent in body language. My palm is tender.

'I'm not your mother, but...'

'You wouldn't want to be her.'

Her raised eyebrow awaits further details but I ignore it. We continue our usual routine of me being elusive while Nicole chips away.

'You fought hard to get sober and clean, Jen. Don't undo it. You'll be a counsellor, working here soon.'

The threat's in my poor choices, not with this conversation. Nicole won't sack me. She's nothing but kind.

'I'll stop. I *can* stop,' I say.

'I shouldn't have insisted on dragging you to the pub after work.'

'Don't be silly. I'm more controlled than that. I can even watch a junkie on the TV without wanting a hit.'

'It's not funny. I'm worried about you.'

'I'm fine. The booze is out of the house and I'm teetotal again.' Not by choice, I don't add, but because it was finished off last night. My mouth salivates at the imagined crispness of Prosecco dancing on my tongue. I replace desire with pain, jabbing my palm with my nails. I mustn't drink again. While this investigation into Kelly's death is ongoing, I need a clear head. If the truth comes out, my life is over.

'Scout's honour.' I give a salute. 'No more alcohol and lots of study. I'll be focused at work and not do too much investigating.'

'Good. Let's go for ice cream later. A mahoosive sundae with sprinkles, chocolate, and anything else we can get on it. I don't see why we can't still have a treat.'

'Sure.'

I was planning to catch up on sleep but she's trying to be a friend. I could do with one. Besides, I've always been partial to ice cream.

28

29TH JULY 1981

'When can I have ice cream?' Jen asked.

'Later. At the party. Stay still.' Patricia jabbed in another pin.

Jen stamped on her mum's foot as a reflexive action to the stab in the head. Patricia's slap resounded against Jen's naked thighs.

'How the hell am I supposed to get this finished if you keep wriggling?' Patricia shouted.

Spittle landed on Jen's face. She dared not wipe it. More movement would make her mum angrier. The lure of promised ice cream helped Jen to focus.

Even an eight-year-old knew it was madness to create an elaborate fancy dress outfit in an hour. Until that morning, the Taylors weren't going to the estate party, held in honour of Charles and Diana's wedding day. It wasn't due to lack of patriotism. Patricia was a staunch royalist and Lady Di fan. She dedicated mirror viewing time to lowering her head and looking upwards, trying to capture the soon-to-be Princess's shyness. For a bold woman, it required plenty of practise.

Patricia initially proposed an estate celebration. She shared a vision of a civilised tea party for the adults, dressed in their finest.

The opportunity to be admired for the resemblance to Diana motivated her. Her hair was recently coloured and the flicked fringe held in place. Children weren't invited, she explained. It wouldn't be a raucous shindig like those happening in other areas of Troddington. Selected adults would be "encouraged" to volunteer their services in looking after the youngsters and sacrificing their time for the sake of others' enjoyment.

At hearing Patricia's ideas, the women at the coffee morning prepared to riot. Cake was left uneaten and coffee went cold. The party couldn't take place without their offspring. They wanted family fun involving costumes, a buffet, booze, and an old-fashioned knees-up. For the first time, they outnumbered Patricia. Suddenly remembering other plans previously made, she withdrew. The others accepted the lie, knowing the wisdom of placating Patricia rather than appearing on a future hit list.

On the day, Patricia reversed her decision. Next door, Porsche and Mercedes strutted in patriotic outfits. Felicity's exclamations of how her daughters were a dead cert to win the fancy dress competition piqued Patricia's interest. She peered over the fence separating their gardens. The Smith girls were walking Union Jacks, in matching flowing blue wigs and white shift dresses adorned with red crosses. Felicity made everything by hand, working on the outfits for months. Patricia yawned whenever she had to hear about it.

Deciding it wouldn't do, Patricia crawled below the height of the fence to avoid Felicity. She grabbed Jen from the armchair, ignoring the cries that Jen was watching cartoons. Patricia got to work. Mike's T-shirts were ripped and transformed into flowers. She didn't care if he still wore them. The fight was on against the Smiths, and sacrifices were necessary. Patricia would never lose out to a woman who couldn't pronounce her own surname correctly.

Felicity and Patricia were often in each other's houses. Theirs was a grudging friendship, fuelled by one-upwomanship. If one got a kitchen gadget or piece of furniture before the other, the world officially ended and the purchase had to be matched. When Jen had the misfortune to enter the Smith household, she could see how people would think they'd gone to the Taylor house by mistake.

A pile of craft items offered Mandy play prospects. Jen removed a pin hanging from her two-year-old sister's mouth. Someone had to be in charge while Patricia disappeared into a fashion designer frenzy. The light breeze from the open patio door made the hairs on Jen's legs rise. She tried to forget the indignity of standing in her knickers, in full view of the estate. As each pin penetrated her scalp, the urge to cry out increased.

Jen knew the outfit would be repulsive, but the finished product was shocking. The red pussy bow blouse was hideous, and the mustiness of its shoulder pads made Jen gag. Remnants of used bath sponges crumbled when she moved. She considered offering her shoulders as serving trays at the party. The indignity of a tomboy being forced to wear a blue A-line skirt was nothing compared to the bonnet. Jen groaned at the girl in the dining room mirror, swamped by a floral abomination. The weight of the head-gear, along with the pins Patricia insisted remained to keep the arrangement intact, made Jen's head ache.

'Stop sweating, you'll make it slip,' Patricia said. 'Tighten the ribbon on Amanda too.'

Mandy hadn't escaped the shame. She wore a matching bonnet which Jen tried to tie under her chin. Considering it a game, Mandy pulled it away. Jen held the ghastly item in place, fearful of Patricia eyeing the glue.

Patricia assessed her handiwork. 'Let's see what Felicity makes of this. Stay clean. We'll go over as soon as I'm dressed.'

Above, wardrobe doors opened and were slammed shut. Shoes were hurled from their racks and thumped on the floor. Jen and Mandy resumed watching cartoons.

Liam appeared and erupted into laughter. 'What on earth do

you two look like?' He scratched his head. Jen hoped he didn't have nits again. He always blamed his sisters.

'Mum did it,' Jen said, awaiting further insults.

'That's priceless. I'm documenting this.' Liam took the camera from the television unit and captured his siblings' misery. Jen wished her dad didn't keep it loaded with film.

'This photograph is going on the wall,' Liam said.

He took over the settee and switched the channel to a western. Jen didn't bother to argue. She was already on a losing streak. Not for the first time, she wondered how they could be related. Liam insisted upon always being impeccably dressed. He was the only kid she knew who wanted clothes for Christmas and birthdays. Today, he wore a linen waistcoat over a crisp pinstripe shirt, resembling a miniature bank manager.

'There you are, darling.' Patricia glided in on a waft of Chanel No.5.

Liam ignored the ruffling of his hair. The sun coming through the windows exposed Patricia's white sheer dress, leaving little to the imagination. Red beads and faux sapphire earrings completed the look.

'Grab the shirt I bought you and put it on,' she instructed Liam.

'I'm not going to the stupid party.' His eyes didn't leave the television screen.

Patricia planted a scarlet kiss upon his forehead. 'For Mummy?'

'No way. I've got other, more important, things to do.' Liam rubbed at the lipstick stain.

Jen leant on the windowsill, pleased her brother was leaving. Patricia applied her game face. Losing the opportunity to showcase her son was disappointing but her daughters were works of art. No one would be able to keep their eyes off her either. Not bad, considering she was nudging thirty. She seized Jen who scooped up

Mandy. Jen prepared herself for the embarrassment of being seen in public.

The residents of the estate, bar Patricia and the less community-minded, had created a feat of patriotism. Embossed paper cloths covered decorating tables. Mismatched dining room chairs, with streamers dangling from their legs, lined the outer edges of the park. Union Jack bunting fluttered from the swings, slide, and climbing frame. Red and white fake carnations stood tall in blue plastic vases.

Vernon Brady, from Munch Drive, had set up his decks. Finally, he could play music without his mum's moaning about disturbing the neighbours. The fact she was footing the electricity bill for this gig remained a secret. Vernon being a part-time DJ was an annoyance for his parent who nagged him to get a "proper job". Vernon hoped thirty-five wasn't too old to meet someone, marry, and leave. Ditching the habit of dressing in a John Travolta white suit in the *Saturday Night Fever* style would have increased his chances.

Patricia's legs made an entrance, kicking high to the *Can Can*. Women sneered at the apparent lack of underwear. Men fell over themselves to get her a drink, a sausage roll, "anything you want, Patricia". Used to her mum's performances, Jen guided Mandy to the shade of the park's only tree. Placing her sister on the ground, Jen sensed him before he spoke.

'Jen, er…'

It had to be the one person she'd always wanted to impress. Jen cursed her life. Johnny, the eternal rebel, wore his usual jeans. The badges covering his khaki jacket glinted in the sun. Jen swore he'd be buried in the garment.

'She made me wear it.' Jen shot a warning glare.

It didn't require further explanation. Eight-year-old Johnny knew Patricia was the devil. Knocking on the Taylors' door was scarier than entering the gates of Hell. He always lingered in the park instead, waiting for Jen to join him.

'Fancy seeing what's in the buffet?' Johnny asked.

Jen moved to the other side of the tree. Mandy had staked a claim upon Liz from Picasso Way. The toddler spiralled Liz's curls around her fingers.

'Have fun,' Liz said. 'Mandy will be okay with us.'

Charlie Pullen, sitting nearby and dressed as a podgy Prince Charles, couldn't resist a jibe. 'Ruddy Nora. Nice afro, Jen.'

Johnny despised the boy. Desperate for acceptance, Charlie became Anthony and Ian's dogsbody. It was the best Charlie could get. He was the estate idiot, due to his constant snitching, buck teeth, and snotty nose.

Incensed Patricia had made her vulnerable to the estate bullies, Jen advanced towards Charlie. He retreated, removing his mask. A glimpse of face disappeared and melded into Patricia's.

Jen formed a fist and engaged with her target.

29TH JULY 1981

J ohnny moved Jen from potentially rearranging Charlie's face. Charlie beckoned her to take a shot, adding "funky flower afro" comments. Johnny shared crude statements about the other boy into Jen's ear. She took measured breaths between laughs. Deciding he wouldn't risk getting smacked in the mouth by a girl, Charlie skulked away.

'Let's get a drink,' Johnny said. He not only shielded Jen, but as a member of the Rose family, it was inevitable someone would blame him for starting the argument.

The buffet table groaned under the weight of an army of foil hedgehogs spiked with cheese and pineapple, accompanied by crisps, jam tarts, and sausages on sticks. A Victoria sponge made of dyed blue sponges, white buttercream, and glossy strawberries took centre stage.

Johnny poured Tizer into plastic cups. Jen blushed at him remembering her favourite drink. Gassiness tickled her nose as she sipped. The bonnet slid. She pushed it back and yelped as the pins pricked her head.

'What's the matter, dear?' Felicity ceased bossing the other helpers. As party organiser and a sight no one could miss, she was in her element. Red, white and blue baubles and sequins lit her up like a Christmas tree. With every movement, she swished and tinkled.

'Nothing,' Jen replied. 'You're, um, very bright.'

Johnny sniggered. Felicity shot him a dirty look that would have felled a lesser boy. He stared her out, used to others' disapproval.

'Couldn't your mother afford an outfit, Jonathan?' Felicity waited for him to decide whether to retaliate or stay silent. When he gave no reply, she believed she'd won.

Johnny knew better. Telling his vengeful mum about Felicity's comment would later even the score.

'I thought your family weren't coming, Jennifer,' Felicity said.

'Mum changed her mind.'

'It must have taken her ages to put that creation together. You and Mandy, I've noticed.' The drumming of Felicity's fingers made the table wobble. Her daughters' chances of winning the fancy dress contest were over.

'She did it this morning, after she saw Mercedes and Porsche in theirs.'

'Right,' Felicity said. 'I see.'

Jen wasn't sure what she'd done wrong but a familiar quaking in her stomach took hold.

Johnny steadied her hand. 'You're spilling your drink.'

She was thankful for his solidarity. The washing machine feeling in her tummy reduced.

'Oh, my…'

Jen and Felicity turned to the source of Johnny's shock.

Doreen drowned in paisley. Her shirt, flared trousers, headband, even shoes, boasted the pattern. Cautious steps helped her balance a collapsed beehive with carrying a glass bowl overflowing with dessert. Beside her waddled Kelly, dressed as a tomato, and with blushing red cheeks to match. A blue and white bow in her hair completed the flag theme.

Jen tried not to laugh. Something inside gnawed away, telling her mocking Kelly was wrong. Jen's underdeveloped conscience caught the laughter of the crowd and she joined in.

Kelly laughed too. She thought joviality showed friendship. Friends did good things and laughing is good. So they must be friends.

Spotting an opportunity to cause trouble, Charlie and Ian rushed at Kelly. The wide girth of the costume, on top of puppy fat, and a lack of glasses, made her a prime target. She landed on her rear. Some giggled at the squashed tomato. Others, who never registered the Pratts' existence, carried on conversations. Johnny helped Doreen to pull Kelly up.

'Thank you, Johnny,' Doreen said. 'It's a shame your brother isn't as decent.' She dusted Kelly off and checked for grazes.

Johnny shrugged. 'No problem. Sorry Ian's such a git.'

Doreen knew when to change the subject. 'Jennifer, you look lovely. That bonnet is so pretty.' She patted Jen's head.

Jen winced. 'Thanks, Mrs Pratt. Kelly looks great too.' Liz had told Jen to always be kind to others. Jen realised she'd lied but decided Patricia wouldn't care on this occasion.

Kelly blushed deeper, surpassing the scarlet tomato. 'Mum got this from the charity shop. It was such a bargain.'

Felicity joined them. 'What have you brought, Doreen?' She wrinkled her nose.

'A trifle. The recipe my nan used.' Doreen beamed at her effort.

Jen loved trifle almost as much as ice cream. She beheld the tower of cream, glistening jelly, custard, and a rainbow of sprinkles.

'Delightful,' Felicity said. She moved the dessert to the edge of the table then wiped her hands on a napkin. Doreen let it pass, as if she had received worse insults.

Felicity scanned the park and blew a whistle. 'Food's ready.'

A scrum of elbows, feet, and grasping fingers launched upon the buffet. Felicity held onto her baubles. Decent parents pulled their children back, determined not to be judged as the producers of ruffians. The others continued necking alcohol, no longer aware they had relatives. Jen stood to the side, wary of the rabble, particularly those making fun of her headwear.

'Take it off. She's too busy to see,' Johnny said.

Jen watched her mum stroking the cheek of a man who must have been visiting.

Patricia enjoyed acting the single woman. Mike had received orders to go to the pub rather than attend the party. He didn't need telling twice. Liz and Freddie rolled a ball to Mandy. *This is how a family should be,* Jen thought.

With Patricia distracted, Jen removed the bonnet. Sweat-soaked hair clung to her head and neck. She raked her fingers through the knots. When Patricia noted Jen's bird's nest appearance, she took an interest in washing her hair. Patricia's knees clamped Jen's head and a steel comb exacted torture. Jen's scalp was already on fire.

The residents dispersed to eat. Jen and Johnny approached the buffet. Pickings were slim, apart from an abundance of salad. No one wanted healthy options for a celebration. In the middle of the park, Patricia and the stranger danced alone to *Green Door*. The man cupped Patricia's rear while she caressed his neck. They became bold under the influence of alcohol.

'Who knew Shakin' Stevens was an aphrodisiac?' Felicity quipped.

'Can I have trifle please?' Jen asked Doreen.

Doreen was elated at the ladies of the Rembrandt Estate allowing her the responsibility of serving. The opportunities to be part of estate life seldom came. Jen's request boosted her confidence.

Felicity had steered each person who'd asked for trifle to another option. Doreen understood the Pratts weren't liked. She tried to get involved in the Friday coffee mornings. The women often cancelled, only for Doreen to find out, too late, it was back on.

'An extra big portion for you, Jennifer.' Doreen held the serving ladle. Felicity was preoccupied, chatting to a gaggle of women. Doreen was determined someone would eat her food.

A shadow cast over Jen's shoulder. 'She's watching her weight. No pudding for Jennifer.' Patricia pushed Doreen's hand away from Jen's bowl. The trifle splotched onto the table. Felicity snickered.

Fuelled by her friend's allegiance, Patricia whispered loud enough to be heard, 'Jennifer, do not eat anything that woman makes. They're not like us. You'll catch something.'

Patricia tugged Jen's arm with such force she feared dislocation. Johnny chewed his thumbnail. Doreen hid behind a stack of pudding bowls.

'Get over there and retrieve your sister,' Patricia slurred. 'Those do-gooder Normans are interfering with my family again.' She lost her footing.

Felicity caught Patricia's elbow. 'Easy does it. No more grape juice for you. Everyone's watching.'

Patricia righted herself as Felicity played on their mutual fear of public embarrassment.

Jen tried to leave. Felicity drew her back; a snake toying with its prey.

'Where's the bonnet your mother worked so hard on this morning?' she asked. 'We wouldn't want all the last-minute work, after checking out my girls' outfits, to go to waste, would we?'

The churning washing machine in Jen's tummy elevated to a spin cycle.

Patricia affected her best "up yours" voice. 'I've been working on it for weeks, Felicity, dear. Can't you tell? Jennifer, get Amanda. It's time to go home.'

Johnny gave Jen's hand a furtive squeeze. He looked as miserable as she felt. Her mouth wouldn't work when Liz asked what was wrong. Pleased to see her sister, Mandy trilled when Jen picked her up. Jen was grateful Mandy wasn't old enough to understand the situation. The walk to join Patricia was a slow one Jen never wanted to end. Being outside meant she wasn't indoors, in private, with a drunk and irate parent.

Out of earshot, Patricia let rip. 'Get your arse inside. How dare you show me up to that snooty cow.'

Patricia's threat clawed at Jen's innards. The washing machine rumbling descended to her feet. Patricia dragged the girls towards the house and the impending punishment for another thing Jen was sure wasn't her fault.

PRESENT

I have a temporary reprieve although it's an unfortunate one. Doreen is in hospital. Ellen sent a text stating Doreen fell down the stairs. She's weakening. Feeling relieved at a person's suffering is wrong, but at least I don't have to face her yet. It's delaying the inevitable though. Until Doreen comes home, I'll spend the time worrying about what she knows. Her threat to go to the police with information she has on me hangs heavy.

On waking, I touched Johnny's "Mods Rule" badge. It's become a habit. Since I took it, when it fell off his jacket, the badge stays next to my bed, wherever I am. A connection to Johnny through a piece of metal sounds foolish, but I'll take what I can.

Last time I stayed at a hotel, I thought I'd lost it. Nicole put on a Christmas party for the practice, including paying for our rooms. The following morning I couldn't find Johnny's badge. I turned the room upside down. Although I'd searched every inch, it wasn't there. It felt like Johnny had left me again. A few days later it showed up. My magpie cat covets shiny things. Doodle hid the prize under his basket.

The cat burglar makes repetitive figures of eight between my

LISA SELL

legs as I stumble to the bathroom. I give him the expected morning chin rubs to tide him over until food hits his bowl. I've become the stereotypical cat lady; destined to be single, with a moggy companion, and stinking of pee. Woe is me. Stuff that. I've decided the direction my life takes. I'll have the cats, not the incontinence.

I'm not alone because of a hatred of men. My dreadful choices are done and buried. I didn't love anyone I was involved with. Maybe you can only give your heart away once. Those who followed Johnny were a poor imitation.

Somehow, I made it to my forties. In the early nineties I considered reaching twenty-one would be a fluke. Memories of most of that decade are hazy due to narcotics, stimulants, and hallucinogens. If it was available, I took it. Dancing at raves in a doped-up world felt like freedom. It was shallow. I have no friends from that era. Junkies and party people tend not to be lifelong pals once they've matured or paid the price for hedonism.

Nowadays I focus on work and my degree. I need to keep focused and not let the past be a distraction. It sounds easy in theory, but it's always on my mind. Whenever I study, guilt creeps in. Kelly never became what she wanted to be, whatever it was. I didn't ask. She knew about my doctor ambition. The entire world would've known, given half a chance. Not long before she died, Kelly gave me an anatomy textbook she'd found in Oxfam. Even though I wasn't interested in her life, she thought of me. When I spouted on about my treasured medical books, she listened.

I place my hand on the bathroom mirror to hide the face of the girl who'd robbed Kelly of her future. My younger self peeks through. I'm haunted by a ghost who will not lay to rest.

I've wrestled with how the head wound I inflicted wasn't an instant death blow. Claire seeing Kelly after the fight makes me consider, for the first time, that maybe I didn't kill her. However, I've read enough to know the injury could have led to a prolonged death. That's even more horrific. I should embrace the possibility I didn't kill her, but I can't. She wouldn't have been lying on the track, weakened and easy prey, if I hadn't put her there.

Kelly gave me a book to follow my dream. In return, I gave her pain and ended hers.

13TH JUNE 1987

'When I grow up I want to be in a girl group like Bananarama, get married, and be a great mum.' Kelly contributed to the Truth Game she was playing with her neighbour, Priscilla Staines.

Kelly looked forward to Graham's visits to the bookies as he'd be there for the rest of the afternoon, followed by the pub. She was able to sit in the garden, lording it over eleven-year-old Priscilla, with her extra three years of wisdom. Finding time together was complicated by Priscilla's mother, Deirdre, banning her daughter from leaving the house.

Priscilla was born with a hole in the heart. Her overbearing mother never failed to remind her, and others, of the fact. Deirdre believed Priscilla was susceptible to germs, which could become illnesses, resulting in death. A recent check-up confirmed the hole was tiny and the heart murmur weak. Deirdre heard the opposite, remembering her fragile baby in an incubator. From Priscilla's birth, Deirdre was intent on encasing her daughter in a protective bubble.

Consumed with cabin fever, Priscilla took advantage of her mum's naps. Chris, her dad, would give the signal when Deirdre's snores began. He tried to reason with his wife that Priscilla's paleness came from a lack of sunshine. It fell on scared ears so he corroborated with Priscilla to give her snatched moments of freedom. Each time, Priscilla shot into the garden, tying a strip of white kitchen towel to the fence post. In a reversal of surrender, it was a message to Kelly of escape. Outside, Priscilla lived life her way.

Kelly sat on a stool she kept in the garden for these occasions. Feeling rebellious, Priscilla lounged on the grass. They united from each side of the fence, making the divide part of their games. They watched their faces flickering in and out of the slats. Their version of Peek-a-Boo always produced hysterics as they slapped each other's heads when they popped above the fence.

The Truth Game was their favourite activity and a means for sharing fears and hopes. Kelly felt confident in telling Priscilla things the other kids judged or Graham would punish. Knowing Priscilla had no other friends to spill secrets to helped. The girls united in being outsiders.

Kelly tried to join in the games the other children played. In desperation, she offered to do the dirty job of being the seeker in Hide and Seek. An hour of searching ended with swallowing the upset at the kids banging on a window and making faces from one of their houses. Once again, Kelly had been left behind.

Being with Priscilla made Kelly feel appreciated and, for the first time, envied. The younger girl commented upon how Kelly wore what she wanted rather than being forced into fussy tartan dresses with satin ribbons. Kelly's "Choose Life" T-shirt caught Priscilla's eye. The slogan flaked and rips formed on the hem. Priscilla wished she could be untidy, but trendy too. Instead she resembled a waif from a Victorian novel. Even the clothes Deirdre chose fitted the era.

Priscilla took a turn at the Truth Game. 'I want to be a singer, like Pat Benatar.'

'Cool.' Kelly gave her friend a high five.

When Priscilla shared her ambition with her dad Chris, a voice mumbled through the *Daily Mail*, 'That's sweet.' Priscilla recognised patronising replies. She resolved to take the rock world by storm *and* hold outside concerts to spite her parents.

Priscilla stood to get a better view of Kelly. 'Who will you marry?'

Kelly squirmed. People usually looked at her to assess how to inflict pain. Friendliness was an alien concept.

Sensing her friend's reticence, Priscilla reached over and touched Kelly's shoulder. 'Who would you like to marry, Kelly? You could marry anyone.'

Kelly smiled at Priscilla's kind ignorance. She was the only person, apart from Doreen, who saw the best in her. 'I'm not sure. Maybe Matt Dillon.'

'Good choice.' They had seen *The Outsiders* and swooned over the cast.

'Or...' Kelly paused.

Priscilla swung her legs over the fence. The gossip was getting too juicy to have boundaries. Kelly moved the stool back, unnerved by their closeness.

Priscilla shook Kelly's shoulder. 'I won't tell anyone. Cross my heart and hope to die.'

'I'm not sure if he loves me too.' Kelly ripped grass from the lawn.

Priscilla bounced, plaits flying in the air. 'Who is it?'

'Priscilla Deirdre Staines, what on earth are you doing?' The sleeping beast had awoken. Deirdre stood by the fence, hands on hips and a snarl on her face. Priscilla enjoyed how smudged mascara ruined her mum's usual perfect presentation.

'We're just talking.'

'You know not to leave the house, let alone go into someone's garden. I'm sure that girl has other things to do with her family.' Deirdre refused to look at Kelly.

The Pratts' reputation travelled through thin walls. With each fight, Deirdre warned Chris not to intervene. She wouldn't get involved in that family's business, no matter how terrifying it sounded. Ignorance, bred by fear, concluded the hatred in the Pratt family was contagious.

'Bye, Kelly.' Priscilla tried not to cry as she returned home.

Kelly understood it would be some time until the girls could meet again. Deirdre was aware Priscilla was chatting with the "urchin next door" – Kelly could hear through the walls too. Deirdre would ramp up her surveillance.

Kelly placed the stool next to Doreen's collection of gnomes. Sometimes her mum talked to them. With anyone else, it would've been amusing. Aware Doreen had no friends, it was pitiful. Kelly decided to spend the afternoon spoiling her mum.

'Oi, Smelly Kelly. You're such a skank. No one wears those tops anymore.' Charlie walked past, holding his middle finger aloft.

Two people within ten minutes had scorned Kelly and she didn't react. At least Deirdre saved her from telling Priscilla the identity of the one she loved. Kelly had nearly slipped up. He wouldn't have been happy about that.

Some secrets were too dangerous to be shared.

32

PRESENT

After thumping her way in, Claire stands in my kitchen. She's a reporter not to be underestimated, seeing as she's found my workplace and home.

'We're going on a field trip.'

'It's 8am on a Sunday,' I say while yawning. 'Why aren't you asleep, like normal people?'

'Come on, Jen. Neither of us is normal.' She sticks out her tongue and crosses her eyes to emphasise the point.

I slump against the fridge, massaging my temples. 'How do you know? We haven't seen each other in years.' The catty tone is a consequence of not getting to sleep until 6am.

'I just do. Do you still dig your nails in your palms when angry or worried?'

I unfurl my fists.

'Do you wear freaking cool T-shirts of bands the populars have never heard of?' She looks at my Throbbing Gristle T-shirt. 'Do you still sing like a goddess, but hide it?'

When we were younger, she caught me belting out a tune in her bedroom. She'd gone for a pee. The Cure came on the radio and I was mid-song when she recorded it. Without my knowledge, she entered the tape for a competition *Smash Hits* magazine held to discover a pop star. Claire was gutted to announce I hadn't won. I was annoyed she'd put me in the spotlight when I wanted to hide. Claire decided the judges were "popster tossers" who wouldn't know a great singer if one smacked them in the chops. I admired her loyalty and chose not to mention her subscription to the pop magazine.

'Bet you do still sing well,' Claire says.

I haven't got a clue. The cat can't hold up scorecards.

She opens the fridge. 'You also still have appalling manners. Are you making breakfast, or what?'

I direct her to the table. The kettle doesn't have the energy to argue with the black pot about *her* rudeness.

'Don't you have food at home?' I ask, rifling through the cupboards.

'I ate hours ago. My stomach feels like my throat has been cut.'

Doodle is in ecstasy as Claire lashes belly rubs upon him. She lowers to the floor and lies on her front. I can't deny the carefree attitude is lovely and I wish I could be more like her. I was once. We were cheeky little blighters. Maybe she can help me find that person again.

'Tea, if you're brewing up.' She moves the blissed-out cat and takes a seat. 'Proper country cottage you've got here. I'd never have thought this was your scene. Didn't you want to be a doctor in a city?'

'Things change.'

'Oxfordshire has a hold on us both.' She tries to create a bond. 'I'm such a loser and even went to Crosston University nearby, to stay close to Mum. I only just got a degree though.'

'What did you study?'

'English and Media, when I wasn't in a coma from nights spent in the Student Union or stoned. We all did it, eh.' She grins at the memory of a misspent youth.

I turn away.

'Did I say something to offend you?'

I face her. 'You looked it up, didn't you.'

'Usually I'm a brilliant reporter, but with people I like, I get flustered.' At least she has the grace to be embarrassed.

I allow the statement she likes me to sink in before I launch. 'I messed up when I was twenty and was arrested for possession of a few ecstasy tablets. I'm not making excuses but it was hardly the crime of the century and I wasn't charged.'

Claire scrapes the chair back. 'Woah there, stress head.' Her hands fly up in mock surrender. 'I was taking the piss. It's no worse than the messes I got into. Mum rescued me from Troddington police station a couple of times. Good job Kev was working there and having a thing with her.'

'Your mum was nobbing Kev Brown?' I never would've believed it of straight-laced Ellen.

'Ew, that's my mother.' Claire pretends to vomit. 'After she chucked Dad out, she decided to live a little. Kev was useful for insider info. Good move really.'

Claire's not lost her mercenary streak. I wonder how she would have fared as the child of my parents. She might have come through it unscathed. I'm glad she had Ellen though. No one deserved my mum, not even me.

'Why are you here?' Gossiping is getting us nowhere. Much as I'm warming to her, it's unsettling having Claire on my territory. This is the only house I've made mine.

'Remember Constance Major? The dotty woman who had a dog called Scruff?'

'Of course.'

Constance was one of the estate's older residents. She walked Scruff twice a day and the kids loved playing with him. Constance always carried chocolates, which added to the duo's popularity. She worked in paediatrics in a hospital in Oxford. I glimpse the anatomy textbooks, stowed beside the microwave. Some came from Constance, who encouraged me to become a doctor. I'd hate for her to find out they were wasted.

Claire sets to work on the toast, spreading a generous helping of jam. I sit opposite, nibbling a more conservatively layered slice.

'Mum says Constance is still spritely, if not more eccentric,' Claire talks around a mouthful of food. 'I think Mum's too nice to say she's nuts.'

'I don't get what it has to do with you being here.'

Claire abandons breakfast. Doodle startles, wary of Claire's sudden pacing. 'Mum sees Constance every now and again. I'm so proud of how Mum's still looking out for people from the estate. She visited Constance yesterday and they got chatting about Kelly. Constance saw Kelly on the train track around the same time I did. How's *that* for a breakthrough?'

Claire's steps become frantic. The cat scarpers. I want to join him. Will this ever end? I wish I'd never got involved. I should've made excuses, emigrated, *anything* to make them go away.

'It's hardly a breakthrough considering how many people went on the tracks,' I say. 'What did Constance say happened?' Knowing what I'm facing is important.

Claire pulls up the sleeves on an enormous bomber jacket. 'She said Kelly was upset. Mum pressed for more info but Constance got distracted by her boyfriend. Older than God and she's still at it.' Her sleeves drop. 'Flipping jacket.'

I couldn't care less about the wardrobe malfunction. 'Did she tell the police?'

'Yes, but they said it wasn't relevant. Idiots.' Claire removes the jacket. She uses her whole body to communicate. Her arms are free to elaborate her points. 'We're off to her residential home to get the full story. Put some clean undies on and spruce yourself up a bit. I'll wait in the living room. Keep the cat company.' She marches through the archway, into the lounge.

It's a done deal. We're going to see Constance. Cruel as it

sounds, I hope in old age her memories have faded and she won't divulge information revealing my guilt.

33

9TH SEPTEMBER 1987

C onstance lowered her head as she meandered along the path running alongside the park. The sight troubled the children, usually assured of a friendly welcome. Constance was older than their parents and had no children. The estate kids adopted her as a surrogate grandmother. She became their chief defender when they were accused of wrongdoing and saw goodness in everyone, refusing to believe anyone could be born bad. Her missionary parents' ways rubbed off, but she refused to embrace all their theology.

Being a sister in a paediatric department was the perfect role for Constance. She had worked hard for the promotion and thrived on helping youngsters. Tending to children satisfied a maternal nature never recognised in her mainly single life. She tried not to consider how she was nearing retirement age. Her job was a lifeline in giving her purpose and companionship. Having Scruff at home, her beloved "bitser" dog – so called because his origins were "a bit of this and a bit of that" – reduced the loneliness. Scruff's absence made her whole body ache.

'Where's Scruff, Mrs Major?' Johnny asked.

'Come here, Johnny Rose, and stop that hollering.' Constance wouldn't abide shoddy manners in any child. They all behaved in her presence, even those who didn't blink at stealing from their mum's purse.

Johnny had watched Constance from his place on the bench. Normally she bounced along the path, with her generous belly jiggling. Shuffling betrayed her advancing years more than the grey streaks in her hair and her clothes looked like she'd slept in them. As she raised her head to greet Johnny, he noted the tear-stained cheeks.

'How many times have I told you to call me Constance?' She mustered a smile. Knowing she'd done so for him pinched his heart.

'Sorry, Constance. Is Scruff okay?'

Johnny doted on the pooch and Scruff adored Johnny. Whenever they met, both strained at the leash, one more literally than the other. Jen was used to Johnny disappearing mid-conversation when Scruff appeared. She wasn't bothered by it, knowing he would be an exceptional vet.

Today, Johnny was going solo. When she'd returned from school, Jen was grounded. The slashing of the throat signal she'd given from the bedroom window signified another unleashing of Patricia's foul temper. Johnny felt powerless seeing Jen trapped behind the glass. He wondered if he was turning soft, imagining scaling the Taylors' greenhouse to rescue the damsel in distress. With his clumsiness, he'd probably break either the greenhouse or his bones.

Constance interrupted his fantasy with a loud blowing of her nose. 'Scruff is with the vet. I'm picking him up later, hopefully.' A tear dripped on the front of her white cardigan, leaving a mascara blotch.

Johnny cleared his throat. 'What's happened?'

'I found him... he was... he...' Powerful sobs made talking

impossible.

Passing by, Ernie Bowers threw his BMX bike to the ground. 'Are you okay, Constance? You better not have upset her, Johnny.'

Ernie collected Constance's newspaper when she slept off the night shifts. He was fourteen, the same age as Johnny, but significantly shorter. Under the tutorage of Johnny's brothers, Ernie's tearaway reputation increased.

'Leave it out. I've not done anything. Do one.' Johnny raised his shoulders and pushed out his chest to assert the Rose boy status.

Ernie rode off, faithful to the code of loyalty between the Roses and their gang. Johnny knew it was flaky, considering how many fights he had with his brothers. Constance turned away from the park. At least no more dubious young knights would try to defend her honour. She beckoned Johnny to walk.

'When I came home from work this morning, I couldn't find Scruff.' Her voice wobbled. 'He's always there, waiting, the second the front door opens.'

'Where was he?' Johnny laced his arm through Constance's. Pollock Road lay next to the park, but they kept a slow pace. It was obvious Constance was in no rush to return to an empty home.

'I searched everywhere, even under the sink – as if he'd fit in there – but I was frantic.' They passed her house. 'Then I saw someone had kicked the back door in. It wasn't sitting flush and I should've got it fixed but I've been doing a lot of overtime.'

Johnny blanched at the thought of a person breaking into Constance's home. An estate rule asserted you never stole from or damaged each other's property. When he found the scroat who did it, he vowed this would be a rare occasion when he'd give Anthony and Ian a nudge to take care of matters.

'Did they nick anything?' Johnny asked.

'No. That's not why they broke in.' Shielding her face, she cried once again.

Johnny offered a handkerchief. Rob mocked him for carrying

one, declaring only homosexuals used them. The attraction the Neanderthal had for his mum baffled Johnny.

Constance continued. 'I went into the garden. Scruff was on the grass.' Johnny held his breath as Constance took a large one. 'Blood matted his fur and his breathing was shallow.'

Johnny held her as she wept. He didn't care if anyone saw and misconstrued the situation.

'On the wall they'd written… I don't like to say.' Constance dipped her chin.

'You can tell me,' Johnny said. 'No one else needs to know.'

She spoke to the ground. 'They'd spray painted "Constance shags dogs".'

'What the hell? Where's Scruff?'

'I took him to the vet in town. He has multiple cuts and possibly broken ribs. Who would do that to an animal?'

Johnny couldn't think of a single person who held a grudge against Constance. She never upset anyone and was widely respected. When her bathroom flooded, the residents helped to clear up and had a whip round for a new carpet. Why would someone attack Scruff? Johnny hoped the guilty party didn't live on the estate. Their life wouldn't be worth living if he found them.

'I'm so sorry.' Johnny fought the tears threatening to come. 'The vet will do his best. I did work experience there over the holidays. They're brilliant with animals.'

'Scruff is in the best place,' Constance said. 'The vet says hopefully the damage shouldn't be permanent.'

'Have you told the police?'

'Yes, but they won't do much.'

Constance understood the police's limitations when a crime occurred on the Rembrandt Estate. Ranks closed and mouths shut.

Whoever had done this wasn't a stupid bored child. The person who'd inflicted the cuts did so with precision, ensuring they were deep enough to wound but not kill. The culprit likely altered their handwriting too, although the police didn't have the resources to check every resident's writing.

'Didn't the neighbours hear anything?' Johnny asked.

'Kelly fed Scruff at eight o'clock and he was fine. She has a key to let him out for a pee when I'm working. When she left, he was sleeping in the lounge. The PC said the attacker must have taken Scruff elsewhere and then laid him on the lawn. There wasn't much blood on the grass.'

It wasn't a spontaneous moment of crazed violence. This was premeditated and frightening.

Johnny scanned the windows of the surrounding houses, realising the person who'd done this could be watching them. Constance widened her eyes, as if drawing a similar conclusion.

'Let's go inside,' Johnny said. 'I'll stay until the vet calls.'

'You're a good boy. Well, young man, really. When did you get so grown-up, Johnny Rose?'

A warm bloom crept across Johnny's cheeks. He wasn't used to hearing kindness. His household was a place built on blokey insults, although his mum tried to boost his ego. The consequences were in his brothers calling him a sissy or Rob being jealous of Rose's diverted attention.

Johnny guided Constance home, desperate to protect her. The estate could get rough sometimes but this was an unknown level of maleficence. He slammed Constance's door and leant against it to guard against what he believed would inevitably come.

34

PRESENT

Constance's current abode is more of a mansion than the average residential home. This is the scenic part of Oxford the tourists flock to; full of historic buildings and green land. Claire's battered Volvo lowers the tone by spluttering up the sweeping gravel drive. I shut my eyes against the strobing sunlight darting through gaps in the trees.

We've covered parts of our lost history on the way here. Rather, I have, under the fire of Claire's scattergun questioning. She now knows I left the estate at sixteen to live in a squat in Troddington. After the police raided it, I shacked up with Deggsy, a dodgy older man, in Oxford. I glossed over that part. Indignation rises whenever I remember how his manipulation almost destroyed me.

I gave Claire the shortened, more sanitary, version of my descent into drinking and drug-taking within the nineties rave scene. We progressed to how I went into a recovery programme after the arrest for possession, with a charity which later provided lodgings.

Claire seemed impressed with how I turned my life around, but I know I'm a fraud. Getting out of addiction doesn't make what I did to Kelly any less horrific. I probably wouldn't have become an addict if I hadn't attacked her.

At an ivy-covered doorway, Claire pulls the tasselled cord to ring the bell. We assess the grounds while we wait. A lake, landscaped hedges, and even the odd peacock, add to its grandeur.

'The butler will appear in a minute,' Claire says. 'I'd live here, let alone Constance.'

A flustered woman opens the door. Her grubby tabard shatters our illusions of waiting staff in tuxedos. A name badge declares she's called Peggy and is "Happy to help". In reality, Peggy looks happy to hurt someone.

'Apologies, ladies.' Peggy smooths her forest of frizzy hair. 'I was dealing with a resident who'd had an accident. We're short-staffed today. All hands on deck.'

She whips off the tabard and scurries behind a welcome desk to rival The Hilton, or what I imagine it's like. Trainee counsellors don't have the budget for swish hotels. Dressed in a black trouser suit and white shirt, Peggy gives a contented sigh at being back in her territory as a receptionist.

'Rather you than me, dealing with people's toilet mishaps.' Claire sniggers.

Peggy's cool stare makes Claire wither.

Ornate touches gild the foyer. Everything has a filigree border, even Peggy's jacket. I consider checking the visitors' book to see if King Midas has been here, such is the amount of gold layering most surfaces. After Claire signs us in, she rolls the golden pen between her fingers. Peggy's open hand suggests prior experience of stationery thieves. Claire slams the pen on the counter.

'Constance is in the Day Room,' Peggy says. 'Knit and Natter should be finishing. It's down the corridor, first on the right.'

We're dismissed as she puts the tabard back on and leaves. I sympathise with the bloke, caked in crap, waiting for an irate Peggy to finish cleaning his backside.

Still bearing a grudge against Peggy for denying her a new

writing implement, Claire says, 'Glad I'm not the old duffer she's probably left with a shitty arse.'

We hold on to each other throughout our hysterics, trying to be quiet in case Peggy returns. I love how Claire's not afraid to speak what others dare not think. Despite the circumstances, I'm pleased to have my thoughts twin back.

Compared to the opulence we've seen so far, the Day Room is a dump. Threadbare chairs sag towards a cracked stained lino. A strong smell of wet dog lingers. As with many things, outer appearances are viewed as more important. My inner justice warrior kicks in, wondering how much they charge to live here. If Constance is being ripped off, I'll be having words.

A cluster of geriatrics huddle in a corner, circling wool around each other's gnarled fingers. A woman snores with her mouth wide open, oblivious to the surrounding chatter. This group definitely has the "natter" part covered. The lone man surveys the room, possibly trying to find the exit. He pulls faces in response to the commands of the lady sitting opposite. Constance has always been bossy.

'Not that wool, Bert. The turquoise one, not the green.'

'It *is* turquoise, dear.' Bert appears to be stifling the urge to strangle the source of the order. He scoops up a navy ball of wool.

I cover Claire's mouth. It's best to begin on a positive note than to incite an uprising of elderly knitters armed with needles.

'Why don't you take a stroll around the lake, love? I've got visitors coming. And here they are.' Constance flings her arms out wide.

She was in her late fifties when I last saw her. Her hair is whiter and more wrinkles etch her face, but she's still the Constance we knew.

'Girls, it's so good to see you. Let's draw up a pew over there.' Constance beckons us to the opposite corner of the room.

The other women take their leave. Constance can still get others to do as they're told. Watching her lower into a recliner is an event in itself. She shifts downward by degrees, bone by bone. How many vertebrae does a person have? I could have answered that once.

Constance indicates the other chairs. 'Don't stand on ceremony.'

I fall into a seat, discovering too late its missing most of its springs. My knees jut towards my chin. Claire's feet hover inches above the ground. It's too awkward to swap seats. I'd make a witty comment if I weren't on the defensive.

Constance shuffles around, trying to get comfortable. Her blue eyes sparkle through their more rheumy appearance. The dimples still indent deep into her cheeks when she smiles. She's lost a little weight, which makes her potbelly more prominent. Constance is thriving.

'Nice gaff, isn't it.' She gives a theatrical swish of her hand. 'A bit dingy in here but they're doing a refit soon. My painting will have pride of place.' She points to a picture on the wall behind her. It might be a vase of flowers. I'm no art expert, but it's obvious Constance is still disillusioned about her artistic skills.

'It's lovely and bright,' I offer, looking away from Claire, who's chewing her fist.

Every Christmas, Constance drew her own cards. The estate joke, never to her face, was in trying to work out what the scene depicted. One year, Claire and I deliberated if the splodge was a monkey or a tortoise. We concluded we were both wrong. Monkeys and tortoises were hardly festive.

Constance beams at my compliment for her latest creation. I realise I've missed her. When I was younger, we spent time together. I'd listen to stories of her early days working as a nurse, and relish the gory details that appealed to my robust stomach.

Claire forces her gaze away from the car crash of a painting. 'You've come up in the world since Pollock Road, Con.'

'Finally, young Claire. Ellen keeps saying you'll visit.'

Claire shrugs. 'Life, you know. Matty's fourteen but acts like she's forty. Seb's more of a boy than a man. They keep me bloody busy.'

'Language.' Constance waggles a finger.

'Sorry.' Claire leans further back, in danger of tipping.

'I can thank my dad for this,' Constance says. 'A businessman he worked with on projects in Africa left him some money in his will. Dad wouldn't take a penny when he was there. This man decided Dad should be paid so he bestowed him a tidy sum. When Dad died, he passed the money on to my brothers and me. He didn't want to spend any of it. I bought a house in Oxford.'

'Nice one,' Claire says.

Constance nods. 'My eyes started to fail and I had one too many falls. Arthritis set in too. It was time to sell up and come here. I like being around people.'

The main theme of our past conversations was loneliness. Having a dog eased it and Constance always encouraged visitors. Kids popped in and returned home with a tummy full of sweets. Adults always left her company with fond hearts.

She shifts forwards as if to conduct business. 'I expect we better get down to it. You're here about Kelly Pratt, right?'

I wish we could continue the informal chat. Being around Constance makes me feel safe again.

Claire straightens. 'Mum said you spoke to Kelly the day she died.'

'I did, back in 1986.'

'1987. Sixteenth October,' I interject. Both turn to me. 'We've been talking about it a lot. I'm good at remembering dates.'

Keep it together, Jen. Slip-ups could be costly.

'Oh yes, that was the Great Storm,' Constance says. 'I remember how my guttering came straight off and I had to run across the park to retrieve it. The council said I'd have to wait for them to fix it so I got your dad to do it, Jen. Flaming council didn't want to shell out as usual.'

Claire gives an exasperated snort. Constance always had a habit of digressing. When I asked for help with science homework, I finished the session knowledgeable in the NHS's problems, but none the wiser regarding chromosomes.

Constance chuckles. 'Sorry, loves. I get sidetracked. It does Bert's head in. He's my current beau. I'm probably ADHD. Should've got diagnosed but there's no point now. When you're old, most people think you're round the bend anyway. I was telling Bert—'

'So, you saw Kelly,' Claire interrupts, before we veer into another unrelated avenue of conversation.

'Yes, I did. She had blood on her clothes and was carrying the worries of the world on her shoulders.'

I concentrate on Constance's painting, bracing myself for what she saw back then.

35

16TH OCTOBER 1987

Constance decided to take Scruff for a longer walk. The scars were healing and his bruising had faded. Thankfully, his ribs weren't broken, as initially suspected. The trauma hadn't erased though. The previously relaxed dog jumped at the slightest noise. Scruff also developed an aversion to males. When a boy from the estate approached, the dog growled and then cowered. The only male he allowed near was Johnny. When they collected Scruff from the vet, Johnny held the dog and he didn't leave until late. Since then, Johnny checked on Scruff and Constance daily.

Constance accepted she was easily distracted but her mind always focused on important matters. The person who'd inflicted harm upon her dog was obviously a man or boy. Both were troubling, especially if it was someone she knew. Determined to be positive and help Scruff enjoy the walk, Constance shook the thought away.

Before, they'd kept to the perimeters of the estate. Today, Constance was resolute Scruff should resume his routine and show the attacker he hadn't won. She understood being on the track wasn't legal, but everyone did it and hardly any trains came through. Scruff enjoyed skipping across the tracks, along with exploring the bushes and hedgerows.

His spirits lifted as they slipped through the gap in the hedge, at the end of Monet Drive. Constance detached the lead, certain of his obedience. The dog took slow steps, looking to his owner for reassurance.

'Go on, little one. You can do it.' She felt like a mother watching their child walk for the first time.

As his confidence increased, Scruff quickened the pace. Looking ahead for potential threats, Constance spotted a figure sitting by the side of the track. Children often played there; throwing stones, building fortresses on the banks, and escaping their parents' supervision. To find a child alone on the railway track was rare. Constance prepared for approaching a male, hoping Scruff wouldn't startle. He returned at her call and she attached the lead.

When she recognised Kelly, Constance exhaled. Kelly never posed a threat to anyone. As a kind neighbour, she'd do Constance favours and often played with Scruff. The girl's need for company was pitiful. Kelly's treatment by some estate kids angered Constance, along with people's determination to write off the Pratts, excluding Graham. Graham deserved everything he got.

Kelly cradled her head. The sight of blood on her hands made Constance move faster. A reluctant Scruff shuffled alongside.

'My goodness. What on earth happened?' Constance asked.

Kelly looked up. The cracked glasses did little to ease Constance's worry. She often worried about Kelly. The fights next door travelled through the thin terraced walls. Constance refused to close her eyes or ears to abuse. Most days she tended to injured and sick children. It was distressing when their injuries were caused by those who were supposed to provide love and care.

Whenever Constance went to the Pratts' house as an argument took place, Doreen attempted to convince her there was no need for concern. Constance never bought it. The cuts and bruises that followed always confirmed her suspicions. Graham almost dared people to report him by inflicting visible marks of brutality.

Most of the estate turned away, as if acknowledging the abuse would taint them. Constance knew the damage ignorance caused and called the police every time. With each visit, Doreen concocted another accident. Kelly always agreed. When the police came to Constance's house afterwards, she didn't care if Graham realised she'd reported it. Even with his later threats to kill her, she held firm against the intimidation. The police vented about Graham getting away with it again but Constance didn't blame Doreen for not pressing charges. Fear governed her life. Shame marked Doreen's cheeks when she refused the women's refuge details Constance offered. Doreen thanked Constance for her concern but insisted she was fine.

Kelly's head lowered. Constance rued how this girl thought she wasn't worth the eye contact. Constance wouldn't have it. She knelt and carefully lifted Kelly's chin.

'Who did this? You can tell me, sweetheart.' She almost whispered, realising Kelly would be ashamed at being brought low again.

'I was being silly. Got over excited looking at what the storm had done and fell.'

Constance detected the stream of lies. She sat next to Kelly and rummaged around her handbag, pulling out a trusty first aid kit.

'Where's the blood coming from?'

Kelly tapped the back of her head and winced.

'Can I take a look? I'll be gentle. Why don't you hold on to Scruff while I do.'

Kelly rubbed her hands together, as if cold, and nodded. Constance lifted Kelly's hair, noting its greasiness. The gash was no longer bleeding.

'When did this happen, love?' Constance started cleaning the wound.

'About forty-five minutes ago. I used my netball skirt to press against it. Did I do right?' Kelly held up the stained garment.

'Absolutely. Well done.' Constance knew Kelly needed praise. 'Seeing the blood must have been scary. Don't fret. Head wounds bleed a lot but I think you'll be okay. It's a small cut and not bleeding anymore.'

Constance finished cleaning up Kelly and, with permission, conducted an overall check of her body. Kelly's eyes darted away when the cigarette burns on the back of her neck were exposed. Hearing Constance's gasp, Kelly moved forward. Constance resolved it was the last time Graham used his daughter as a vehicle for channelling hatred. Social Services would pay a visit. Noting the girl's distress, Constance didn't mention the burns.

'Do you feel dizzy or sick?' She checked Kelly's eyes.

Kelly wrapped an arm around her waist. 'No. I'm okay, honestly.'

'I'll take you to the GP. It doesn't look serious, but best to check.'

Kelly stood. 'I sent Claire to get Mum. She'll be here in a minute.'

'Why didn't you go with Claire?'

'I wanted to be alone to think.' Kelly tried to straighten the frame of her broken glasses. The right lens fell out and smashed on the track.

'We'll go to the optician to get that sorted.' Constance understood Kelly was dreading Graham's impending anger. 'Don't fret. I'll sort your uniform out too. I'm an expert at getting blood out of clothes.'

'Thanks for always being so kind to me.'

Scruff pulled away and whined at the bushes behind them. Kelly tilted forward, trying to keep a hold on the dog.

Constance acknowledged the walk was too much too soon. 'What on earth is the matter, Scruff?'

'Take him home.' Kelly handed over the lead. 'Mum will be here soon.'

Constance had never heard the control in Kelly's voice before. Maybe she was growing up.

Constance was torn. Leaving Kelly alone on the track felt wrong. However, Doreen would arrive and although she may have been downtrodden, she always tended to Kelly. Scruff howled. Constance feared a relapse. If she didn't leave, he'd never venture outside again.

Battling self-loathing for the decision she had already made, Constance asked, 'Is Claire definitely getting your mum?'

'She's coming. Please go. Scruff's upset and I can't bear the noise any longer.'

Neither could his owner. Constance picked Scruff up and soothed him. 'Come round later and tell me what the doctor said.' Constance kissed Kelly's cheek and walked away.

With every step they took, Scruff's anxiety abated, as Constance's increased. She wanted to believe Doreen would arrive because it was convenient. Realistically, she knew Kelly would sit there, summoning the courage to go home.

Constance's unease didn't fade. Not when Scruff snuggled on her lap. Nor when she watched the television and waited for Kelly to knock on the door. Not even when she scrawled a reminder to phone Social Services in the morning. Most certainly not when she fell asleep in the armchair.

Constance's guilt returned the next day with force, when she heard Kelly was dead.

36

PRESENT

'I let Kelly down.' Constance stares at her slippers. I wish I could share how the blame is mine, not hers.

The moment of contemplation breaks as a group of men enter, preparing to play dominoes. They bicker over who won last time and who is the best player. Claire shoots them a filthy look. The room quietens.

Constance doesn't register the disruption. Her mind seems to be in 1987. 'I should've stayed. At least then she wouldn't have killed herself.'

'Do you reckon that's what happened?' Claire squeezes Constance's knee and receives a shrieking response. 'So sorry, Con.' Claire remembers too late she's dealing with an arthritic woman.

'I left her, which I regret, but the cut had stopped bleeding.' Constance turns to Claire, daring her to challenge the diagnosis. 'Head wounds are worrying to see because they bleed a lot. Kelly's was a small cut. She may have slipped and gashed her head on the broken bottles. Glass was everywhere.'

'You don't think the head wound killed her?' The attempt to keep my tone light fails. I sound like I'm being strangled.

'I've dealt with many head wounds. Kelly's probably wouldn't have needed stitches. I checked for concussion too. She was more upset than anything else.'

'So the head wound wasn't fatal?'

Claire gives me a shove. 'Pissing hell, Jen. You'd make for a crappy detective, asking the same question repeatedly.'

Constance taps Claire's hand. 'Language.'

Claire buries her face in a months-old copy of *Woman's Own*.

'The head wound, in my opinion, didn't kill her.' Constance's familiar eyes fix upon mine. What does she see? What does she know?

Recovered from chastisement, Claire throws the magazine aside. 'Doreen believes something happened to Kelly. She's convinced that even though Kelly went through some rubbish, she'd never have killed herself.'

'She had a tough life,' Constance says. 'Living next door, I saw and heard everything.'

'Maybe she'd had enough of the bullying and Graham's abuse,' I add. 'It's too much for any young girl to deal with.'

Although Constance's version lets me off the hook, it's still beneficial if we decide Kelly died by suicide or blame it on Graham. I'm ashamed of the part I played. Whether it attributed to her death or not, I can't allow anyone to know. There will be consequences.

'Doreen said she told Kelly about a great uncle who'd died from an overdose. Kelly swore she'd never take her own life, no matter how bad things got.' Claire offers information I didn't know.

'But knowing of others who've died by suicide can sometimes be suggestive to those in a vulnerable place.' My counselling studies and work at Listening Ear are often useful.

'True,' Claire says. 'We do need to consider Kelly dying another way as well though. We're left with an accident or someone did her in.'

We make eye contact, silently agreeing not to share with Constance our suspicions about Graham.

'You must look into every option,' Constance says. 'As much as it could've been suicide, I still wonder what frightened Scruff. He was such a well-behaved dog. The way he acted that day was strange. I've often thought… Forget it. It's silly.' She waves her hands away to dismiss the idea.

'Go on.' I have to know.

'Maybe someone hid in the bushes,' Constance says. 'Scruff was okay at the beginning of the walk. When I checked Kelly over, he was fine then too. The howling came from nowhere. Perhaps the nasty piece of work that hurt him was hiding.'

The atmosphere grows thick with possibilities. We sit in contemplation.

Constance eases herself up. 'What do I know? I'm not a reporter or a smart counsellor lady. Ellen said you're going to be one, Jen. I'll leave the detecting to you two.'

Claire is poised to ask more questions. I pass over her jacket. Constance is done and I'd rather this conversation finished before anything incriminating is revealed.

'Thanks so much, Constance. It's great to see you again.' A wave of nostalgia passes between us as we hug.

'You too, Jen. You showed 'em, love.'

I should have realised she wouldn't think less of me for not becoming a doctor. Telling her what I did to Kelly is too risky though. Tolerance and friendship only stretch so far.

Bert's face emerges around the doorway. 'Coming for refreshments, treasure?' He rabbit twitches his nose to hold up steel-rimmed glasses.

Constance winks. 'Try and stop me, lover boy. There's nothing like a cuppa and a slice of cake to keep your strength up.'

Claire and I share a look of revulsion. It's similar to considering your parents doing it. You don't if you'd rather not be psychologically scarred for life. When I was a child, I considered if Mandy and I were adopted. Mum letting Dad anywhere near her was surprising, let alone three times. Being adopted had the bonus of not being related to Patricia Taylor. Unfortunately our birth certificates confirm her parentage.

After Constance plants a kiss on Claire, Bert grabs Constance's hand and they wave goodbye. Their singing travels along the corridor.

'Come on, plonker.' Claire pushes me towards the door. 'Let's get out of here before the stench of antiseptic and boiled cabbage makes me hurl. We've got work to do now Constance has given us the goss.'

'Do you reckon Kelly didn't die from the head wound?' I need someone else, other than Constance, to place me in the clear.

'You're obsessed with that. It sounds like she didn't.'

We leave the foyer, and Peggy, mopping a puddle. She mutters, 'Chuffing piddle. I'm not a flaming carer.'

I move Claire along, saving Peggy from getting sacked if she has to respond to one of Claire's sarcastic comments.

As we get into the car, I continue the conversation. 'So, we're looking at suicide?'

'I don't buy it. Kelly was upset but didn't appear suicidal when we spoke.' Claire crunches the car into gear. I grip the dashboard in preparation, aware of her racing driver tendencies.

'How do you know what feeling suicidal looks like?'

'Thankfully, I don't, but the evidence is moving away from suicide being the cause of her death. You're the counselling expert and it's why I value your opinion. Kelly doing that doesn't feel right though.'

'Okay.' I'm learning to be economical with words so as not to make mistakes.

'It leaves us with an accident,' Claire says, 'but that doesn't sit well with me either. Kelly said she'd already had a mishap. How unlucky can a person be? It's also odd that she told me someone was there when she fell but she told Constance she was alone. It bothers me.'

'Why? She probably got confused.'

'A person is either there or they're not. You don't forget that. I think someone else *was* there when she hit her head and she didn't want to say who.'

'Right.' I fiddle with the stiff window handle, trying to let in some air.

'It might be the same person who Constance thinks was hiding,' Claire adds.

Oxford passes by in a speedy blur.

'We can't say for certain anyone was in the bushes,' I say. 'Scruff was nervous anyway, after what happened to him.'

Claire looks at me rather than ahead. The intensity is scarier than the prospect of a crash. 'I'm convinced it wasn't an accident. She looked frightened. Someone was with Kelly and they caused her initial injury. That person is the key to this and I *will* find out who they are.'

I don't reply. What can I say? She's right next to you.

37

17TH JULY 1987

Johnny watched Jen sleep. He knew most people would view it as creepy, but it was the only way to be with her. Besides, Jen looked so peaceful and being asleep meant less noise. Being in the Taylors' house for the first time, and potentially being discovered by Patricia, was terrifying.

Mandy poked her head into the room. 'Wake Jen up if you want to talk. Mum will be home soon.' She left to resume her command on the other side of the door.

Mandy's unease at keeping watch troubled Johnny. If Jen weren't ill, he would never have dared to be there. He'd already taken a few days to summon up the courage to arrange with Mandy to visit while the rest of the Taylors were out. An eight-year-old tending to her sick sister alone made him angry, although Mandy was doing a sterling job. What teenage girl wouldn't want the 1984 edition of the *Twinkle* annual and a packet of Fruit Gums when battling tonsillitis?

The sleeping beauty awoke. 'What the hell?'

Johnny smiled at his whimsy in imagining Jen as his princess. He was hardly a prince. Princes were manly and poised. A kooky gangly teenager didn't match up.

. . .

Jen pulled the duvet higher, hoping he hadn't seen her baggy flannelette pyjamas. Usually she didn't care about fashion, but certain looks weren't allowed in the public eye, especially Johnny's eyes.

'How did you get in here?' Jen rasped. Sweat-soaked hair clung to her neck and forehead. Her inner thermostat cranked up a few notches.

'Mandy is on guard outside.' Johnny tried to find a suitable spot on the bed. He slipped off the edge and landed on the rug.

Jen gripped her throat against the pain of laughing. 'Clumsy idiot. Only you could fall over your own legs.'

Not for the first time, Johnny cursed the limbs he was often tangled up in. He hoped to either stop growing or discover the advantages of being tall. Rose said he should be a policeman because of his height. Rob threatened to leave if one of their clan joined "the enemy".

Jen shifted nearer to the wall to make more space. Johnny lying beside her wasn't a big deal. For years they'd laid side-by-side in the field by the railway track, deciding what objects clouds resembled and chatting nonsense.

Johnny took the opportunity to look around the room, knowing he'd probably never be there again. The demarcation between Mandy and Jen's sides was obvious. While Mandy's area exploded with powder pink, George Michael posters, and mountains of cuddly toys, Jen's side could have been filed in the dictionary as a definition for *organisation*. Alphabetically ordered books, an empty desk, and a noticeboard full of reminders confirmed her orderly nature.

'Can you get my dressing gown out of the wardrobe please?' Jen asked.

A pile of clothes landed on Johnny's feet. 'Jen Taylor. You messy cow!' Despite the teasing, Johnny liked seeing the chink in her regimented armour. Jen needed to lighten up sometimes.

'Get stuffed. You're supposed to be nice. I'm poorly.' She sat up and put on the dressing gown.

Johnny took his place next to her and presented a carrier bag. 'I've got goodies.'

Jen worked through the contents. The mix tapes he'd compiled made her tearful. Whenever she was ill, Jen always felt more vulnerable.

'Don't be mopey,' Johnny said in response to Jen's eyes welling. 'I need you to listen to this stuff to learn the words. Then we can sing tunes from your Walkman again.'

Claire's card instructing her to "Hurry up and get well because I've got no one to take the piss out of" cheered Jen. She missed their banter, but Claire tagging along could have caused problems. Unlike most people, Claire didn't have a problem with responding to Patricia's barbs in kind. For that reason, Jen always went to the Woods' house and never invited Claire to the Taylors'.

'Who's this from?' The weighty tome on anatomy wobbled within Jen's grip.

'Kelly said to give it to you.'

The book became a heavier burden in Jen's hands, symbolising the shame for the unkind thoughts she'd had about Kelly.

Johnny leafed through it. 'She apologised for it being second-hand, but I said you wouldn't mind.'

Jen knew she'd have to hide the gift, along with her other medical textbooks. Patricia didn't respond well to reminders of Jen's ambition to be a doctor. She tolerated second-hand items in her house even less.

'I hope you like this book too.' Johnny held a copy of *Jane Eyre*. 'Ian took the mickey when he saw it. He asked why I was reading books written by dozy birds about dappy bints. Quite the intellectual is my brother.' Johnny gave Jen a glass of water from the windowsill to ease her laugh-coughing.

'I haven't read this one yet.' Jen had developed an obsession with the classics and devoured works by women authors. Johnny wasn't so stupidly macho that he refused to read them.

'Just to ruin the ending a bit, that bloke shouldn't have been forgiven,' Johnny said.

Jen hurled a pillow at his face. 'Why do you always do that? I've yet to read a novel or watch a film without you giving away the ending. Anyway, what did the man do that was so bad?'

Johnny grinned at how Jen's curiosity always won over annoyance. She hated surprises as much as he did. Coming from unpredictable backgrounds, neither wanted to be unprepared.

'Rochester was going to marry Jane even though he already had a wife. He convinced Jane he was on the level and let her down big time.' Johnny became more animated explaining the plot. 'He gets his comeuppance when he goes blind but still, why he's allowed to get the girl is beyond me.'

'The poor man can't see. What more do you want?'

'His sight begins to return at the end. So he's not punished at all.'

'Cheers. I don't need to read this after you've shared most of the story.'

Jen winked to cover her unease in hoping she'd never do anything so terrible that Johnny couldn't forgive her.

The door opened. They held their breath.

'You'd better go, Johnny.' Mandy crossed her legs, demonstrating how the scariness of fending off Patricia affected her bladder.

Johnny kissed her on the forehead. 'You've done a brilliant job. The guards at Buckingham Palace have got nothing on you.'

Boosted by the validation, Mandy resumed her post.

Johnny turned to Jen. 'I'm off. It's best not to give Patricia any more reasons to be a bitch.'

. . .

Jen's open vulnerability made Johnny want to comfort her with a kiss on the forehead too. As Jen looked up to say goodbye, Johnny's lips hit the side of hers. She jolted her head back. Johnny startled. The awkward kiss, that wasn't a proper kiss, but both hoped was a real kiss, surprised them.

'Er, sorry.' Johnny looked everywhere but at Jen. 'That went off target.'

Jen chewed her lip, willing her happiness not to show. 'Let's hope you don't get tonsillitis too.'

'Look after yourself.' His overgrown fringe covered some of Johnny's embarrassment.

After he left, Jen felt she was floating on air and not because of the strong medication. It might not have been an intentional romantic kiss, but it was *something*. She touched her lips.

'Thanks, little one,' Johnny said to Mandy.

Mandy broke away from listening to Teddy Ruxpin telling a story. 'You're very red.'

Johnny left the Taylors' house touching his lips and grinning too.

PRESENT

'Why won't you help me, Jen?' Kelly lies on the ground. A pool of claret forms around her head. 'I only wanted to be your friend.' She rises from the track. A train slams into her body.

I scream awake. The dream replays every night. For years I had nightmares of Kelly in different guises: crawling from a grave, condemning my pride or emerging from under the bed, like childhood's imagined monster. When I became settled at work and found the cottage, the dreams disappeared. This investigation has brought them back.

It's 5.15am. My mobile shows seven missed calls from Doreen, beginning at 2am. In the hope of achieving uninterrupted sleep, I'd silenced the phone. Doreen obviously didn't sleep well either. She probably knows about our meeting with Constance.

I decide to caffeinate and go for a run before phoning Doreen. My mind needs to be straight because my innocence isn't definite yet. I believe Constance's diagnosis that the head wound didn't kill Kelly. I have to. A wave of doubt still niggles in how I contributed to her death. If I hadn't retaliated, she wouldn't have lingered on the track. I told her to shut up and I didn't want to hear what she was saying. Still she persisted, desperate to forge a common link between us. If Kelly had known when to stop, she might be alive. I bunch the duvet in my hands, stretching out the tension.

It's time to face the day. Doodle swats my legs, playing a game he never tires of. I carry him downstairs, unapologetically aware I'm indulging a grown cat. If they got me on the couch, I'd be a psychologist's dream. Seeing a counsellor is a condition of the training. Knowing how to play the system helps. When you've studied non-verbal cues, fillers, and voice, you know how to blag it. I will never share my past with another counsellor. It's hypocritical but I have too much to lose. I push the memories away, always a master in compartmentalising.

My phone rings. It's Doreen. Buoyed with confidence at the possibility I didn't kill Kelly, I answer. 'Hello. How are you? Are you still in hospital?'

'No, I'm not.' Her words are clipped. Perhaps she's tired.

'It's great you're home. Did Claire mention we visited Constance Major? She's given us important info about Kelly. I expect Claire's shared it with you already. You know how excited she gets when—'

'I couldn't give a toss about that. I haven't spoken to Claire but I will when you're both at my house, today at ten.'

The uncharacteristic demand throws me. 'I can't. I'm working.'

'You *will* come, you murdering bitch, or I'll go straight to the police. Then you'll not get the chance to explain to me how you murdered my daughter.'

'What?'

'Be there.' The phone connection ends.

Was I wrong to start believing it wasn't me? Did I kill Kelly as I've always thought?

29TH DECEMBER 1982

Many of the households on the Rembrandt Estate wished the festive period would end. Days off work were always welcome. Having to spend more time with relatives often wasn't. Children wore adults down with complaints of boredom, demands for broken toys to be fixed, and batteries replaced. Some parents regretted past accidents or decisions about stopping birth control. They threw another selection box at their offspring and prayed for sugar-induced comas.

The Taylors' house also lacked festive cheer. From the moment the school holiday began, Patricia had been in even more of a disagreeable mood. She was likely to maim the next person who played Slade or Wizzard in her presence. Her Christmas memories made it a less than wonderful time of the year.

Growing up, she'd hated living above a pub run by her parents. The hospitality of the landlords led to the pub's popularity. The patrons of The Cat and Fiddle often lingered after hours. Most mornings Patricia discovered strangers sleeping in the snug. Her parents didn't see the problem in a customer who spent a fortune having an overnight stay.

Every Christmas, Patricia performed a song and dance routine

LISA SELL

in the bar. She rehearsed for months, making the act good enough for her father's approval. After her performance, the clientele applauded while her father demanded she return upstairs. When money was hitting the tills, Patricia became invisible.

Patricia rebuffed her mother's attempts at showing affection. The girl only wanted her father and refused to share him with the bawdy woman who wore revealing outfits. Her mother's insistence on calling her Patty added to the shame. Whenever Patricia offered her full name in correction, others scorned her snootiness. Patricia then became "Duchess", a nickname given by a regular. Whenever the clientele used it, Patricia raged. Her family adopting it, making it her name, didn't help.

Patricia's four older brothers worshipped her. Nothing was too much for their Duchess. They bought her gifts and placed her on a pedestal far higher than their mother. *Fat lot of good it does me now*, Patricia thought, lowering the sleep mask. She'd left her siblings behind. Satisfied with council house existences, for them climbing the social ladder was unnecessary and laborious. Patricia wouldn't be dragged down by her relatives. She also shunned her parents. The geographical distance that arose when they retired to Blackpool made it easier. Family was an overrated concept.

Her own elder daughter was sulking somewhere. Patricia figured it served Jennifer right for breaking Patricia's Wedgewood ornament, a wedding gift from her godmother. Violet had led the local W.I. and lived liked a queen, thanks to her banker husband leaving her a fortune in his will. Patricia idolised Violet until she died of a stroke while sitting on the toilet. The shine of knowing a prestigious woman dulled afterwards. Patricia refused to mention someone who passed away in such vulgar circumstances.

Jen tried to hide the breakage of the cuckoo ornament. Hearing the smash, Patricia slipped into the living room and drank in Jen's fear. She felt no guilt at scaring her nine-year-old daughter. Carelessness led to consequences.

Patricia seized the dustpan from Jen and sprinkled the collected pieces of china, with an order to pick up each piece. If Patricia found a single speck, Jen would be grounded for two weeks. Patricia knew it was an impossible task. White china in a deep pile white carpet was the proverbial needle in the haystack.

While Patricia settled into her beauty sleep, Jen sifted the debris from the carpet. Mandy played drums on the highchair table. Jen was thankful Patricia didn't know Mandy had dropped the ornament by the fireplace. The punishment her mum could inflict upon a three-year-old was uncertain. Jen didn't want to find out and decided to take the blame.

Liam watched a war film, ignoring Jen scrabbling around. He jabbed at Mandy's chest.

Hearing Mandy's earlier happiness become a whimper stirred Jen's temper. 'Leave her alone.'

Liam stared at Jen and poked Mandy harder, inviting a fight. Jen took Mandy from the chair, attempting to soothe her before the crying began. Too late, she bounced the sobbing child on her knee.

'Shut that brat up,' Liam said. 'I'm trying to watch this.'

'If you hadn't been irritating her, she wouldn't be upset.'

Liam had been lounging around all morning, demanding refreshments. Jen wanted to smash them into his smarmy face. She only waited on him because he knew who really broke Patricia's ornament.

'Do you want Mum to tell you off again? I'll give her a shout.' Liam rose from the sofa.

'No! Don't. I'll calm her.'

Mandy showed appreciation for Jen handing over her favourite toy elephant by chewing Ellie's leg.

'What's going on in here?' Mike asked as he entered the room.

His dungarees, marked with plaster, signified another day of working. He had only taken Christmas Day off. Customers praised his dedication in getting their plastering done. He didn't tell them he'd rather be in their houses than his own.

He lifted Mandy and made silly faces. She squealed and played with his nose. Jen found the interaction difficult to watch, wishing he was always so attentive. His fleeting appearances in the Taylor house hurt. The only time he spoke was to either reprimand them for upsetting Patricia or give warnings not to.

'What's this on the floor?' Mike flicked a shard of china from his sock.

'Jen broke Mum's cuckoo ornament,' Liam said, sneering at his sister.

Mike's forehead settled into its usual frown. 'Flaming hell, Jen. It's her favourite. Can't you be more careful?'

Liam folded his arms. 'She did it on purpose.'

Liam's malice confused Jen. He thrived on causing trouble. She considered her fist as a replacement for the Wotsits he shovelled into his mouth.

'I didn't! It caught on my sleeve as I swung round.' She glared at Liam. He waved in return.

Mike sagged against the wall. Jen tried not to be a disappointment. One parent's approval shouldn't have been too much to expect. Mike fought exhaustion. Lack of sleep was standard as Patricia often kicked him out of bed. The weariness came from being in his situation. He couldn't be the husband his wife demanded, and had proved to be an ineffectual father. If Liam spoke to him, his words were riddled with sarcasm.

For self-preservation, Mike distanced himself from Mandy. The shattered relationship with Jen dealt the heaviest blow. He never told her she was his best girl. If Patricia knew, her viciousness would increase. Once, he naively thought she could change, believing his affection would soften her. It didn't take long to realise the woman he married lacked the ability to love and controlled everything.

. . .

Patricia planned Liam's conception and her mission paid off. She bagged herself a husband and underplayed the part Mike had in Liam's creation. Their son was *her* success.

Jen was the next project. Patricia longed for another son. When the midwife declared they had a daughter, she passed the baby to Mike and left Jen mostly to his care.

Mandy was a slip-up Patricia soon regretted. After hearing of the death of her oldest brother, vulnerability made her careless. Heart complaints were common in her family. Patricia's fears for her mortality led to the hasty decision to create a new life. As Mike did his business, her mind drifted to the prospect of her next son.

Another girl became another disappointment for Patricia. She decided six years was old enough for Jen to help look after the baby. Patricia believed she'd done Jen a favour in teaching her the harsh realities of life. When Jen complained, Patricia highlighted her ingratitude at having a playmate.

Noticing Jen's hurt at his earlier scolding, Mike stroked her cheek. 'Let's get this cleared up before Mum comes downstairs.' He leant over and whispered, 'We'll have ice cream later, when she goes to the Tupperware party. Chocolate with hundreds and thousands, right?'

Jen contained her excitement. Her dad actually knew what she liked.

Patricia's spy, Liam, was in the room. Mike kept his voice low. 'It will be our little secret.'

40

PRESENT

'When were you going to tell us your little secret?' Claire stumbles over the words.

To have caused such a confident person upset, adds to my heap of shame. I take a seat at Doreen's dining room table. Doreen, Claire, and Ellen huddle at the opposite end. Placed alone, I'm the defendant at a hearing. Before I even speak, the judges have reached a verdict: guilty.

'*Little?*' Doreen's legs wobble with the effort as she stands.

Ellen guides her back to her chair. 'Take it easy. You've only just got out of hospital.'

'I'd hardly call murdering my daughter *little*.' Doreen slaps the table.

The force of the reverberation startles me. Claire and Ellen ignore it. They've been here for a while and know why Doreen is raging.

I must make this situation right but I can't find the words. I want to ask what Doreen knows and how. More than that, I wish I could disappear. I swear Doreen would kill me if she had the energy. Claire's expression suggests she'd willingly do so on her behalf.

'I'm not sure why I'm here.' I sound pathetic. The time for stalling is over, but still I try.

Doreen reaches across the table. 'You were seen that day, Jennifer, Jen, whatever you call yourself.'

She knows what happened. 'Who saw me?'

Doreen smirks. She knows hearing the name will destroy me. 'Johnny Rose.'

Fatigue and stress collide. A cloud descends over me.

41

21ST MARCH 1981

'Friends forever?' Johnny hooked his little finger around Jen's to confirm the oath.

'Always,' Jen replied, overjoyed to have found this kind boy with an oddness that matched her own.

Since their families had moved to the Rembrandt Estate two months earlier, Johnny knew they'd be friends. Jen was seven and a loner too.

In the first week, he'd left the house to escape family rows over who should unpack boxes that remained untouched. If he hung around, it would inevitably fall to him. Venturing to the top of Turner Road, Johnny understood not to leave the estate, much as he sometimes wanted to run away.

This was the third time the Roses had moved in the last year. Trying to settle into a new area over and over was exhausting. He hoped they would stay. Wherever they went, the Roses became unpopular. His roguish brothers terrorised people and Rose made a habit of stealing other women's husbands. The succession of men who appeared in the kitchen every morning ended when Rob Morgan moved in. Although his gruffness and sexist ways didn't make him a prize catch, at least he was consistent.

The day he met Jen, Johnny discovered a bush on Turner Road. It stood alone and offered the privacy he needed from a chaotic household. He vaulted over the bush, landing on top of a girl. The Johnny and Jen alliance formed from a sore head, giggles, and shared sweets.

Most of their following days were spent together. Johnny ignored Anthony and Ian calling Jen his girlfriend. Johnny didn't understand the things they said he should do with her. With how icky it sounded, he resolved to never want to.

Every day he looked for Jen. When she wasn't outside, Johnny stood in the park, visible from her bedroom window.

Johnny and Jen became collectively known on the Rembrandt Estate as J&J. Throughout the next six years, they believed their relationship would last forever. They even later dared to dream, albeit separately, for more.

Then came 16th October 1987 when Johnny decided he couldn't trust or understand a killer. When Jen struck Kelly, she shattered their friendship.

42

PRESENT

Claire places a glass of water in front of me. 'I can't believe you lied. I thought we were mates.'

'We are. I'm so sorry.'

I take slow sips, glad I didn't faint. They're looking at me like I'm a drama queen. Sympathy in this room is limited.

'Finished with the dramatics?' Doreen asks.

I'm resigned to letting her lead. I can hardly ask the mother of the girl she thinks I killed to have mercy. Doreen throws a coaster over as I put the glass down, disgusted at the animal staining her pine table.

'So, Jennifer.' Doreen no longer considers me a more amiable Jen. 'I saw Johnny in town. He lives in Aylesbury too.'

I was convinced he'd moved far away, not to the next county. The distance between us seemed like thousands of miles.

'What's he doing nowadays?' Claire receives my silent gratitude for asking the question.

'He's a vet,' Doreen says, 'and a partner in a practice. The bloke's done well for himself.'

'He always wanted to be a vet.' I can't resist staking a claim on knowing Johnny's dream. They're talking about *my* best friend.

Doreen scowls. 'Getting back to the actual reason for this meeting...' Coughing overwhelms her. Ellen rubs her back. Doreen ignores it, determined to continue.

'Johnny walked past the shop I was in. One of the carers took me out in that thing.' Doreen looks towards the wheelchair in the corner. 'A tall man strolled by. I wondered if it was Johnny Rose but thought not because of the flecks of grey in his hair. You forget children grow up. Well, *some* do. When he glanced over I knew it was him. Those blue eyes are unforgettable.'

They certainly are. Many times I looked into them and found my home.

Doreen continues. 'It shocked him to see me so frail. I told him I have cancer. He was sad to hear it, of course. We then went to a café. His treat.'

That's my Johnny; still kind to others.

'I asked about his life. He's divorced.'

My mind whirs with lost possibilities as I try to concentrate on Doreen's words.

'No kids. He focused on being a vet. Why am I spouting Johnny's life story? This isn't a reunion.' Doreen coughs again.

I want her to talk about Johnny forever.

Doreen looks my way. The harsh stare of an older woman brings back disturbing memories. I take another sip of water to unglue my tongue from the roof of my mouth.

Doreen gathers her composure. 'I shared with Johnny how we're investigating Kelly's death. When I told him you're helping, Jennifer, he looked ready to throw up. He was there when you were with Kelly on the railway track. Johnny heard you arguing and witnessed you pushing her. Then he saw the blood.'

'What were they rowing about?' Ellen asks Doreen. I'm no longer reliable enough to discuss events in which I played a key role.

'He couldn't hear well. The bush he hid behind was on the other side of the track. He'd gone to pick up Benny but Rob had already done it. Johnny said he remembers being excited at having a day off, and took the shortcut home to catch up with Jennifer.'

I conceal my joy in hearing how he wanted to be with me. Besides, it's not the case anymore.

Doreen takes a breath. 'As he approached the tracks, it sounded like someone was being attacked. He tiptoed around the trees that remained after the storm.'

'Why didn't he come out when he saw us?' I ask. Is my anger really that frightening?

'He was going to. Poor kid was terrified when you shoved Kelly and she lay bleeding on the ground.' Doreen's words are razor-sharp.

'Did he help Kelly?' Claire asks.

'No. He's regretted it ever since. The boy saw his best friend kill a girl. He was so tortured by it he didn't tell anyone.'

'It must have been awful,' Claire says.

'I've forgiven him. But I will never forgive *you*.' Doreen's finger points at me.

I seize a last opportunity for leniency. 'But Claire said she spoke to Kelly after it happened. Kelly was conscious.'

Doreen hugs herself. 'It doesn't mean she didn't eventually die. Stop trying to wriggle out of it.'

'Did Johnny's family move because of me?' I'm pushing my luck, but I have to ask. Although Doreen said Johnny kept it a secret, I wonder if he told Rose and she scooped her clan away.

'For a while afterwards he was in a bad way and wouldn't leave his room. *You* did that to him.' Doreen raises the accusing finger again. 'Rose fretted. When Rob got the opportunity to go into partnership at a garage in Little Parston, she jumped at it. Johnny practically begged her to get them off the estate. He couldn't face me or bumping into Jennifer. The family moved on a few months after Kelly died.'

My heart shattered that day, watching them filling up a van and Johnny refusing to acknowledge me. The Roses didn't go far though. The information is useless. Still, something else nags at me. Knowing Constance's version, this needs to be put into context.

I grasp a fragile lifeline. 'Did Claire tell you what Constance shared with us yesterday?'

Claire startles as the pieces slot together. 'Call myself a reporter? I was so wrapped up in you lying, Jen, I forgot. Constance spoke to Kelly after I did. Kelly was alive.'

'She could have died slowly and painfully.' Ellen's face confirms the error of her harsh statement. 'Sorry, Doreen.'

'But that's just it.' I must speak now I'm convinced I'm not a killer. 'Constance checked her over thoroughly. The wound was small. Head wounds sometimes bleed a lot but Kelly's had stopped.'

'Really?' Doreen raises an eyebrow.

Claire stands and squeezes my shoulder. I wonder if it's excitement or a show of solidarity. 'It's true. Constance was great at her job, right, Doreen?'

She doesn't reply, probably recalling the times Constance patched her and Kelly up after altercations with Graham.

Claire returns to reporter mode. 'Constance was adamant Kelly didn't die from the cut in her head. The one Jen caused, and which she needs to explain why she's never mentioned it.' She removes her hand from my shoulder. I'm still not forgiven for lying to my old friend.

'Claire recorded it.' Ellen passes Claire her mobile phone. 'We need to listen to it.'

Shaken by the series of revelations, Doreen visibly weakens. 'Before we do, Jennifer owes us the truth about why she attacked Kelly and abandoned her.'

It's time to tell them what happened. There's nothing left to lose. I allow my mind to travel back, taking these three women from the past and present with me.

43

16TH OCTOBER 1987

Jen pounded out her hatred for Patricia with every step she took back from school. She'd told her mum it would be shut because of storm damage. As usual, Patricia ignored her. She banned Jen from turning on the radio to listen to closures updates. The disruption to her sleep when Jen asked if they had to go to school was bad enough. A string of curses served as answers from under Patricia's duvet.

Approaching the estate, Jen decided she had an advantage. While out of the house, she was away from Patricia. Mandy would be safe with Liz, who'd no doubt listened to the announcements and kept her at the flat. Liz had a week off work. She said she was looking forward to not delivering bouquets on behalf of guilty husbands and boyfriends. Jen knew she was joking. Flowers and people were Liz's favourite things.

On the way home, Kelly was chattier than usual. The noise went straight through Jen who'd woken in a foul mood. Facing Patricia's bitchiness first thing did nothing to reduce it. When Kelly shrieked at the sight of the tree lying across the entrance to Troddington Secondary, Jen wanted to gag her. It was a tree. They fell in storms. Kelly could be so immature.

. . .

Mrs Newton slouched against the gate, instructing parents and children to go home. She rued being the designated emergency member of staff this time. The head of department role had its drawbacks. She'd rather have been marking a stack of ever-increasing maths homework. Instead, she hoped another natural disaster happened soon. The science department were next on the cover list.

'Mrs Newton, look at the tree!' Kelly sought her teacher's mutual enthusiasm.

Mrs Newton's disdain for Kelly pointing out the obvious was a thing of beauty. Jen liked her maths teacher even more as she reflected on the earlier scene.

'Why are you laughing?' Kelly asked.

Jen didn't reply. On approach to the Rembrandt Estate sign, Kelly skipped. Jen wondered if she had been dropped on her head at birth. The girl wasn't normal. Kelly beckoned Jen to catch up, frustrated with her slowness.

'What's the matter?' Kelly asked.

'Lay off the constant questions.'

Kelly interrogated Jen all the way home. She was nearing learning Jen's inside leg measurement with the information she'd collated.

As Kelly dropped behind, Jen knew she'd taken it too far. 'Ignore me. I'm having a rubbish day.'

Kelly smiled forgiveness. 'I'll try to be quieter. Mum says I'm a chatterbox and...'

Jen signalled a zipping of the lips. Kelly giggled at her error. She tugged her sleeves, stretching an outgrown jacket Graham insisted still had plenty of wear.

'Shall we see what the storm's done to the railway track?' Kelly said. 'I bet loads of trees have fallen there.'

'I need to check if Mandy is at Liz's.' Having a younger sister was useful for making excuses.

'Okay.' The excitement disappeared from Kelly's face.

'Only for a few minutes then.' Jen didn't want to upset her again. For the whole of their walk she'd inflicted her annoyance for Patricia upon Kelly. Kelly craved attention. She spent too much time alone.

Kelly bolted across Turner Road, through the field of over-grown grass, and towards the railway track. Her flabby thighs rubbed against each other in tight trousers. Jen jogged behind, figuring the quicker they got there, the sooner she would see Mandy and Johnny. She wondered if he'd attempted to go to school.

Hurtling down the embankment was always a thrill. They slipped down, with the momentum throwing them onto the track. An unguarded flash of affection hit Jen as she watched Kelly spin-ning in a circle with her arms wide open. Kelly's impulsive delight was charming.

'Look, so many fallen trees!' Kelly became Dorothy seeing Oz; no longer in a dull life but captured by a strange and wonderfully altered world.

None of the trees were on the line as the banks were set far back. The odd train still using the route would make it through. Jen studied timetables so she could watch them pass by. Creating stories for the commuters fired her imagination. As fewer trains passed through the stretch of track, the opportunities to be creative there dwindled.

Jen's childhood had seen many changes in the estate's landscape. Over the years, park equipment was removed, never to be replaced. All that remained were a set of swings with broken chains and split tyres. The square of concrete that once housed the park now memorialised a playful past. Depending on their occupants, houses were either neglected or extended. At its heart though, it was still the Rembrandt Estate. Jen hoped the community would endure against the supposed progress.

Kelly examined the gravel at the side of the track, kicking away pieces of glass. Finding what she sought, she took a box of matches from the inside pocket of her satchel and lit the dog end of a cigarette.

'That's grim, Kelly.'

'Want a puff?'

'No way. Buy them from the ice cream van, like the other kids do.' As Kelly dropped her hand, Jen realised she couldn't afford it. 'Don't smoke. It's not nice and you'll stink.'

'My dad smokes,' Kelly said.

Jen decided not to state Graham was no one's role model.

Kelly regarded the cigarette. 'I don't smoke much, only when he leaves longer bits of fags in the ashtray. I like seeing the smoke trail into the air.'

'You can do that watching someone else smoking, you goon.'

A visible lump forced its way down Kelly's throat. Jen was tiring of the girl's fragility. Kelly deserved to be bullied if she didn't toughen up.

'I enjoy stealing Dad's ciggies. It makes me feel stronger than him when I do.' Kelly paused then crushed the cigarette under her foot. 'You're right though. Smoking is bad for me.'

'Wouldn't Graham do his nut if he found out?' Jen heard the rumours about the Pratts. She wasn't usually bold enough to discuss the family dynamic with Kelly.

'He'd lose it big time, but he's not sussed it out yet,' Kelly said.

Jen didn't reply. The conversation about domineering parents was taking a difficult turn.

'He hits me a lot anyway, so it wouldn't make much difference.' Kelly shrugged and then jumped over the tracks. It reminded Jen of the game they used to play. If you stood on a crack, you broke your mother's back. She willed Kelly to hit the line if they could change it to disabling your abusive father.

'Does your mum try to stop him?' Jen's curiosity won against her uneasiness.

'She does her best. Sometimes I don't tell Mum when he hits me so she doesn't get walloped too. Mum always defends me, you see.

I'm an expert at holding in tears. Dad hates it because he likes to see me upset.'

Kelly plucked a robust white flower bursting through from the gravel. A single flower bloomed in autumn. A girl spoke of violence inflicted upon her as a normal occurrence. Jen felt heady with the world around her no longer making sense.

'Does Patricia enjoy making you cry?' Kelly asked.

Jen pretended not to hear. 'I'm going home.'

'Does your mum like hurting you?'

Kelly's second question dripped poison in Jen's ears. The storm inside her gathered momentum.

Jen swivelled around, stomping towards Kelly. 'You'd better shut your mouth or I'll shut it for you, permanently.'

44

16TH OCTOBER 1987

K elly stared at Jen. 'I'm sorry Patricia hurts you. That's not nice.'

Jen moved closer. 'Mum's never touched me. I don't know where you got that idea from.'

'My mum said Patricia's been hitting you and Mandy for *years*. Mum says when you're being hit yourself you can spot others who get belted a mile off. She's seen the bruises you try to hide.'

The space between Jen and Kelly's faces narrowed but Jen couldn't see the person in front of her. Kelly disappeared and became another obstacle to living a normal life.

'What the hell are you talking about?' Jen tried to focus on the other girl. 'You don't know me or my family, Smelly Kelly.'

'There's a bruise on your wrist.' Kelly looked at where Jen's sleeve had ridden up.

Jen gripped the cuff. 'I did it in P.E.'

'I use that excuse too. Do you tell people you have accidents as well?'

'We're not the same. My parents love me and we're a decent family. Not like you weirdo Pratts.' Jen refused to unite with Kelly on the basis of being a punch bag.

Kelly stepped away.

Jen lost reason. A girl she'd been kind to was taunting her. The rage Jen harboured for Patricia unleashed.

Jen snatched Kelly's collar.

Kelly propelled forwards.

Jen saw ridicule in sympathetic eyes.

Kelly's ankle rolled.

Jen pushed.

Kelly toppled back.

Silence descended.

Kelly lay upon the track. Blood spooled from her head. Her eyes were shut.

Jen slumped to the ground to check if Kelly was breathing. Glass pierced Jen's palm as she steadied herself. Panic diagnosed Kelly must be dead. Scarlet stained the stones. Kelly's chest appeared still.

Jen's survival instinct directed her to Liz and Freddie, her protectors. They would know what to do.

Running through the estate, her mind spun with how to confess. Would she lose the only adults who cared about her? Would Johnny no longer be her friend? Would she be arrested? Sobbing made sprinting harder but she continued, afraid of discovery.

I'm evil, she decided. *I'm worse than Mum. She's never killed anyone. She has the perfect reason to hate me.*

Her thoughts turned to Mandy. Resting in an alleyway, Jen took a moment to think. If she went to prison, what would happen to her sister? Patricia wouldn't allow Freddie and Liz custody. With Jen locked up, Mandy would take the full brunt of their mum's spite.

Jen had a sickening decision to make between Mandy and Kelly. Mandy was alive and reliant upon her. Devastating as it was, Kelly was probably dead. Jen hated herself for the lie she made in that moment, and one she'd always have to tell. She ran once more.

...

Liz opened the door. She gasped at the sight of the sweating and injured girl. As Jen recounted how a group of kids tripped her and she'd landed on glass, Jen hoped Kelly still had a chance. Liz poured out love, along with TCP, upon Jen's wounds.

Jen grieved for the end of childhood innocence.

45

PRESENT

The room is heavy with confessions and revelations. I've given my version of the altercation with Kelly. Claire has also played the recording of our meeting with Constance. Lying for decades has taken its toll. My speech will be more economical and I refuse to offer excuses. Kelly's death began with me and I accept responsibility.

Doreen gathers strength. 'Kelly always was chatty. I said her mouth would get her into trouble eventually.'

I daren't ask what she means. Stretching my limbs, I check if I'm real. I've shared my biggest secret and I'm no longer sure who I am. Killer and liar were my main identities.

Claire fidgets with her hair. Ellen focuses on Doreen. We look to Doreen for a final verdict.

'You hurt Kelly,' Doreen says.

'Yes, I did.' Their stares make me conscious of showing weakness. I remove the fingers curled into my palm.

'But you didn't kill her.'

All heads turn from me to Doreen. I await the dramatic gasps of the courtroom spectators, astounded at the judge's leniency. Nothing comes.

The masochist within me has to ask, 'Do you really believe that?'

'I do. God help me, I do. Constance should've been a doctor. She said the senior staff admired her work. If she says Kelly's wound wasn't life-threatening, it must be true.'

It's callous to show relief when Doreen's sobbing. Instead, I go to her, offering a hug she might rebuff. She lifts her arms and I kneel. The embrace feels right this time.

'I can't forgive myself for pushing Kelly and leaving her there.'

Doreen touches my cheek. 'Don't you see? You were a kid.'

I've never allowed myself to consider how I was a fourteen-year-old impetuous abused girl. When I told the story to Doreen, Ellen, and Claire, the terror I felt back then returned. I didn't want to be like Kelly and couldn't bear the similarities of our circumstances. The truth is though, she was stronger than I ever was.

Aware that kneeling appears as if I'm begging for leniency, I stand.

'I should've told someone Kelly was hurt.' I can't allow myself to go unpunished. Losing part of years to addiction and self-hatred isn't enough for what Doreen has endured.

'Yes, you should have,' Doreen says, 'but you were scared and protecting your sister. You thought it was the right thing to do, but you could've told us. If anyone is to blame for this, it's your mother.'

I can't speak. It will take time to unlearn defending Mum.

Claire places an arm around me.

Ellen blows her nose. 'I should've done something about Patricia.'

I shake my head, asserting everyone needs forgiveness for what we did and didn't do. We need to begin the process of moving on.

'That was intense,' Claire says, as we sit.

Doreen yawns.

'Let's get you to bed.' Ellen moves to help.

'Let Jen do it,' Doreen says.

I hold her elbow as she negotiates the stairs. The care assistant is due soon, but Doreen needs to sleep. She insists I wait outside

LISA SELL

the bedroom while she undresses, intent on keeping her dignity for as long as possible.

'You can come in.' Doreen's faint voice battles through the closed door.

She sits on the edge of a bed topped with a duvet of chintzy flowers. The pattern explodes across the room, covering walls, lampshades, and cushions. Doreen takes pride in her home. Many council estate women aimed for a showroom standard. Their houses were their palaces.

I help Doreen swing her legs onto the bed. I wonder if she'll wake tomorrow. She's broken. I let go of the shame I've contributed to it, knowing she doesn't want that for me. Shifting up the pillows, she puffs out exertion. I refrain from helping, guessing she wants to be independent for as long as possible.

'We'll have to give up,' she says.

'Why?'

'It looks like suicide, doesn't it? Now I know Kelly was on the track in those circumstances, and was upset.' Doreen sees my discomfort. 'It's hard to say but Kelly probably took her life.'

'Don't be hasty. You said before you believed Kelly wouldn't do that. I still think it's right. I'm not trying to absolve myself, but she was so strong in taking relentless blows and insults from people. Would she really have killed herself over a childish spat?'

'I'm not sure anymore.' Doreen's eyelids droop.

'Let Claire and me continue investigating. Don't give up yet. We'll do our best for you and Kelly.' I'm trying to atone for the past, but a new empathy for this woman sits alongside it.

'Okay, if you're sure. There's nothing left to lose anyway. You *are* a good person, Jen. Trust people more.'

I swipe away tears. I needed the approval. She offers a piece of paper from the nightstand.

'What's this?' I ask.

'It's Johnny's telephone number and e-mail address. He told me not to give it to you. You've shared what happened and you must reunite with your soulmate.' She falls asleep with a smile on her face.

The precious slip of paper burns in my hand. Johnny still thinks I'm a killer. I've tried to make contact. Until I can prove how Kelly died, I must leave it. I remember how, after the awkward kiss when I had tonsillitis, Johnny behaved strangely. Maybe he was pulling away from me before I hurt Kelly. Too much time has passed anyway.

Claire and Ellen wait at the foot of the stairs.

'What have you got there?' Nothing gets past Claire, particularly knowing I'm a liar. I can see she's hurting but trying to hide it.

'Not much.' I slide the piece of paper into her rear jeans pocket. It's too late for Johnny and me. 'You can have this. It's more use to you.'

She unfolds it and frowns. I open the front door, ending any further conversation.

We've got work to do.

46

PRESENT

Everyone who heard the name thought Rose Rose's parents were drunk or having a laugh when they named her. Rose asserted being a double Rose meant she was twice as lovely. She also lived life in double time; fast, loose, and taking every scrap of happiness she could grasp.

Rose valued the surname so much, her sons had it too. None of the fathers protested until she became pregnant with Rob Morgan's child. Rob was six years younger than Rose, but more than a match for her formidable character. Their son, Benny, carried the Morgan name and was the likeness of his father. Rob believed in lineage and heritage, even if he could only scrape together a couple of pounds for his offspring.

Having a toyboy boosted Rose's ego. She accepted she wasn't a conventional beauty, but knew how to make the most of her assets. Her ample cleavage and trim figure had served her well. Gravity hadn't set in yet, despite having four children.

The Rose boys were renowned on the Rembrandt Estate. Anthony and Ian were a handful because of Rose's weak parenting. They spent their days around town and returned home when hungry. Rose often forgot to get food in. Her boys, apart from

Johnny, often stole from the shops. A growing boy's stomach demanded immediate sustenance.

Rose's domestic skills similarly lacked. The house never saw a duster unless Johnny intervened. Provisions ran to a sour bottle of milk, gin, and a plentiful supply of knock-off cigarettes. Rose figured she'd done her family a favour in teaching them self-sufficiency.

On the Rembrandt Estate, the Rose boys were the group you joined or avoided. Responsible parents tried to shield their children from the Rose influence. They often failed. The allure of shenanigans with the Roses was tempting, except for one child. Although a Rose by name, Johnny didn't belong. Not since Eliza Doolittle had a person puzzled over why they lived in such an alien environment. Johnny's kindness, desire for justice, and quiet disposition made him a stranger within a family of delinquents. He was the thorn among the Roses.

Rose doted on Johnny, certain he would "do good" in the world. Lying in bed at night she devised plans, picturing Johnny's high-flying career as a businessman. Rose watched the smoke of a cigarette fade, hoping her son's prospects had more substance. She feared being a Rose and living on a council estate meant Johnny would always fight against the odds. Rose continued to dream. Johnny *would* move on from the estate and, perhaps, away from the family too. If the sacrifice had to be made, she would let him go.

Johnny decided from an early age to avoid family scams and scuffles. He hid within the security of friendship with Jen, hoping to find the courage to make it something more. Jen understood the embarrassment of bearing the burden of your family. When he recounted his family's escapades, Johnny cringed. Jen expressed horror or laughed until she gasped for air. Sometimes the Roses' adventures were hilarious, even Johnny had to admit it. Maybe he'd eventually crack jokes about that afternoon's events, later known as the "War of the Roses".

It began when Rob lost his temper at the lack of dinner to soak up the booze from a day in the pub. He threw saucepans to show Rose what cooking implements were. Used to his rants, Rose lit up and watched cutlery fly.

Anthony found Rob useful for keeping him in cigarettes and beer, but his allegiances always lay with his mum. He threatened Rob with a smack in the chops. Ian joined him, brandishing a rounders bat. The two boys stood either side of their mum; a wall of double denim and malice.

Taking it into the garden, every piece of Benny's play equipment inflicted cuts and bruises. Rob discovered swingball's ability to make a black eye. When Ian stated it wasn't the first time Rob had balls in his face, he narrowly escaped drowning in the paddling pool.

The police arrived, greeted by the wounded Roses and Rob, seated on the lawn. Apparently, nothing had happened and people were clumsy. Rose made a mental note to flush out the nosey neighbour who'd interfered.

Benny emerged with Anthony's makeshift shuriken and Rob's stash of pills as the police were leaving. He'd found the booty in a kitchen cupboard. Benny became a grass at the tender age of three.

Johnny squirmed as he related the incident to Jen. They were taking a stroll into town to escape the neighbours' judging looks. He questioned why he didn't have a decent family and not the one residing at Troddington police station.

'Where were you when it happened?' Jen asked.

'Getting a bottle of wine for Mum.'

The owner of the corner shop neglected to check the ages of those buying alcohol and cigarettes. Being the nearest shop to the estate, it made a roaring trade from kids sent to buy their parents' legal highs. The owner had banned Anthony and Ian for stealing, and Rob for being mouthy. With Rose's added laziness, it left Johnny to do the family's shopping.

Johnny continued. 'I saw the police car as I came up our road. They let me go inside to get Benny's stuff. The coppers took him in too.'

Noting Johnny's annoyance in the telling, Jen tried to be serious. 'What the hell are they going to find out from a three-year-old?'

'Fingerprints on Ant's ninja weapon. They need to eliminate a toddler.' Johnny shook his head. 'Mum phoned earlier to give me an update. Benny was checked over to see if he'd taken any of Rob's uppers. He didn't. I'd have lost it with Rob if Benny had.

'Rob's being questioned for possession. They may charge Ant with having a dangerous weapon. I've had enough of my lot. Poor Benny doesn't have a hope. I wish I could get him away from them.'

'I feel the same about Mandy,' Jen said.

Johnny halted. 'When exams are over, let's find somewhere to live and take Benny and Mandy with us.'

'The council won't help teenagers with two young kids get a place.' Jen was always the realist to Johnny, the dreamer.

Johnny rubbed his chin. 'Ant's dad is a top bloke. He keeps in contact even though Ant's a git to him. His dad lives in Cornwall and might put us up for a while. We could get jobs and then have our own place one day.'

'Maybe.' Jen didn't want to quash his enthusiasm. The thought of being with Johnny forever was too wonderful not to embrace. 'Would he take us in?'

'Possibly. He feels bad for Ian and me because our dads aren't around.'

Mark died from leukaemia when Johnny was two. Rose hid an envelope containing photos of Mark behind the crying boy picture in the hallway. She refused to scrap the portrait in the midst of the media scare of its cursed nature. Rose made her own luck. Johnny found the photos when he'd knocked the painting after running away from Ian.

Rose found Johnny flicking through the pictures and explained Mark was his father and "The One". She begged her son not to tell perpetually jealous Rob. Since then, Johnny often considered how his life would have been if Mark had lived.

Unable to change the past, Johnny made a firm decision about the future. 'Let's try to get out of here. Mum will understand it's best for Benny not to grow up with Ant and Ian. It'll give us something to hope for too.'

Jen moved to the side as a woman with a pram tutted and asserted a perceived right to the whole path.

'Okay, we'll do it and not allow anyone or anything to stand in our way,' Jen said.

'I'll never leave you.'

But by the end of the year, he had.

47

PRESENT

We're gathered in Ellen's lounge. Doreen is resting at home. Now they all know the truth, hopefully we can start over, if Claire will stop sulking. She has a face like a slapped arse and gives only monosyllabic answers. I forgot what a diva she can be.

Ellen has assumed the role of co-ordinator. 'So, Jen, you'll contact the Roses?'

'I'll do my best.'

It's obvious I have this job as a ruse to bring me closer to Johnny. Refusing to ruin his life again, I've insisted I won't phone him. There's too much hurt and I doubt he'll forgive me anyway. Johnny's intolerance for injustice was something I admired. I'd be a hypocrite to condemn it. Besides, Johnny has given his full version of that day already.

'Claire, you're okay with making a list of who lived on the estate and following potential leads?' Ellen coaxes her surly daughter into action.

'Yep.' Claire taps her phone against her knee.

'What on earth's the matter, young lady? I'm getting fed up of your attitude.'

'Me?' Claire leaps up. 'You've got a problem with *me* when Jen's been lying all along?'

'Watch your tone, Claire Florence,' Ellen says.

I dare to speak. 'I thought we were sorted.'

'Yeah, well.' Claire sits and perfects the parody of an affronted teenager. 'I'm pissed off. When we were younger, we promised never to lie to each other. You can't make a huge confession like that and expect us to forgive you straight away.'

'I'm so sorry.'

'That's what Dad said every time he cheated on Mum. He let us down too. I hate liars.'

Ellen's shoulders rise. 'Jen doesn't need to hear about that.'

'It's relevant, Mum. He wrecked our trust. It took years to rebuild. What you've done, Jen, is just as upsetting.'

'Please forgive me, twonk.' Using our old humour is a risky move. 'The last thing I wanted was to hurt you. I was a numpty who believed you'd hate me if you knew what happened. Losing your friendship after finding it again would be awful.'

Determined to stay grumpy, Claire fights the tweaking at the corner of her mouth. 'Give me some time to get over it. I'll probably forgive you, in time. Don't ever lie again. Pinky swear?'

We stand, lock little fingers, and chant the rhyme, 'Make friends, make friends. Never ever break friends. If you do, you'll catch the flu and that will be the end of you.'

'Florence, eh?' I grin. 'I forgot it's your middle name.'

'Get stuffed.' Claire sticks out her tongue. 'It's not my fault.'

Ellen gives us a light-hearted cuff around the head. 'That was my grandmother's name.'

We fall onto the settee, laughing at Ellen's annoyance and our silly adult selves.

Claire becomes more serious. 'I've got a contact who can dig into Kelly's coroner's report.'

'Be careful,' Ellen says. 'You're a great reporter, but your insistence on using methods I would never have contemplated is worrying. Don't get arrested.'

I'm amused a parent's standard advice is to continue risky practices but avoid prosecution. Ellen and Claire are tenacious in the pursuit of the truth.

'It's all good,' Claire replies. 'He owes me a favour.'

'I'm getting concerned about the number of blokes who owe you one,' I say. 'What do you do that leaves them owing you something?'

Claire gives a guttural laugh. 'Wouldn't you like to know? Not in front of the mother though.' She glances at Ellen. 'I'm joking, Mum. It's a bloke I met in the coroner's office when I was investigating the last mayor's death. The papers reported it as a stroke. Strokes *were* involved. The paramedics found him in bed with his mistress, back full of lashes and trussed up. The excitement killed him.' Claire confirms her sensitivity chip is still missing. My old friend has clearly evolved from the days of carrying a tape recorder and a stack of cassettes.

'How does this bloke at the coroner's office owe you a favour?' I ask.

'I did some P.I. work on his missus, last year. She was having an affair and he wanted shot of her. It made the divorce a lot easier.'

Ellen steers us back to our investigation. 'So, everyone knows what they're doing. I'll keep talking to Doreen and see if there's more to look into. It's time for you youngsters to do the groundwork. I'm getting too old for this palaver.' She places her feet on the coffee table.

Claire and I wink at each other. Despite the circumstances, we relish reforming our duo. We're picking up where we left off; a little foolish, but determined and together.

48

20 SEPTEMBER 1987

J en dreaded Sundays. Patricia was always more testy than usual, due to a hangover brought on from a heavy Saturday night. She insisted on Mike accompanying her to a pretentious wine bar in Troddington. He favoured the local where shoes stuck to the carpet and men talked nonsense without being accused of womanly gossiping. The Crafty Goat was hallowed turf Mike hoped his wife would never enter.

Every Saturday Patricia got wasted on house white, flirted with men, riled their wives, and spread malicious rumours. *That* was a successful night. Mike found it excruciating. His presence was required only to support the illusion of a solid marriage, along with a wallet to keep his wife in alcohol.

Patricia's middle-class aspirations forbade her from working. As a lady of leisure, she ploughed her energies into visible acts of charity, keeping the estate's residents in order, and honing the Taylors' golden image. Saturday nights were a treat for alleviating the stress of organising others.

On that morning, she languished in bed, clothed in a cream silk nightie and her face sunk into a pillow. Mike was working and

Liam was missing in action. Jen and Mandy knew not to be around when the hungover ogre awoke.

Jen, Claire, and Mandy sat on a pavement on Picasso Way. Claire decided today's news should focus on this road. Armed with her tape recorder, she awaited a significant event. It remained unspoken between the girls that the Pratts would likely provide Claire with fodder. Their rows always got the estate talking. Jen felt conflicted waiting for the Pratts' misfortune. She'd heard the rumours but kept out of their business. Doreen rarely allowed her into the house in the mornings when she collected Kelly. Jen suggested meeting in the park but Doreen insisted Jen came to their home. The decision was odd, considering Jen usually had to wait outside. The few occasions she'd entered their abode, she dreaded seeing Graham. He was a threatening figure, often swearing and chasing after kids, as best his tarred lungs would allow. Thankfully, he'd never been there when Jen went inside the Pratts' house. She realised that was the point.

'Slow news day,' Claire said. 'I thought Picasso Way would be newsworthy gold. Not much has happened on the estate since the "War of the Roses". We should've gone to the folk festival.'

Troddington held an annual celebration of Morris dancers, folk singers, and maypole dancing. Its appeal had long worn off for Jen and Claire. Most of the estate kids attended to mock the participants or for something to do. The estate could get claustrophobic.

'I'm sure there'll be a punch up when people return or someone will call someone else's mum a whore,' Jen half-teased.

'What's a *whore?*' Mandy ceased drawing a chalk princess on the pavement.

Mandy's exemplary behaviour made it easy to forget her. Jen wished her sister had the freedom to be boisterous. Making her follow the rules of a quiet life could prove stifling. Jen worried she'd taken the control too far and would morph into Patricia.

'*Whore* is a nasty word I shouldn't have used,' Jen said. 'Best not call anyone that. Great drawing, by the way.'

Warmth spread in Mandy's chest. 'It's a picture of how I will be the princess of the estate one day.'

'Aim higher, kid,' Claire said. 'Get out of here as soon as possible. Marry Prince Harry.'

Mandy's eyes and mouth widened. 'He's only a toddler.'

'He won't be when you're eighteen, idiot. Shitting Ada, don't you teach her anything, Jen?'

'Watch your gob. I'm trying to make sure she doesn't swear. She's spending too much time with the ropey kids as it is.' Jen turned from Mandy and whispered, 'I caught a boy from her class in Mandy's bedroom, showing her a porno mag. I soon booted his backside out the door.'

Aware of Jen's annoyance, Claire tried not to laugh. 'He must be only six. Hey, can I interview Mandy about it?'

'No, you flipping well can't. Do you have any scruples?'

'Isn't that a game?'

'That's Scrabble, you donkey.' Jen shoved her friend.

As Claire fell off the kerb, a pained sound came from behind them. Mandy looked to Jen.

'What the hell was that?' Jen asked Claire.

Before she could answer, the door to the Easts' house burst open.

Lorraine East gripped the doorframe, displaying a ballooned belly. 'Baby's coming. Geoff's taken the kids to the festival. This one's in a hurry.'

Jen ran to help. Mandy trailed behind. Claire chewed her cuticles.

'Don't worry,' Lorraine reassured them. 'I've done this seven times. The baby is breech though and it's early.'

Jen understood breech births were tricky. She'd read about labour but wasn't ready to become a doctor or midwife yet. An adult needed to take charge.

'Have you phoned anyone?' she asked Lorraine.

The woman clasped her stomach as a contraction took hold. 'Geoff forgot to pay the bill. I told him to sort it out.'

'Mandy, knock on doors and ask to use someone's phone,' Jen instructed, confident of her sister's maturity for an eight-year-old. In their family, she had to be. 'Claire, see if Scott Reilly is in.' Jen figured an ambulance driver would have more of a clue than she did.

Claire wasted no time darting towards Turner Road. She wasn't keen on bloodshed and was glad to be far away from it.

Jen guided Lorraine to the lounge. They chatted around each contraction. Mandy and Claire seemed to take forever. Eventually, voices came through the open front door.

Kelly bounded into the room. 'How are you doing, Lorraine?'

Jen's hope of rescue faded. What could this fellow fourteen-year-old do that she couldn't?

'Why did you bring her?' Jen snapped at Mandy.

Mandy cowered behind a chair, chewing her plait. 'She's the only person who answered. I did my best.' She squeezed her eyes shut and bit down on her lip. Patricia had drilled into them the vulgarity of shedding tears in public.

Jen was torn between a woman struggling and her sister hurting. She approached Mandy. 'You did a great job. I'm so proud of you.'

Mandy gave a beauty-queen grin.

'Did you phone for an ambulance?' Jen asked Kelly.

Kelly focused on Lorraine.

'Kelly,' Jen yelled, 'did you call 999?'

Kelly broke from her spell. 'Yes. I know what to do.' She had never shouted at Jen before. The sight of someone in labour troubled Kelly. Jen attributed it to inexperience.

'Will the baby be okay?' Kelly asked. She sat beside Lorraine and stroked the woman's stomach. Lorraine appeared unfazed even though Kelly's blank-eyed stare gave the gesture a sinister edge.

'Sure she will,' Lorraine said with her Scottish lilt. 'I've had a breech birth before. I can do it again.'

'It's a girl?' Kelly's hyperactivity made Jen wonder what she'd had for breakfast.

Lorraine forced her words out through the pain. 'I'm not certain but when you've had a lot of kids, you get an inkling.'

'I'd like to have a girl,' Kelly said.

'Not yet I hope,' Lorraine replied. 'There's plenty of time for that.'

Kelly blushed. 'Of course.'

A contraction hit. As Lorraine gripped her, Jen hoped her hand would still be operational afterwards.

Mandy sat on the front doorstep. There were things a young girl wasn't ready to learn. Jen had told her about reproduction. Seeing it in action though wasn't part of Mandy's education.

Claire appeared and took Mandy outside. Scott Reilly rushed past.

Jen welcomed the cavalry. She had resigned herself to blagging it, but the prospect of delivering a baby was terrifying.

Scott addressed Jen. 'You've done a great job. You'll be a brilliant doctor.'

Jen hardly ever received praise. Few believed in her ambition. The words of encouragement from a man who helped the sick and needy gave her the validation she needed. She stood tall.

'Ladies,' Scott said, 'can you go outside to wait for the ambulance? Lorraine and I can take it from here.'

Lorraine grimaced thanks. Jen left, checking if Kelly was following. The girl seemed to be in a trance. Jen touched her shoulder. 'Come on, Kelly, let's go.' They joined Mandy and Claire on the pavement.

Claire punched the air. 'I got my story.'

'You certainly did,' Jen said.

'Some things are private.' Kelly's acerbic tone dampened the jubilant mood. 'It should only be between the mum and her baby. Not everyone needs to know.' She returned home, slamming the door.

'What bit her arse?' Claire asked.

Jen couldn't see the humour in the situation. Watching Lorraine in labour had disturbed Kelly. Jen ignored the ridiculous idea forming in her mind and began her star interview for *Into the Woods Radio*.

49

PRESENT

'Kelly was pregnant.' A hush falls over Doreen's lounge as Claire drops the bombshell.

Ellen pales. Doreen lies back against the shock. I trawl through memories to when Lorraine East was in labour and how I'd considered if Kelly was pregnant. Back then I dismissed it as ridiculous. I'm sickened I attacked a pregnant girl, but how was I to know? Kelly hid it well.

'I'm stunned,' Doreen says.

She can't manage the stairs anymore so we've formed a semi-circle around the bed downstairs. There is a communal need to be close, like when animals die in the wild and their tribe stays with the body. I hope for Doreen's sake the similarities end there.

'Kelly was nine weeks pregnant when she died.' Claire keeps her voice soft. 'My contact from the coroner's office showed me the files on her death. The pregnancy was on record. Didn't you know?'

'No,' Doreen says. 'I should have gone to the hearing but I couldn't face it. Graham went. He said the verdict was open, nothing else.'

'Perhaps he didn't want to upset you,' Ellen says.

Doreen blanches. 'Graham wouldn't have spared me the grief.

He enjoyed making my life a misery. Knowing him, he was ashamed.'

'Or there may be another reason why he said nothing.' Claire twiddles the bee pendant on her necklace around her fingers.

I can see where she's going. There's an elephant in the room and Claire's jumped on it, ready to charge through.

'Like what?' Doreen asks.

'Maybe Graham had something to do with it?' Claire holds up her hands, prepared for the backlash.

We wait for Doreen to interpret the suggestion. A few beats behind, she forces herself up from the pillows. 'So, you believed those disgusting rumours too?' She regards each of us. 'I expect you all did.'

Knowing Claire and I have considered Graham's violent history as evidence for being Kelly's killer, I beg my cheeks not to tinge with shame. When other investigative avenues appeared, we put it to one side. Claire has pushed it back into the foreground.

Doreen clenches the blanket. 'Graham was an evil man. After he died, I vowed never to defend him again. I lied to the police when people reported him. For that, I was a fraud.'

'Calm down, love,' Ellen soothes. 'You'll make yourself ill.'

'Ill? I'm dying, Ellen. If my husband had been sexually abusing our daughter, I'd tell you. I would *never* allow that to happen anyway. Confused as they sometimes were, I had boundaries. I was at home most of the time because he wouldn't let me out. Not much passed me by in our house. Graham didn't need to satisfy himself with Kelly.' Doreen's breathing hitches. 'He raped me, not her.'

Showing alarm isn't an appropriate response to her bravery. Doreen has more strength than a herd of those proverbial elephants. She deserves praise, not pity. I give a nod to signify my admiration for speaking out.

Claire is red-faced. 'I shouldn't have suggested it.'

Doreen's anger ebbs into acceptance. 'I can see why people

thought it, but physical violence doesn't automatically lead to sexual assault. Graham violated me because he viewed sex as a husbandly right. It took years to accept it wasn't my fault. His past actions don't affect me anymore. I swear he didn't rape Kelly.'

'I'm so sorry for what you went through.' Claire couldn't look more distressed if she tried.

'Let's move on to what we should consider,' Doreen replies. 'Who was the father of Kelly's baby?'

None of us has an idea, let alone the answer. I'm still reeling that Kelly was pregnant. Even in the eighties, teenagers got themselves in the family way. Kelly though? It became a craze in my school to get up the duff and demand a council house. I was already living on a council estate and raising my sister. Much as I loved Mandy, I would've advised those foolish youngsters it wasn't worth the hassle.

'Why didn't Kelly tell me she was pregnant?' Doreen says. 'I prided myself on how open we were with each other.'

Ellen touches Claire's knee. 'Daughters often keep things from their parents. I bet this one has.'

Claire looks at me. 'So do best friends.'

I let the comment pass, knowing it will take time to regain her trust.

'What a secret for Kelly to have,' Doreen says.

'Why didn't you go to the inquest, Mum?' Claire asks.

'Out of respect to Doreen, I wouldn't report on Kelly's death. I asked the paper to give the story to someone else. The reporter must have omitted Kelly's pregnancy as a kindness to the family. I wish I'd gone, Doreen. You would've known.'

'Her death wasn't in any other newspapers. I checked.' Claire squirms at the small impact Kelly's death had on the world.

'We must find out who got Kelly pregnant,' Doreen says. 'It may help us understand how she died. I know for definite she wouldn't have killed herself. Although she respected people's right to choose,

Kelly didn't support abortion, let alone doing that to her child. Not only have I lost my daughter but my grandchild too.'

Claire clears her throat. 'We have to consider if Kelly got pregnant because she consented or if it was…'

'Rape.' I complete the sentence, refusing on Doreen's behalf and for those who've shared with me at Listening Ear, for it to be taboo.

Doreen mouths her thanks.

'Kelly's pregnancy could be linked to why she died,' Claire says.

'Do what you need to do.' Doreen presses the button on the control pad to lower the bed. 'I've had enough for one day. Would you mind if I sleep?'

'Not at all,' Ellen replies. She stays to check Doreen has what she needs. Claire and I go into the hallway.

'I hate my job sometimes,' Claire says.

'Try being a counsellor.'

'Must be tough. You'll be great though.'

'Thanks.'

'Nut sacks.' Claire's range of swear words are vast. 'I forgot to say, I've tracked down Priscilla.'

'Who's Priscilla?'

'Priscilla Staines, the scrawny kid who lived next door to the Pratts. Her mum, Deirdre, kept her locked away, like some kind of fairy tale witch. Priscilla used to talk to Kelly.'

I visualise a thin girl with dishwater brown stringy hair. 'Oh, yes. She was born with a hole in the heart. Deirdre believed if Priscilla got excited playing with other kids, she'd die on the spot.'

Claire slaps me on the back. 'Maybe *you* should be the reporter.'

'No thanks. I was interested in other people's medical issues. The Rembrandt Estate provided plenty of interesting case studies.'

'I never saw Priscilla outside the garden,' Claire says. 'She's finally free. I found her online and we were messaging last night.'

'What did she tell you?'

'Deirdre is dead. Priscilla stayed on the estate until her mum snuffed it. Her dad's still there. Priscilla's working at Mabel's Parlour in Troddington and lives in the flat above.'

'Mabel's Parlour?' It's a long time since I've been to Troddington.

'It's a tearoom. We're going to see her tomorrow.'

I consider making excuses for how I can't duck out of work. Since this investigation began, I've taken quite a few days off. Nicole's been tolerant as I never use all my annual leave. Claire will only reschedule if I refuse.

'Fine,' I say as my stomach knots.

I'm returning to Troddington. For decades I've vowed never to go back. Now, I must.

50

27TH NOVEMBER 1987

S t Peter's Church was full. Doped up on tranquillisers, Doreen saw only a sea of blurred faces. A cry of hysterics escaped from her mouth. Kelly would love this. She was finally popular and Doreen couldn't wait to tell her. Since Kelly's death, Doreen had moments when she forgot her child's absence. She wondered if a breakdown was coming, then decided she didn't care.

Graham pinched her thigh. 'Don't show me up, woman.'

She ignored him. Even if he tried to kill her, she wouldn't fight back. At least she'd be with Kelly again. Graham hadn't struck Doreen since Kelly died. He vented his fury on inanimate objects instead, trashing their house. Graham was a pressure cooker, waiting to go off. When he did, Doreen knew she'd be incapacitated for weeks.

Graham regarded the gathering. How dare they pretend to care after making his family's life unbearable? He loathed their smart clothes and fake sorrowful expressions. Later, after a few pints, he'd take them down a peg or two. This he would do for his daughter.

Doreen stared at the Order of Service, stroking Kelly's sunshine smile radiating from the front cover. The photograph was taken a few months earlier. Kelly had laid out a spread of sandwiches, scones, jam, and cream, on the lawn as a treat for her mum. When she revealed the feast, happiness danced across Kelly's face. It became Doreen's most treasured photo. She kissed the paper cheek of her thoughtful girl.

Ellen sat in the pew behind and squeezed Doreen's shoulder. Graham's warning glares didn't deter Ellen. No one knew what had happened to Kelly. Under loud speculation, the truth remained silent. Ellen decided to no longer be quiet about Graham's violence. If she learned he'd so much as raised his voice, she'd call the police. Ellen would be a better friend to Doreen.

Seated next to her mum, Claire wriggled. The wooden seat and crushing remorse made settling impossible. The hypocrisy of kids who'd bullied Kelly and were acting up in the back rows annoyed her, along with the adults who gossiped about the Pratts. With each of Claire's stares, they looked away. *Let them feel ashamed*, she thought. *I do.*

Claire couldn't forgive herself for leaving Kelly alone on the track. Ellen tried to reason she'd done her best, but Claire refused to accept it. Alex took her to lunch as a ruse to extract what troubled her. Considering his lying tendencies regarding his affairs, he was the last person she could confide in.

Claire legitimately wore Ellen's cashmere jumper to the service but she felt no joy. Shame twisted her gut. She had no right to nice things. Kelly would never experience goodness again. Guilt gnawed at Claire throughout the day. It manifested as an ache in the evening. Every night she awoke, screaming. Ellen's hugs and soothing words to eradicate nightmares of a mutilated Kelly helped.

. . .

The vicar began the eulogy. Patricia tuned him out. She'd never been interested in "religious clap trap". The only time she attended church was for weddings, christenings and funerals.

She checked her skirt, hoping the spillage didn't show. Amanda chose to have a tantrum the moment they were leaving. Patricia swallowed anger at her now-cherubic daughter. Amanda's punishment would be severe. Why the brat behaved like her sister was beyond Patricia. Jen refused to attend the funeral. Even when threatened with discipline, Jen didn't budge. The stricken expression at mentions of the funeral confused her mum.

Patricia told her to stop being a sissy. People died every day. Jen asserted she wasn't going. In response, Patricia proposed three weeks of grounding. Catching Patricia unprepared, Jen accepted the fact. The threat of not seeing the dreadful Rose boy usually made Patricia's daughter obedient. Patricia scowled at him for daring to look at her across the church.

Jennifer was God knows where. Patricia sniggered at her blasphemy, bold at being a bitch to the man upstairs on His patch. God was for losers. She didn't need an emotional crutch. Patricia had it covered.

Jen's defiance had unnerved her though. To reassert authority, Patricia had threatened to punish Mandy instead. Jen kicked a wall and dictated Patricia would pay if she touched a hair on Mandy's head. Patricia enjoyed Jen's feistiness. It confirmed her belief of her daughter's hidden violent streak. Unable to concede defeat, Patricia stated Mandy had to attend. Having the family at public events was important. Two out of three children would do. Jen left. Patricia made plans for how to deal with her later.

Bored with the service, Liam yawned and pushed away his mother's incoming hug. The female need to be tactile was irritating. He was seventeen and no longer a mummy's boy. As the vicar continued his speech, Liam gave a louder yawn, not bothering to cover his mouth.

Mike touched Patricia's knee. She inspected his hand and then dropped it. He berated himself for the unchecked moment. The girl inside the coffin was the same age as Jen. He thought the woman who'd carried their daughter shared his sadness, forgetting who he had married.

Mandy had never been to a funeral. Although Jen explained death, she couldn't grasp how Kelly was alive one minute and gone the next. Minds older than hers were struggling to comprehend it too.

Without her anchoring sister, Mandy was adrift. Before she could make sense of the fight that had happened earlier between Patricia and Jen, she was bundled into the car, not having a chance to set down her glass of milk. The liquid splashed over Patricia's black skirt. There wasn't time to change in order for the Taylors to secure a coveted spot at the front. Patricia's face since the spillage rivalled the milk stain in its curdling. Mandy knew it signified trouble. Anxiety fluttered from her stomach to her throat. It lodged there and pulsated. She concentrated on breathing, pushing the butterfly of panic away. Jen taught her well.

Johnny offered a twitch of the mouth at Mandy's smile. His discomfort at attending Kelly's funeral was obvious. He was only there to please his mum. Rose insisted the family "show those pricks we're as good as them". She'd even made the effort of wearing a top that didn't graze her nipples.

Rob donned a natty suit, let down by shoddy hemming. Anthony's only concession to the occasion was to put on a clean pair of black jeans, along with his usual white vest and a denim jacket. Ian scooped up the previous day's slashed jeans and Sex Pistols T-shirt from the floor. Benny wore a white shirt, black waistcoat, and trousers. Rose figured she'd done well with at least two of her sons looking the part. Johnny wore his school trousers and a black shirt, with a tie.

He flicked the pages of the Bible, ignoring its contents. He didn't know what to make of God normally, let alone when someone his age died. Shifting his anger towards God was futile. Johnny blamed Jen and himself for leaving Kelly on the track.

After, he took to the safety of his room. Rose brought meals, trying to be the mother she'd neglected to be. He appreciated the gesture but could never share what happened. When Anthony and Ian called him moody and other choice terms, he didn't respond. Benny played alone. Rose and Rob thought he battled puberty. Their questions were excruciating. Johnny felt far from a man. He was a coward.

Patricia gave Johnny a hard stare as he glanced at the Taylors. He ignored it, focusing instead on his relief that Jen wasn't there. If she'd decided to come, he might have lost it in public. Then everyone would know he was almost as bad as her in covering up how Kelly died.

The moment Jen struck Kelly, she'd severed the relationship with Johnny. He drew the curtains as a barrier when Jen stood outside his house. At first, she sat on the pavement for hours. Johnny instructed Rose to get rid of Jen when she braved knocking the door. Jen got Rose's brutal message and hadn't come near for the past few days. Johnny was torn between love and justice. He mourned his Jenny Wren, not the unimaginable killing version.

A couple of rows ahead, Constance sang the hymn with gusto. Singing of how the Lord was her shepherd usually brought her solace. In moments such as this, however, faith was confusing. It was a cliché to ask where God was in times of strife, and yet, she asked. She'd prayed for explanations for Kelly's death but no answers came. Constance feared seeking God's forgiveness for not taking Kelly home. She reasoned the girl wasn't bleeding, couldn't have died from the head wound, and wasn't concussed. Constance was assured in her diagnosis but also believed Kelly might be alive if she'd stayed with her. Whatever happened after she'd left had led to Kelly's death.

Many decided it was suicide. Constance found it hard to grasp. Kelly had been upset but not distraught. Her home life was undeniably difficult but still, Constance couldn't accept Kelly leaving Doreen to live alone with Graham. The possibility of an accident didn't ring true. Falling over twice and being injured was unlikely. It left only one verdict. Someone had killed Kelly. Constance wasn't ready to explore it. She sent a prayer for the inquest to lay uncertainty to rest.

Mrs Newton glowered at the Pullen boys, tussling over a prayer book. Having the misfortune of teaching Charlie and Glen in the past, she knew they weren't trying to connect with God. She waggled a finger, considering it enough of a warning. Glen responded with an obscene gesture. Yvonne Newton mentally applauded Porky when he cuffed Glen around the head.

A woman stood to read Scripture. Her confident tones filled the church, reaching Yvonne in the back pew. She knew youngsters always sought the cheap seats. Ever the efficient teacher, she considered keeping an eye on them the least she could do for the Pratts. Yvonne was one of the last people to see Kelly alive. Recriminations niggled in how sharp she'd been with Kelly. She recalled the girl marvelling at the fallen tree that landed on the school, excited by the aftereffects of the storm. Kelly's childlike qualities were charming. Yvonne blew her nose, accepting she'd never witness Kelly's innocence again. An elbow struck Yvonne's knee. She prepared to reprimand an errant child.

A mousy voice spoke, 'Sorry, Miss. I dropped my money for the collection plate.'

Priscilla Staines was a sweet girl who Yvonne enjoyed teaching. She may not have been clever but Priscilla was always keen.

She retrieved the coins and swung her legs. Sitting next to Mrs Newton, her favourite teacher, was a treat. Deirdre insisted they sat at the back in case the church gave Priscilla a chill and they had to leave. For once, Priscilla followed her mother's instruction without argument.

Chris's assertion they must pay their respects confused Deirdre. He ignored her string of excuses not to attend. Priscilla understood he felt guilty about turning up the television to drown out the Pratts' altercations. Realising she couldn't win, Deirdre dosed Priscilla with vitamin C and gave her a tissue to place over her nose and mouth.

Priscilla missed her only friend. Kelly may have been three years older but she never made Priscilla feel inferior. They'd shared many secrets; some silly, others of a greater magnitude. Kelly left Priscilla with her most damning secret. Priscilla wondered if trying to keep it would break her.

51

PRESENT

When I phoned to ask for a day off work, Nicole said to take a few weeks instead. Cover is arranged. Deciding I was facing the sack, I panicked. When dealing with people in authority, I often think the worst. Nicole knows my weaknesses well enough to assure me I won't lose my job. I shared with her the basics of the investigation so far, excluding the argument with Kelly. My boss doesn't need to know everything.

I'm hunting for a parking space in Troddington. Claire's supposed to be helping. Instead, she's focused on playing a game on her phone that emits regular irritating bleeps accompanied by Claire's profanities.

Troddington town is almost unrecognisable. Most of the functional shops are gone. It's become a middle-class oasis of overpriced clothes shops, delicatessens, estate agents, and hairdressers. Come back Woolworths, all is forgiven.

Claire loses the game and stamps the dashboard where her feet lay. At least she removed her boots. I can't be bothered to ask her to move. Old Jen would have threatened to chop her feet off. It's taking all my strength not to mention how her big toes have made a bid for freedom. I'll buy her some designer socks. The way to Claire's heart is always via clothing.

'When did you leave here?' Claire asks.

'1990. After what happened with Kelly, I lived with Freddie and Liz, and–'

Claire interrupts. 'Patricia must have had a fit when you moved out.'

'She didn't care. In fact she packed my bags.'

'Patricia was one nasty bitch.'

I mumble agreement, still learning not to support the myth of the perfect family. 'She said I could leave, but not Mandy. It broke me. I was sixteen, thinking I'd killed Kelly, and had to leave my sister.'

'Mandy was okay though, wasn't she?'

'Most of the time, from what I heard. I expected Mum to take my leaving out on Mandy. She must have got bored and concentrated on worshipping Liam full-on instead.'

Claire puts on her biker boots. 'The obsession with your brother was creepy. You'd have thought she was married to Liam, not Mike.'

There's no answer for that. It's the truth.

I pull into a narrow gap, wondering if we'll need a tin opener to get out. Claire smacks the passenger door into the car parked next to us. I pretend not to notice. She checks for damage and gives a grin guaranteed to save her from reprimands.

'Mabel's Parlour is up here.' Claire marches ahead.

I dawdle to take in the surroundings. Being in a place that was once familiar and feeling like a stranger is weird. I spot the shoe menders where I took Mum's shoes for reheeling. Strutting the estate and looking for places to interfere wore down her stilettos. I didn't mind the chore as I enjoyed chatting to the owner, Warren Myatt. Hoping to see him, I peer into the window. An unknown man sits at the counter, accompanied by a sullen teenager. The man has Warren's receding hairline and bulbous nose. After checking the shop sign, I decided the son of Warren Myatt and Son must be in charge. I move on, leaving nostalgia behind. Claire waits outside the tearoom, waving me in.

Mabel's Parlour aspires to be a country-style kitchen and parlour. It's stuffed with Welsh dressers full of teapots and porcelain cups. Embroidered pieces hang over an unused fireplace. Everything screams shabby chic. Nothing is authentically aged. On the surface it has an old-fashioned charm. Closer inspection exposes fakery. People lap it up though. The place is heaving. Even the hammering and swearing of workmen outside isn't putting them off.

Priscilla Staines was a scraggy thing but always welcoming whenever I ventured to Pollock Road. The prisoner welcomed any interaction. She reminded me of a waif. If a gust of wind came, she'd fall over. Adult Priscilla made up for lost time. She leads the way to the only available table, swaying an ample rear. Gone is the delicate girl. Across from us sits a woman wearing a tight leather waistcoat, enhancing a deep cleavage and beefy biceps. Piercings line the edges of her ears and a floral tattoo snakes along her neck. I want to applaud her for rebelling against her mum too. The thought of my mum makes me wary though. I watch the entrance, hoping someone familiar doesn't come in. Rembrandt Estate reunions are happening too often for my liking.

Priscilla summons a waitress to take our order.

It arrives quickly, pleasing Claire who attacks a huge eclair. Where she puts it all is a mystery. She deserves to be the size of a house, yet remains dainty.

'Thanks for seeing us,' Claire garbles around a mouthful of cake.

I indicate there's a dollop of cream on her nose. She scrubs it away with a napkin. Kate Adie wouldn't conduct an interview with food on her face. It will not do for our intrepid reporter either.

Priscilla slams her elbows on the table, asserting she's no longer a meek child. As she arranges her hair into a ponytail, I focus on her eyes and see hints of the friendly girl she used to be. Her brown hair is streaked blonde, probably the result of a dodgy home dye job. I hush my inner snob.

'So, what do you want to know?' There's mischief in her smile. 'I'm not sure why you're digging this up.'

'As I wrote to you in my messages,' Claire says, 'Doreen's asked us to investigate what happened to Kelly. I thought you'd have information about her state of mind back then. You said you spoke to her fairly often.'

'She was a great kid who always had time for me.' Priscilla's smile looks more genuine.

'Fair enough.' Claire checks her watch. 'Anything in particular she told you?'

Priscilla drums her fingers on her thigh. 'Chill out, Miss Marple. Give me a minute. It's been ages.'

The bell rings above the door and a group of men enter.

Priscilla gives an enthusiastic wave. 'Hello, fellas. Up for a ride tonight?'

The tearoom quietens. An elderly couple aim for the exit, moving as fast as their walking sticks will allow. The woman at the till, likely Priscilla's boss, appears ready to commit murder.

Priscilla notices it. 'I meant a ride on our motorbikes, you dirty-minded lot.'

She's making it worse. I hold a menu to shield my face. My inner snob is winning.

'You're a one, aren't you, Priscilla?' Claire's false laugh isn't fooling anyone.

Priscilla false laughs with her, whacking Claire on the back. Claire splutters.

I take over. 'Was there something Kelly said that could be useful?'

'She was pregnant. Bet you don't know that.'

'We do, actually. Got anything else?' Claire refuses to hide her annoyance any longer.

Priscilla assesses her. 'Still not had your ears fixed then.'

The cords in Claire's neck tighten. I don't fancy her chances against Priscilla, even with Claire's amateur wrestling past. Priscilla is twice Claire's size.

'Anyone married you yet?' Priscilla will not quit.

'Yes.' Claire shows off her ring. 'I see you don't have a husband.'

'Men are rubbish at commitment. They love you and leave you unless you obey them.' Priscilla's childhood vulnerability returns. I wonder how awful her relationship history must be to hold such a cynical view.

'Seeing anyone at the moment?' Claire won't allow Priscilla to win.

'Might be.' She giggles like a schoolgirl and winks at me. I'm not sure why she thinks I care.

I return to the task. 'Did Kelly say anything about the pregnancy?'

'You two have a nerve. If you'd been better friends to Kelly, she'd still be here. I was eleven. What could I do to help a pregnant teenager? Kelly wouldn't let me tell anyone. She wanted to have her baby and settle down. It's not much to ask for, is it.'

'She was lucky to have a friend like you.' Claire musters compassion.

Priscilla fiddles with the tears in her jeans, snapping off frayed cotton. 'I felt honoured she trusted me.'

Claire's armed with more questions. I nudge her. Priscilla won't be rushed and looks like she needs to feel she's in charge. A childhood of being dominated does that to you.

'Kelly had such a crush on the father of her baby,' Priscilla says.

Claire grips my leg under the table, excited at the direction in which we're moving. I remove her hand, fearful of being crippled.

Priscilla continues. 'It was an older man from the estate.'

She's making us work for it. It's my turn to put the screws on Claire's kneecap as a deterrent for shutting Priscilla down.

'Yeees,' Claire squeaks.

'They were having it off regularly,' Priscilla says. 'They did it in secluded places around the Rembrandt Estate. Kelly was in love with him. He was definitely a catch.'

'Who?' Claire's fighting not to get annoyed with Priscilla's slow reveal.

'Rob Morgan, Rose's fella.' Priscilla practically takes a bow at delivering the shock announcement.

Claire chokes on her second cake. Game over. Priscilla wins.

52

15TH OCTOBER 1987

A lex Woods was in a difficult situation. He agonised over how to end it, not expecting to have become so attached. No rules had been set for their affair but he thought she understood he'd never leave his wife. What could she offer that Ellen couldn't? The estate would also be in uproar if he chose his bit on the side.

Alex marched along Turner Road, contemplating how she would take the rejection. Her devotion was surprising. People didn't see how funny and engaging she was. The residents of the Rembrandt Estate focused only on appearances and they had written her off years ago. Alex knew her hidden gentleness. When they kissed, she softened and became beautiful, not just an estate joke.

Jen and Johnny sat on their wall. Alex wished he could go back to the uncomplicated age of fourteen. His only concerns then were how to get rid of acne and the chances of Oxford United ever winning a game. Having a mistress made him feel young again when, in truth, he was an ageing lothario.

He waved to Johnny and Jen, determined to appear composed and not show his fear. As his arm quivered, he dropped the deceitful limb. Circling around, he prepared to face her.

Lust and stress filled the past few months. Alex never imagined she, of all people, would want him. Their union was wrong but when they were together, nothing else mattered. With her, he became more than a husband, father, and a postman.

Compared to his intelligent reporter wife, Alex acknowledged his insignificance. Ellen chased the story, not his validation. While he was certain she would lay down her life for him, he accepted she wouldn't lie on their bed and oblige. Their sex drives differed. Alex cajoled and pleaded but Ellen knew her own mind. If she didn't want to have sex, she wouldn't fake a headache. Ellen was a believer in the power of words; *no* meant just that and her husband would have to live with it. Alex reasoned he'd done her a favour by seeking fulfilment elsewhere.

Ellen discovered the first affair and eventually forgave him. The second indiscretion led to the brink of separation. He remained thankful she decided she couldn't be without him. Ellen would never forgive this though. It was close to home and the person satisfying his needs too shameful to confess.

The darkness of the alleyway beckoned. She arched her back and lifted a leg to lean against the opposite wall. The scarlet lipstick was more clown-like than seductive. She resembled a prostitute, waiting for business. Alex considered when fourteen-year-olds had become sexual. He noted his hypocrisy, considering he'd been chasing skirt the moment he discovered girls could be more than friends.

'Fancy seeing you here,' Kelly said.

...

Her world tumbled. She knew he wasn't perfect but had never expected this. Her hero became a villain.

'How could you, Dad?' Claire wept.

Alex slumped against the wall where Jen and Johnny had sat,

relieved they'd gone. His daughter knowing was embarrassing enough. He considered how to recover their relationship.

Claire caught them in the act.

A reporter never lets go of a story, even if it brings personal loss and pain. Claire suspected Alex was hiding something and she recorded each time he left the house. His "just popping to the shop", "going to see a mate", and "my legs need a stretch" were regular occurrences.

Ellen's alarm bells also rang. She noted her observations too, which Claire found when rooting through her mum's wardrobe for a blouse. The thought of Ellen discovering Alex in such an uncompromising position made Claire nauseous. Although she'd never trust Alex again, at least Claire spared her mum the humiliation.

After following Alex, Claire braced herself to look into the alleyway, knowing her life would change. Below tangled limbs, Alex's trousers gathered around his ankles. His lover extended her legs against the opposite wall, used to having sex in this location. Their all-consuming passion made Claire invisible.

She froze. What should she do? Only a clichéd cough came to mind. The groans and pants ceased. The bitch spotted Claire before Alex. If it had been a news scoop, the fear in the bitch's eyes would have been satisfying. This was Claire's life though, and that thing in the alleyway wrecked it. Any sympathy Claire previously had for her as a person others sniped about disappeared as the bitch adjusted her skirt, winked, and left. Claire vowed to confront her later.

Alex emerged from the shade, zipping his trousers. Trees swayed. A storm brewed, outside and within the Woods family. A birch lashed its branches into the wind. Claire considered it falling upon Alex as retribution.

'It isn't what it looks like,' he began.

'Are you kidding me?' Claire said. 'It's exactly how it looks. You're shagging *her*.'

Alex trotted behind his daughter, desperate to salvage his

family. Claire sat on Johnny and Jen's wall, nibbling her cuticles. Alex slumped to the ground, trying to summon any fight he had left.

'Why her?' Claire swiped at her betraying tears.

'It was madness. She bewitched me.'

He didn't see the punch before it connected.

'Don't blame her.' Claire inspected her knuckles, astonished at her fast reflexes. 'It takes two.'

Alex nursed his jaw, half proud of Claire's fighting prowess, half afraid of another blow. 'Are you going to tell Mum?'

Claire blew on her sore fingers, remembering how Ellen used to blow on cuts to "heal" them. How could she tell her mum? Alex and Claire were her world. Claire didn't want to destroy it. In that moment, she hated her dad.

Alex touched Claire's face. 'Angel, please don't tell your mum.'

Claire shook her head to release the caress. She never wanted him to touch her again, knowing those hands had been on *her*.

'I need time to think. It's the best I can offer.' She jumped from the wall. Alex followed. 'Don't you dare come home for a while. It won't hurt you to sweat it out for a bit, wondering if, or when, I will expose your grubby little secret.'

She walked away, her body aching with each sob.

...

Alex returned to the scene of the crime, grateful the alleyway shielded him from sight. He was a disgusting creature and wished he could disappear. He hoped Claire wouldn't say anything to Ellen and then despised himself for the thought. Placing such a burden upon his beloved daughter was worse than having an affair. Her eyes showed his fallen idol status. Another pair of teenager's eyes had judged him earlier.

When Alex first entered the alleyway, he'd startled Kelly. She covered her embarrassment with a saucy line and made to leave.

Unfortunately she hadn't moved fast enough. His mistress appeared.

Unable to see into the dark space, she offered herself. 'Alex, I'm wearing the stockings you like.'

Alex didn't know who was more stunned when the three of them noticed each other: him, Kelly or Felicity.

After Kelly left, Alex considered finding her and devising a lie. Then he reasoned, no one spoke to Kelly, so who would she tell? Felicity had to be dealt with first. Kelly could wait for tomorrow. He'd beg her to stay quiet, even apply pressure if he must. There was nothing Alex wouldn't do to hold his family together.

At seeing Kelly, Felicity decided if a Pratt was going to expose her secret, she might as well have fun first. Knowing it was their last encounter, she used her magic on Alex. Felicity had ways and means of dealing with Kelly too. Silencing girls didn't challenge Felicity's morals. No one would shatter the reputation she'd worked hard to build on the Rembrandt Estate. Alex was weak but she knew he could placate Claire. As she sauntered away, high on the thrill, Felicity considered her strategy for sorting out Kelly.

Claire didn't tell her mum about Alex's affair with Felicity until Ellen finally left him, years later. Kelly never had the chance to share what she had witnessed with anyone.

The next day her silence was permanent.

53

PRESENT

The customers of Mabel's Parlour continue their idle chatter and chinking of cups and saucers. Priscilla's sharing of Kelly's secret has no impact on them. Claire and I are stunned.

Priscilla smirks. 'Straight up, it's true. Rob Morgan was the father of Kelly's baby, and that's not all.'

'Go on.' Claire knocks over a salt cellar as she leans forward.

'I saw Rob by the tracks that day.' Priscilla hams up the intrigue. 'He was hanging around the crossing, looking like he was up to no good. It was about the time Kelly was supposed to have been there. Mum grounded me for getting my ears pierced, thinking it would keep me in. As soon as she was having another one of her epic kips, I went for a walk and spotted Rob.'

'It doesn't mean he killed Kelly.' My defence of a man who made my skin crawl is surprising. Priscilla's aggressiveness brings out the worst in people. I remember though how faithful Rob seemed to be to Rose, probably because she was the boss in their relationship. Even though Johnny disliked Rob, he never doubted the man's loyalty to his mum.

'Wake up, Jen.' The force of her bitchiness causes spit to hit my face. 'You're supposed to be brainy. Of course Rob did it.'

I wipe the spit away. A group of ladies shake their heads and tut disapproval of Priscilla's volume. How she keeps her job is a mystery.

Claire checks her phone is recording the conversation. 'Got anything else?'

'Isn't that enough, Dumbo?'

Claire's lunge over the table confirms she's still not a fan of her childhood nickname. The woman at the till approaches us, notices Priscilla's snarl, and steps back. *This* is why, despite her lack of social skills, Priscilla remains employed. She scares her colleagues witless.

'Is there a problem, ladies?' the woman asks.

'We're fine. Why don't you concentrate on getting those lazy sods doing the extension to keep the noise down. Off you go.' Priscilla waves her away. The woman scuttles off to safety, behind the coffee machine.

Claire simmers. Priscilla better not have any secrets because my reporter friend won't rest until she gets revenge. Seeing Claire tensing her fists, I hope she doesn't whack Priscilla. Explaining to the police why we were talking to Priscilla could make matters trickier.

'This chat is over.' Priscilla stands. 'Your drinks and grub are covered.' She flicks her hands, summoning us to leave.

I'm close to punching her too. Smiling through clenched teeth, I give her one of my business cards instead. 'In case you remember anything else.'

She holds the card as if it will explode. 'Someone thinks their shit doesn't stink, with their fancy cards.'

We aim for the exit, relieved to be free of this good kid turned bad.

'Jen,' Priscilla blasts across the room, 'give my regards to your family.'

I ignore her, seeing as Priscilla had nothing to do with us. I

don't allow her the satisfaction of replying but the comment turns
around in my mind on the way home.

54

8TH OCTOBER 1987

Despite Deirdre Staines's efforts, she couldn't keep her daughter, Priscilla, away from Kelly. After Deirdre caught Priscilla in the Pratts' garden four months earlier, their friendship was threatened. Deirdre ramped up her surveillance. Even going to the toilet wasn't a private affair. Whenever Priscilla flushed, her mum stood outside the door. Deirdre couldn't maintain the regime for long though, and the afternoon naps beckoned. She fancied herself as a lady from a bygone era. Her delicate constitution demanded rest and a dose of smelling salts for frazzled nerves. Deirdre's old-fashioned fancies worked in Priscilla's favour.

Kelly and Priscilla became bold in taking their adventures outside the confines of the garden. At first, they ventured only as far as the railway track. Chris's loud whistle served as a warning for Priscilla to return. The witch had returned to her lair.

That day Deirdre was away from home, tending to her mother. Priscilla couldn't grieve for her dying grandmother who was a vicious woman. When Priscilla felt generous, she understood why her mum developed neuroses. Her grandmother ruled the family with antiseptic and fears of fatality. The germ phobia began with her. Even in the summer she wrapped up in a scarf and cardigan to keep out stray chills. If a person so much as cleared their throat, she barred them from her company.

Deirdre endured a childhood of medical tests, prodding and poking to find an affliction that didn't exist. If she hadn't repeated history, Priscilla could have pitied her. If Priscilla was malicious, her grandmother genuinely dying would have bordered on comical. Instead, she empathised with Deirdre, sitting by her mother's bedside, hoping to be set free. Priscilla wondered if her future involved waiting for the freedom that came from Deirdre's passing. At eleven, she probably had years to wait. It was the time to escape, whenever the opportunity arose.

...

Kelly beckoned Priscilla over. Resembling a plump bumble bee, in neon yellow leggings with black stripes, Kelly glowed. Priscilla attributed the attention-seeking outfit to the affair. They always referred to it as an affair rather than the more basic truth. Priscilla knew it couldn't go anywhere. Although she still didn't know who Kelly's object of affection was, it didn't sound like he viewed their relationship as long term. Priscilla watched enough soap operas – Deirdre's guilty pleasure – to spot a dud coupling.

Priscilla assessed Kelly's clothes against her own. The daring threads would swamp her skinny body. Her jeans and hooded sweatshirt that she hid from Deirdre, and wore that day, were frumpy in comparison. Priscilla considered putting her school uniform back on. At least she'd blend in with the other pupils milling around town.

Priscilla thumbed lipstick from above Kelly's top lip. 'You went over the line.'

In thanks, Kelly slathered Steamy Scarlet over Priscilla's mouth. It was a special day, being Priscilla's first time into Troddington without her parents. Chris hesitated in deciding. Priscilla worked her dad a charm, detailing her rotten life, captured in a council home prison. He soon caved. Priscilla was more cunning than people realised.

...

The pink explosion of Fruity Beauty invited them in. The cerise building jarred against the more traditional white shops with their muted awnings. Kim, the owner, insisted on using the brightest pink paint to set the tone. Troddington's residents remarked upon its garishness. Petitions did the rounds, demanding a change of colour. Kim refused to budge.

'Dare you.' Kelly pointed at the salon. Her crop top rose to expose rolls of flesh. Priscilla pulled it down.

She was torn between pleasing her friend and obedience. Deirdre would ground her for the rest of her natural life if she went through with the plan.

'They won't let me do it,' Priscilla said. 'Not without an adult.' She had a stronger constitution than Deirdre credited her with, but ear piercing was a brutal form of rebellion.

'Are you scared?' Kelly asked.

'No.' Priscilla inspected her flaking nails, affecting boredom.

A group of teenagers surged past, jeering at Kelly's appearance. Priscilla wondered why the girl didn't help herself by making better choices. As Kelly read the salon's price list, Priscilla felt remorse at the lack of loyalty to her friend. Kelly was her hero. She cared for Priscilla with a fierce passion and wore what she liked with no apologies. Priscilla wanted to be more like Kelly without being a victim.

'I'll do it,' Priscilla said.

Kelly performed a jubilant dance. The lines on her leggings wobbled along with her early bloomer breasts. A woman trailing a shopping trolley advised, 'Put it away, sweetheart.'

Kelly rearranged her top, realising that cutting the length of her top in half was ill-judged. Graham would go mad if he caught her exposing her body in public.

'We need an adult to get my ears pierced though,' Priscilla said.

Kelly led her towards the premises. 'No problem. My mum knows Kim. They were at school together. I'll tell them Mum said it's okay.'

Kelly hoped Kim wasn't working. The proprietor didn't allow children to have unsupervised ear piercing. Kelly knew if she told Priscilla, she wouldn't do it. Noting the absence of Kim and that Charlene, the dippy junior appeared to be in charge, Kelly led Priscilla into the pink palace.

...

'I chucked him because he felt me up when I wasn't in the mood.' Charlene was in her element, detailing her short-lived relationship. Kim had given her a verbal warning for gossiping in the salon but she figured Kelly and Priscilla were only kids and wouldn't say anything. Charlene tightened her side ponytail and checked her reflection in the gold and pink-framed mirror. 'I told Gaz, my tits are my own and I decide who touches them.' To emphasise her conviction, Charlene smoothed the chest area of her baby-pink dress.

'I agree,' Kelly said. 'Only one special person is allowed near my body.'

The plastic beads around Charlene's neck jingled along with her hysterics. Priscilla moved away, afraid of the piercing implement in the woman's unsteady hands.

A lady with a colossal bouffant turned up the dryer to drown out the crass talk.

'You're too young for that,' Charlene said. 'Wait until you're fifteen, at least.'

'Too late,' Priscilla said. Realising the error, she awaited Kelly's annoyance.

Instead, Kelly said, 'I'm pregnant.'

Charlene gave a nervous titter. The impact of Kelly's bombshell left Priscilla unprepared for the piercing gun hitting her ear.

...

'Don't puke on the chaise longue. It's velour. Kim will go ballistic.' Charlene hovered over Priscilla, holding a bucket under her chin.

Priscilla pushed it away. 'I'm fine, thank you. Where are we?'

'In the back room,' Charlene said. 'We needed to get you in here. Unconscious customers are bad for business. Your secret is safe with me by the way, Kel.'

This was true, mainly because Charlene couldn't retain information for five minutes. She left to attend to a customer.

'Who's the dad?' Priscilla asked Kelly.

Kelly fiddled with a highlighting cap, trying to force her fingers through the pinprick holes. 'My mum says these are instruments of torture.'

'Don't change the subject.'

'We'll talk about it later so the nosey cows in here don't overhear. I haven't told Mum yet.'

Priscilla felt proud but uneasy in knowing Kelly's secret. It confirmed their closeness, but how could she help Kelly? Asking Deirdre for advice wasn't an option.

Charlene reappeared. 'I've got a perm waiting. We need to do the other ear if you don't want to look like a bloke.'

Having endured enough shocks, Priscilla didn't flinch.

...

'He's older than me,' Kelly said.

They sat on a bench outside the shoe menders and sipped Panda Pops. Both whispered. Fearful of voicing her truth, Kelly insisted

Priscilla guess the father's identity. She listed almost every male resident on the estate, even the ridiculous. Kelly's hesitance to give straight answers became tiring. Priscilla had to go home soon. Deirdre phoned every day, at the same time. Many of the names Priscilla offered received a negative response. Some suggestions made Kelly more guarded.

Charlie Pullen exited the shoe menders, swinging his repaired shoes by the laces. He hovered behind the girls, clearly lacking spying skills. Kelly wouldn't speak openly while her nemesis lingered. Priscilla decided to later explore Mike Taylor, Henry Ponting, Anthony Rose, Ian Rose, and Rob Morgan, as candidates for Kelly's boyfriend. At the mention of each of their names, Kelly was more uneasy than with the others Priscilla suggested, especially Rob Morgan.

Priscilla hoped for both their sakes the father of Kelly's baby wasn't Rob. Their friendship wouldn't survive it.

55

PRESENT

Claire and I have spent the last few days tracking the Rose/Morgan family. I didn't do it alone as originally planned, as we decided to share the abuse between us. Rose being the most difficult wasn't surprising. Claire found their telephone numbers then begged me to phone Rose. Our fear of the formidable matriarch hasn't reduced. Claire thought because of my closeness to Johnny, Rose would be more receptive to my call. It's *because* Johnny and I were best friends that Rose resented me. She viewed me as competition for her son's attention.

I tried to be friendly to her. On the rare occasions I was in her house, I offered to help with chores or looking after Benny. She viewed it as an attack on her domestic skills, declaring not everyone had it as easy as those on Renoir Road. I couldn't confess I'd rather have her as a mum. Rose was lazy and occasionally on the wrong side of the law but she loved her children without question.

I took one for the team and phoned her.

My ears are still ringing from Rose's convincing imitation of a banshee. I was informed I'd always been a stuck-up tart like my mum, was asked why I upset Johnny, and where the hell did I get her number? In closing, she warned me to stay away from her family or else. It's what I expected. I didn't get the opportunity to ask if she and Rob were still together.

Claire had the tasks of contacting Ian and Benny. We spent an afternoon trawling through the Internet as we're aware, barring Johnny, you don't approach a Rose or Morgan without ammunition. An article from 1992, reporting Benny's disappearance, was upsetting. After reading the Buckinghamshire newspaper archives, we learned he'd never been found. Anniversary reports in the first few years revived the story. After, Benny became a memory and no longer news. Perhaps this explains Rose's harshness on the phone. Maybe speaking to someone who reminds her of back then, when Benny was still around, is too painful. He was the centre of the family. Even Anthony and Ian softened around their little brother. Rob and Rose adored Benny. I cannot contemplate how it affected Johnny. Benny was Johnny's shadow. I wish I'd been there to support Johnny, but maybe Benny wouldn't be missing if Johnny hadn't seen me hurt Kelly, and then his family moved away. No. I won't take the blame for this too. This isn't about me.

Benny's disappearance makes me think of Mandy. She's in her late thirties. I can't imagine what she looks like. Is she married? Does she have children? Did her life turn out well? As soon as we find out what happened to Kelly, I'll try to reconcile with Mandy. I need to fill the missing part of me.

Ian was his old offensive self when Claire called. Rose had prepared him as he lives with her. None of the records Claire collated showed him as being resident there, confirming Ian is still shady. Before Claire could ask a single question, he warned us to stay away from his family or we'd find ourselves cut into small pieces. Claire brushed it off. In her line of work, it's nothing she hasn't heard before.

I struck gold with Anthony if that means being told he couldn't refuse such a stunner. He scorned how Rose and Ian said he

LISA SELL

mustn't talk to us. No one tells him what to do. I'm meeting with him for a chat. He said he'd rather talk in person.

Anthony made me want to take a shower after being near him, to wash off the filth of his stare. Even though I was a kid, he mentally undressed me and remarked upon my "hotness". Johnny always defended my honour. Anthony's references to how we must be having sex embarrassed us. His crudeness was another reason to avoid their house.

Anthony will learn he's no longer dealing with a timid girl. Much has happened since we last saw each other. Jen Taylor has grown up. I'm ready to face him.

PRESENT

The car park of The Weary Ox is full of pimped-up BMWs, motorbikes, fat exhausts, and, oddly, a new Fiat Panda. My Astra doesn't stand out, which helps when you're already feeling conspicuous. Anthony chose the renowned ropey pub for our meeting place. It's on the Burtonfields Estate, Oxford's hotspot of crime, and where Anthony lives.

I assured Claire that coming here on my own is fine. She was torn between investigative duties and attending Matty's drama club's play. I'm a stickler for parents not disappointing their kids. Even if Matty was backstage, Claire should be there. Her daughter has a main part so Claire has no excuses. Seb avoided it due to a client's financial disaster. Claire joked about marrying a geeky accountant, bitter at having to endure the musical alone. I promised to call if Anthony got out of hand. I scroll to her number, making sure it's ready if needed.

Anthony plays on a fruit machine while gulping a pint. A bull-mastiff lies on its back next to him. I hope it's friendly as I stopped being a dog lover when I was bitten by one. On a rare occasion of Mum's parents visiting, they brought their Jack Russell. The snappy thing growled throughout and when I hugged Nan goodbye, it bit my shin. I still have a scar where Pixie took a chunk out of my leg.

Anthony's dog is more interested in sleeping than attacking. Its owner could learn from his mutt. The notion that pets resemble their owners holds true. Anthony is built like the proverbial brick outhouse. He was always chubby, but now he's really stacked on weight. His hard man image remains with the close-shaven haircut. The ill-fitting suit is a strange choice. I approach, determined to be confident and in charge.

'Out the way, Nuts. Lady coming through.' Anthony nudges the dog with his foot.

Anthony points to a booth more suited for a date. I hope he doesn't think this is a romantic meeting. The idea is so comical I pretend to get something from my bag under the table, to hide the amusement.

'What are you having?' Anthony's grown into his gruff voice. As a teenager it sounded ridiculous.

I shift along the bench, away from the sticky patch, origin unknown and best it remains that way. 'Lemonade please. I'm driving.'

'Have a proper drink with me, for old time's sake.'

To keep him happy, I agree to a small white wine, intending not to drink it. I haven't broken my sobriety in a while and I'm certainly not going to do so for Anthony Rose. He returns from the bar and places a goldfish bowl glass on the table. He waits for me to sample the wine. As I fake taking a sip, I resist sucking in my cheeks. The smell confirms it's more suited to being sprinkled on chips.

'Nice?' he asks.

'Lovely.' I hope there's no trace of sarcasm. 'Thanks so much for seeing me, Anthony. How are you?'

'It's Ant, remember? Let's make it nice and friendly.' He straightens his tie, covered in burlesque dancers. 'Life is good. Your phone call was unexpected. I couldn't believe you wanted to meet with me. You always preferred Johnny.'

I keep it professional. 'Are you working at the moment?'

'No. Why? Are you from social services?'

'The suit. I thought you might've come straight from work.'

He sticks out his chest. 'I scrubbed up, for you.'

Damn it. He *does* think we're on a date. Do I continue so I can gather information or say I wouldn't go near him if he were the last Neanderthal on earth? I decide for a variation of the former: be nice, don't crush him, and find out what he knows.

'That's kind of you, Ant. But you needn't have bothered.'

'Like your men tougher?' He winks. 'I'm not a fan of suits either. Rough and ready is more my style.'

My mind is screaming "leave", but I have to talk to him. 'You said on the phone you knew what Rob was up to, the day Kelly died.' I neglect to mention how he also said he'd only provide more information in person.

'Why are you so interested in Rob?' The offence taken at me talking about another man is noticeable.

'I saw Priscilla Staines recently. She shared something interesting about him.'

He lets out a booming laugh. 'That old slut? A few blokes I know in Troddington had a dose of the clap from her.'

'I have no interest in male bravado regarding sexual conquests those men probably never had.' Priscilla and I may not be friends but I won't allow him to shame her.

He chuckles. 'Look who got fancy with her words.'

'Anyway.' I steer it back, desperate to escape this oik as soon as possible. 'Priscilla said Rob was having sex with Kelly and got her pregnant.'

I await Anthony's indignation. Instead he almost chokes, trying to breathe through hysterics. 'Are you having a giraffe? Rob wouldn't have touched her if his todger depended on it. Priscilla didn't mention how she was stalking Rob, then?'

I'd rather he was laughing than this hard-faced seriousness.

'Priscilla posted cards through our letterbox, telling Rob she loved him. She even wrote her name on them, the dappy cow. Mum and Rob put up with it for a while. Then she began hanging around our gate. Rob told her to do one. He tore up the cards in front of her and she still kept on. It kicked off when Mum found a teddy bear under Rob's pillow, with "Priscilla" sewn on it. I think it was just before Kelly died.'

'What happened?'

Anthony swipes lager foam from his lip with the back of his hand. 'After giving Rob grief and checking he wasn't a kiddy fiddler, Mum marched round to the Staines's house and had it out with Priscilla. It was classic.' He sniggers.

I move along the bench, no longer caring about the stickiness if it means I have a rapid exit route.

'The rest of us, apart from Johnny, joined Mum,' Anthony says. 'Priscilla's mum blew her conkers. Priscilla said she asked Kelly to slip the teddy under Rob's pillow when we were out. Kelly did it because no one ever noticed her. Mum threatened to whack Priscilla. Priscilla's dad was ready to deck Rob for leading a young girl astray. Nobody got hit, more's the pity. That nutter never went near Rob again.'

Johnny didn't tell me this story. I expect he grew weary of sharing his family's embarrassing escapades.

'Why would Priscilla say that about Rob and Kelly?' I ask. 'I don't get it.'

'She's lying, you stupid cow. Priscilla's still bitter but it won't do her any good anyway.'

'Why?'

'Rob's dead.'

PRESENT

'I didn't know about Rob. What happened?' I ask Anthony.

'Dickhead smashed his bike into a lorry on the opposite side of the road, back in 1993.' Anthony remains impassive.

'Sorry to hear it.' The Roses have been through so much.

'Don't be. Rob was an arsehole. He was good for getting the drinks in but not a lot else.' Anthony pulls the dog's lead and Nuts lies on his feet.

I decide not to mention Benny's disappearance. Anthony is riled enough already. 'Do you know where Rob was the day Kelly died? Priscilla said he was lingering by the train track around the same time Kelly was there.'

'For a brainy bird, you can be so dumb. Priscilla's trying to get Rob into trouble. That's sick, doing that to a dead bloke.'

I worry I may have put Priscilla at risk. Anthony always settled scores. 'Leave it, Anthony.'

'I told you, it's Ant. Don't tell me what to do. If you must know, Rob was waiting for me. We were sloping off for a few pints. Then he took me to a strip bar in Oxford. There were tits and arse galore.'

I teeter on the end of the bench in response to the licking of his lips. 'Why did you meet at the track?'

'Out of respect for Mum.' Ant's frown relaxes. 'She'd have lost the plot if Rob and I had left together and she found out I was going there. As for Rob, she would've made earrings out of his "nads".'

'Right.' I need to move on from the strip club topic considering he's looking at me like I work in one. 'You don't think there was any way Rob could've been the father of Kelly's baby?'

'You haven't drunk your wine. That cost more than a pint, you know.' He pushes it closer to me. 'Apart from Rob not touching Kelly with a bargepole, he had the snip after Benny was born. Mum wanted more kids but he didn't. He confessed when we were pissed and then threatened a slow death if I told Mum.'

This avenue is closed. 'Thanks so much for your time. I must go as I've got an early start tomorrow.'

He grabs my wrist. 'Finish your drink.' Fanciful pretences disappear. *This* is the real Anthony Rose.

I move the glass aside and pull away from his grip. 'I'm leaving, right now.'

'Suit yourself,' he grumbles.

Anthony moves to my side of the booth. My finger hovers over dialling Claire's number and I'm ready to shout for help. Anthony clasps me into a smothering hug. Foul breath accompanies the whisper calling me a prick tease who stringed Johnny along.

The repressed anger of the last few weeks rushes to the surface. Anthony will not intimidate me further. I raise my knee, aiming – on behalf of the female race – to put him out of action. He performs a footballer dive, cupping his crotch. A crescendo of laughter ripples across the pub. I pick up my bag and step alongside him.

Through the pain, Anthony shouts, 'You're a stuck-up slag, like your mum! I had her once.'

I shake my head. Mum was many things, but she wasn't blind.

...

I'm still laughing as I get into my car. Turning the key in the ignition, I relish speaking to Claire. Voicemail messages play as I drive. Claire asks if death by show tune is a thing because she's approaching it. I chuckle and move on to the next message. It's Priscilla.

'Hello, Jen. Sorry I was off when we met. Seeing you two looking so good and having done well made me feel crappy. I'm just a waitress, lugging bags of rubbish outside at the moment. My life is rubbish too. It's time to tell you the truth.' She pauses. 'Oh, shit. You're here. I didn't know we were meeting today.'

I can hear rustling and a muffled male voice.

Priscilla returns. 'Stop calling me. I'm not interested in making an accident claim. Goodbye.'

Why did she end the call when she was ready to share something? She sounded terrified.

I try to phone her throughout the evening. An announcement the number isn't available is the only reply. My unease turns to horror when Claire appears on my doorstep, at 4am.

Priscilla is dead.

9TH OCTOBER 1987

Charlie Pullen teased and harassed Kelly for years. Everyone was convinced of his hatred. In trying to conceal his crush, Charlie shifted too far in the opposite direction. The attraction to the girl many loved to hate scared him, but the time for waiting was over. He needed to declare his feelings for Kelly and ignore others' opinions.

Charlie accepted he wasn't a catch. Numerous takeaways increased his girth. Since his mum left, a house of males led to little housekeeping and poor nutrition. His dad's nickname, Porky, was apt for a man who thought nothing of eating a double portion of fish and chips, washed down with lager. Trying to be healthy, Charlie once made a salad for dinner. Porky called him a poof as limp as the offensive lettuce on the plate.

Charlie realised he wasn't attractive but figured it meant he was suited to Kelly. They held their attributes inside rather than relying on an outer veneer. Her kindness to others moved him. When he insulted her, she never retaliated. Kelly was a lady, reminding him of his mum's gentle manner. Charlie wished his mum, Annette, was still around to ask for advice.

Weary of being married to a slobby alcoholic with a volatile reputation, Annette left Porky in 1985. Her letter, blaming Porky's slovenly ways for her decision, offered little comfort for Charlie and his brother, Glen. Annette's prolonged absence confirmed she'd left them too. The last they'd heard, she lived with an ex-criminal in Abingdon. A man from the pub told Porky, who shared the news with his sons, triumphant at not being the only crap parent.

Glen took Annette's departure hard and made all females the enemy. At twelve, he swore off the opposite sex for life. It wouldn't last long. Charlie didn't hate women, not even Annette. He planned to find her and move in. The only obstacle was never seeing Kelly again.

Charlie held his unrequited love tight. If Porky or Glen found out, their mocking would reach a new level of nastiness. For sport, they often ridiculed the estate's residents. Charlie seethed when they discussed Smelly Kelly, a specimen so ugly you'd have to put a bag over her head to kiss her. To avoid suspicion, Charlie joined in and continued as Kelly's chief bully. It had backfired. Convincing her of his worthiness would be difficult, especially after over-hearing her confession the previous day.

...

Seeing Kelly and Priscilla sitting on the bench outside the shoe menders was unexpected. Charlie always tried to prepare for Kelly's appearances. The girls' conversation caught his attention. He hovered near the bin, swinging his dad's shoes by their laces and casting glances at his watch as if waiting for someone. Priscilla gave him suspicious looks, unconvinced of the subterfuge.

As Kelly chatted, Charlie beamed. He loved hearing her voice even though she talked for England and a few other countries. For a supposed thicko, Kelly spoke well. Charlie worked on his speech every evening, with an etiquette tape he'd found in a box Annette had left behind. He considered joining the girls to show off his enunciated vowels. Before he could move, Kelly dropped a bombshell.

Charlie stooped over the shoes that slipped from his grip. If he stood, Kelly would have seen his face. He swallowed hard, begging humiliating tears not to surface. When he rose, Kelly looked over. Her bitter stare pierced his heart on the way home.

Later, Charlie reasoned Kelly was afraid he knew her secret. He would show her his loyalty by offering to be her boyfriend and a father to her child. Fourteen was young but his intentions were honourable. Whoever had made Kelly pregnant didn't sound reliable, from what Kelly told Priscilla. Charlie decided to find out the father's identity so the Rose boys could get to work on him.

Soon, Kelly would understand Charlie wasn't the enemy but someone who adored her. Soon, Kelly would be his, whatever he had to do to make it happen.

59

10TH OCTOBER 1987

The top of Renoir Road became the youngsters' new spot to congregate, much to Patricia's annoyance. Jen knew her mum's explosive temper fed her peers' desire to be there. Patricia's rages as she stomped the pavement in feathered slippers kept them amused. Jen wished they understood the strife created when she had to return home. Patricia punished Jen for the other children's behaviour, citing guilt by association.

'Your mum's a witch,' Claire said as Patricia's kitten heels clicked away.

Jen didn't argue and concentrated instead on stripping chewing gum from Claire's hair. Nervous at Shane East, her current object of affection, coming towards them, Claire chewed her hair. When Shane looked over, Claire spat out her plait and tangled it in the gum.

'He thinks I'm a dumb cow.' Claire flung her arms around Jen.

Johnny prepared a concoction of washing-up liquid and water in a jug. 'Stop being so melodramatic.'

'I had chewing gum stretching across my face,' Claire said. 'He saw it.'

Johnny threw the soapy water at her head, partly as a fix but mostly to silence her.

'Blimey.' Claire rubbed her stinging eyes. 'You could've used warm water.'

Jen worked at the knotted mess, ignoring the expressions Johnny made at their drama queen friend.

Johnny tried not to touch Jen's fingers as they scrubbed Claire's hair.

Charlie waited for Kelly to appear. Sometimes she was bold and tried to join in with the others. Often, she either stayed in or walked the estate alone.

'Catch, durr brain!' Anthony shouted as the tennis ball sailed past Charlie's head.

They commandeered the road for a game of cricket. Anthony threatened any drivers who dared to disrupt. Most waited for permission to pass, aware of the consequences of arguing with a Rose. Jen was grateful for the cricketers' decision not to use a cricket ball. Patricia would do more than mouth off if they smashed her greenhouse again.

Preparing to bat, Roxanne McDonald, from Turner Road, lifted the peak of her cap and said, 'Freak show coming through. What the hell does she look like?'

Kelly exited from Pollock Road. Charlie sniggered as Roxanne slipped, from leaning on the cricket bat, and fell on her knees.

Kelly dawdled near Jen, Claire, and Johnny. A hair clip slid down her head, making her pineapple ponytail lopsided. Her black and white polka dot shirt strained at the waist and buttons threatened to pop. Demonstrating the saying of showing what she'd had for dinner, Kelly's miniscule denim skirt skirted her backside.

While the others ignored her, Charlie couldn't see anyone else.

Kelly never looked more beautiful, and not because of the revealing outfit. Charlie recalled the boy from the Ready Brek advert, who radiated heat. Kelly shone too. His mum used to say pregnant women glowed. Expecting girls apparently did too. The girl's confidence gave Charlie the courage to decide to make his pledge straightaway.

He watched as she lingered around Jen, desperate for acceptance. Charlie couldn't tolerate Jen and Claire. They were unobtainable and he certainly wouldn't go near Patricia's daughter. Claire's mum being a reporter was off-putting too. No one messed with the Woods family if they didn't want to feature in the local rag. Jen and Claire were snooty bitches anyway. He glowered as they ignored Kelly, focusing instead on playing with Claire's hair. Even Johnny joined in. Charlie couldn't accept Johnny as a true Rose. What sort of bloke hung around with girls?

Kelly said goodbye to the three as if they'd been socialising. Charlie empathised with the rejection. Not being accepted was familiar. He was only in Anthony and Ian's gang because no one else wanted to be with him. Charlie knew he was an "annoying shit", as his dad so eloquently put it, and he had little intelligence to offer. He believed though, if people saw the real Charlie, they'd learn of a tender-hearted boy who used to make his mum breakfast in bed. They would discover the comedian who told jokes that made his brother and dad hold their sides. The problem with living in the same place for years was you became a set of labels. Change proved impossible. Charlie would always be the Rembrandt Estate's resident bully. He hoped to convince Kelly to see beyond it.

Charlie followed at a discreet distance as she ambled along Turner Road. Blisters formed on his heels from Porky's three-sizes-too large brogues. Every day, Charlie slicked his hair and put on the smart shoes, preparing for an encounter with Kelly. He'd used his pocket money for reheeling, such was his dedication to Kelly and fear of Porky discovering his son had stolen his best shoes.

Kelly adjusted her skirt. Charlie welcomed the extra coverage, feeling protective of her and the baby. He wondered how this girl bewitched him. Once, he'd despised her. Over time, an alien emotion crept inside and lodged there. As Kelly grew, he noticed her warmth and exuberance. Even though her life was difficult, she maintained a cheerful disposition.

Kelly's face wasn't so radiant now. Furrows lined her forehead when she glimpsed behind before stepping into the alley. People avoided the alleyways unless they were up to no good. Charlie retreated and stood outside the McDonalds' house to consider his next move.

Noticing a figure entering the top of the road and not willing to explain his loitering, Charlie vaulted a fence and landed in the McDonalds' garden. He hoped "Macca" wasn't at home. Trespassing on the tough nut's premises was suicide. Charlie peered through a hole in the gate, trailing the person walking past.

When it was clear, Charlie climbed over the fence. A nail caught his leg mid-clamber. Although his flesh tore at the knee, he ignored the pain and prepared to declare his feelings for Kelly.

A male spoke from the alleyway. 'Stop asking if I like you. Being here should be enough.'

Charlie hoped the male was talking to anyone but Kelly. Maybe she'd left while he was hiding. Kelly couldn't possibly be with *him*.

'I want to hear you say it.'

Charlie's hopes plummeted as he recognised her voice. He heard it in his fantasies, telling him of her love. Now, Kelly cooed at someone else; *him*, of anyone she could have chosen. Why would she choose such an unsuitable person? He was sick in the head for getting involved with her.

'I love you,' Kelly said.

Charlie's courage disappeared. He peered around the corner. Curiosity made him stay. Listening to their passion was torturous. When Kelly protested the bricks grazed her skin and her lover paid no attention, Charlie's murderous impulses flared. He numbed at the cry of ecstasy and zoned out as the couple chatted afterwards. Then Kelly mentioned his name.

When her partner commented on her weight gain, she replied, 'It could be worse. I could be a huge, disgusting slob, like Charlie Pullen. He makes me want to puke.'

Their laughter remained with Charlie as he stomped home, ignoring Anthony's command to get his arse back into the cricket game.

...

The following week, Charlie punched Glen in the face for calling him a whale, after Charlie gobbled a second bowl of cereal. Remembering Kelly's taunt about his appearance made the blow more forceful than he'd intended. The brothers tussled on the living room floor until Porky came home to wrecked furniture and broken sons. For the first time, Porky locked them in their bedrooms. Porky didn't care if school was shut or not, due to the aftereffects of the storm. Family did not fight each other. Charlie wasn't bothered by the incarceration. Being shielded from sight meant no one could witness his distress.

Within days, his love for Kelly splintered and then shattered. Revenge took its place. He vowed she would feel the humiliation of being made to look a fool. His campaign of abuse would escalate to the more personal and real.

Kelly Pratt was dead to him.

60

PRESENT

'Priscilla's dead?' I'm asking for clarification again because I cannot process it.

When Claire got here, neither of us could speak. We sit and drink coffee, hardly in need of caffeine to keep awake, even in this early hour.

Claire received a call from a reporter friend. She'd missed it due to being tortured by Matty's drama club's production of *Cats*. The rest of the evening was family time. Tired of seeing the back of his family's mobiles rather than their faces, Seb issued instructions to silence their phones. Unable to go cold turkey, Claire got up at 3am, listened to the voicemail, and sped over to my house.

'How do you get out of bed, looking the same as always? Seb says I resemble Alice Cooper when I emerge from my pit.' Claire tries to lighten the mood but neither of us feels jovial. Someone we used to know and recently saw has died.

The owner of Mabel's Parlour found Priscilla in the alleyway, alongside the premises. Her body was by the bins she mentioned in her phone call.

'Maybe it's linked to our meeting with her,' I say. 'The way she shouted her mouth off wasn't inconspicuous.'

'Why would someone kill her for talking to us?'

'You didn't say she was killed.'

'What did you think happened?' Claire's sarcasm never hides under civility.

'Suicide? An accident?' The irony of how we've considered Kelly's death similarly isn't lost on me.

'Unless she smacked her own head in repeatedly with a brick, we can safely assume Priscilla was murdered.' Claire punches one hand into the other. 'Who the hell would do that? Priscilla was a right royal pain in the arse, but didn't deserve that.'

'She called me. Listen to this.' I play the message. Hearing someone who's no longer alive is chilling.

'She wanted to make amends,' Claire says. 'Did you hear someone in the background? Sounds like a man, although it's faint.'

'Yes. It's weird how Priscilla pretended to be taking a call. Perhaps she didn't want the other person to know who she was phoning. Maybe the male voice belongs to the person who killed her.' The image of Priscilla's head covered in blood won't shift. I let Kelly down but I *can* help Priscilla. 'I need to play this to the police.'

'Murder in Troddington. Who would've thought it?'

'We would. It might have happened before, remember? Could Priscilla's death be linked to Kelly's? It seems too much of a coincidence.'

Claire rakes through her hair. Her husband is right. She's a mess. Lazy cow didn't even remove her mascara before going to bed. Panda eyes trail to her cheeks.

'Don't tell the police about our Kelly investigation yet,' Claire says. 'Coppers don't take well to reporters and the public playing amateur detective. It may not be connected to Kelly anyway.'

I'm inclined to agree as I'd rather not confess my part in Kelly's death. Doreen has given me forgiveness. If I speak to the police, they might pursue me as a suspect, no matter what Constance says about the blow not being fatal.

'Do we continue?' I ask.

'If you need to duck out, I won't hold it against you.' Claire grabs my hand and smooths her thumb over it. 'This is getting complicated and you've been through so much. Priscilla's death has made me realise life's too short to be angry about something you did as a kid. I understand why you couldn't tell me. You must have been so scared. If it makes it easier, I can take the investigation from here.'

I've always been stubborn. Sometimes it's my downfall, other times it's an asset. I can't quit. Doreen and I need peace. I owe it to Priscilla too. She phoned because she trusted me.

I extend my little finger and Claire latches hers to mine. 'I swear I'll stick with you in this, until the end.'

She smiles at my vow. 'How did it go with Anthony?'

'Flaming hell. He's more of a sleaze than ever.' I recount the evening, taking pleasure in detailing the moment I spoiled his plums.

Coffee spurts from Claire's mouth. She wipes it on her Mickey Mouse nightie. 'Anthony tried it with me once. I was walking home from school and he was in his front garden, which was odd since it was the size of a postage stamp.'

'The front gardens were rubbish on the estate. Good job we had huge back gardens.'

Claire shudders at a memory. 'Anthony was sitting on a foldout chair, scratching his bits, and smoking. The second I saw him, I regretted going that way.'

'I hated being in their house,' I say. 'When Rose barred me, I was relieved. Whenever I sat in their living room, Rob and Anthony leered at me. Johnny always made excuses to leave.'

Claire makes a disgusted face. 'Anthony walked alongside, then offered for us to go somewhere private, to show me a good time. I was thirteen, the dirty bastard.' She's incensed, not only for her younger self but probably for her teenage daughter too.

'What did you do?' I ask.

'I stamped on his foot and legged it. After, I avoided Turner Road. It shook me up. Do you think Anthony was Kelly's boyfriend?'

'No way. She was scared of him and Ian. Kelly wouldn't have gone anywhere near Anthony. It took a while for her to even talk to Johnny. Hearing she risked putting the teddy bear under Rob's pillow for Priscilla was surprising.'

'She was a good kid,' Claire says. 'Twisted as it was, she was helping her friend. I can't see Kelly and Anthony having a thing either. I can't imagine *anyone* going near him.'

'You can rest assured he'll be out of action for a while.'

We laugh at the thought of Anthony nursing sore balls. Death still lies heavy between us and cuts through the merriment.

Claire paces the kitchen. 'This is so frustrating. We have so many loose ends and no logical way to tie them up. Mum and I have tried contacting everyone on the estate. They're either dead, we can't find them, they know nothing, or have told us to do one.'

Estate law rules, even when you leave. You must never speak a word of what happened on the Rembrandt Estate. We are making ourselves unpopular in resurrecting the community's most tragic event. After the theories faded, Kelly's death became a legend people feared mentioning. As in life, Kelly was invisible.

'What about Charlie Pullen?' I ask. 'He was always picking on Kelly.'

'I considered him too. Mum spoke to his brother. Remember Glen? He works in the breakers yard in Troddington and is more polite than he used to be.'

Glen Pullen turned nice? I find it hard to believe. 'Where's Charlie?'

'He's moved on. Glen doesn't know where. I'm not surprised considering how much those two fought. Glen knew where Charlie was when Kelly died though. Porky locked them in their rooms for scrapping. None of the Pullens left the house that day.'

Porky being a responsible parent was unheard of. He must have been sober for once.

Our options have run out.

'There's my dad, seeing as he still lives on the estate. I could talk to him.' The words feel like they're coming from someone else's mouth.

'Do you really want to see him?' Claire traces a finger around the rim of her mug. 'Would he be of much use? Mum tried to speak to him, but he didn't answer the phone.'

Dad has always hidden away.

'He knew lots of people on the estate from doing odd jobs for them. Mum gave him grief for it as he never got paid. Dad did anything for a pint. There's the pub too. Those blokes shared a lot of gossip. He might have heard something there.'

'I can speak to him,' Claire says.

I appreciate her kindness for sparing me potential hurt. If you'd told me a few months ago I'd return to the Rembrandt Estate to talk to Dad, I would've called you crazy. Now it's necessary, not only to discover what he might know but also to confront my demons. I've lived with them for too long.

'I need to do this alone,' I say. 'You understand, don't you?'

'I do. Be careful. I'm not sure about this.'

Bravado won't allow me to confess I'm terrified.

I have to go back.

61

12TH SEPTEMBER 1989

In 1989, after losing Johnny's friendship, Jen hung out at Troddington's youth club. It became a refuge and where she found a temporary tribe. Jen was reborn as a child of the shiny and colourful rave revolution. Her former uniform of black and more black died, along with her dreams. Jen signed up to the ravers' dress code of baggy jeans, body suits, patterned hoodies, and bold jewellery. She didn't recognise herself. That was the point.

The group was there to be seen. In belonging to them, Jen became invisible. Moving in crowds offered the perfect hiding place for harbouring a secret. When the pain of losing Johnny was too much, Jen listened to The Jam on her Walkman and imagined Johnny on the other side of the headphones.

Claire's life had changed too. She honed her snooping skills to become even more of an avid reporter. Jen had to avoid her. The last thing a killer needed was an inquisitive friend. Claire was the editor of the school newspaper, and with it, enjoyed a sudden popularity. At school they acknowledged each other as acquaintances rather than friends. They never saw each other on the estate. Jen made sure of it.

Jen's life was more bearable, living with Freddie and Liz for the past two years. In December 1987, she left the Taylor house, after Patricia's nastiness escalated. Traumatised by sixteenth October, Jen was easy prey for physical and verbal assaults.

One day she knew she must leave. Patricia decided Jen's mopping skills were inadequate. For her failings, Patricia threw the bucket of dirty water at her daughter. Jen caught her soaked reflection in the kitchen mirror and saw a pathetic being nearing destruction. It had to stop. Either Jen left or Patricia would; in a coffin.

After the altercation with Kelly, Jen swore never to let anger dictate her behaviour again. Patricia's renewed campaign of hatred compromised her resilience. When Jen moved into the Normans' flat, no explanations were necessary. Freddie and Liz knew it would be a matter of time since Johnny had left. Always fair, Liz sought Mike and Patricia's permission. She did so trying not to scratch Patricia's eyes out. Patricia remained disinterested throughout the conversation. Her daughter could live on the moon for all she cared. Jen expected a fight. Patricia didn't allow others to win. Later, Jen realised Patricia *had* won. Jen was gone.

Jen checked the clock. Freddie and Liz were at work, which gave enough time to pack and consider the plan. A group she hung around with in Troddington market square squatted in a house in town. A few of the road's residents grew suspicious of the abode, whose occupants multiplied. The police might turn up but it would do as a first step to getting away from the past.

Jen received significantly lower grades than predicted in her exams. The ambition to become a doctor shattered and her life prospects sank. Before exam results day, she'd refused to drink from the bottle of vodka doing the rounds in a friend's car. Previously, the smell of cigarettes made her queasy. Now, drinking and smoking blurred the sharp edges. The harder stuff followed. If she died, so be it.

Freddie and Liz tried to reason with her, explaining the potential consequences of Jen's dubious choices. Jen cringed when Liz asked about her sex life. Believing Jen wanted to be intimate with anyone was ridiculous. Men flirted with her. They sat outside school in their vans, picking up their teenage girlfriends and trying to add Jen to the list. She resolved never to be so easy. The barriers she'd created were impossible to overcome anyway.

The girls teased that Deggsy had his eye on her. He was in his twenties and had a reputation with the ladies. The only male she wanted near her was Johnny. It felt unfaithful to consider a relationship with anyone else, even if she'd never see Johnny again.

Deggsy served a purpose by waiting in his car. Jen refused to let him into the flat. Her seedy life didn't belong in the Normans' home. She needed to break the habit of letting them down.

Deciding to leave had been torturous. Leaving Mandy with their parents even more so. Jen wished she could take her sister away but a squat wasn't a suitable place to raise a child. Besides, Patricia would never let Mandy go. Two missing daughters didn't lend well to the perfect mother persona.

Jen hated herself for taking the coward's way out in writing Mandy a letter. It sat in the hallway, alongside another for the Normans. Knowing no amount of words could make it right, Jen kept them short.

She pulled out the tin tucked behind a fish ornament and emptied it of the notes. Freddie and Liz were saving to take Jen to New York. She played along, knowing it would never happen. Allowing them to believe in a future with her seemed right but it could never be. Since Kelly died, Jen felt sick with dread at the Normans discovering the truth. Each morning she woke, wondering if it was the day Freddie and Liz cast her out. Living in fear became exhausting. She knew stealing from them was wrong, but hoped they would understand it was an act of survival.

Deggsy's car gave a pathetic toot. Jen sniggered at how the souped-up BMW lacked oomph. She wondered if it reflected on the owner; all show and not much to back it up. For the meantime, she needed him. He led the squat and offered her a place to stay, with a new family. The prospect of living with druggies and ravers was paradise compared to the Taylor household.

Liz's scarf hung on the coat stand. Jen inhaled its scent and faltered. Could she leave? She had no choice. The Normans lived on the estate. Distressing reminders smothered her every day. She had to get out. Freddie and Liz deserved to have their uncomplicated lives back.

Comforted by the token, Jen wrapped the scarf around her wrist. She posted the keys through the letterbox and vowed never to set foot on the Rembrandt Estate again.

PRESENT

The drive through Troddington is familiar this time. My stomach clenches at the sight of Mabel's Parlour. There's a sign on the door, "Closed due to bereavement".

Shoppers and cars bottleneck, desperate to glean information from the cordoned off alleyway. Priscilla deserved better than this. I want to open the window and shout that a person I knew died there. Instead, I turn up the stereo. The Jam sings *A Town Called Malice*, summing up Troddington past and present. The link to Johnny strengthens my resolve to continue.

I need to focus more on the earlier good times before a single impetuous act ruined everything. The Rembrandt Estate used to be my place of belonging. Television programmes that use council estate residents as viewer bait are annoying. To the outside world, those who live on council estates are often portrayed as spongers, addicts or workshy.

My heart remains within the council estate. I had to leave, but will always be a part of the Rembrandt Estate's 1980s community. We looked out for each other. The woman next door could be having an affair with your husband but if an official turned up, you'd say she was out. You'd bawl her out later but never grass.

Upon approach, it's clear the estate has altered. There's an imposing sign, similar to ones you see at holiday parks. It extends a welcome to the Rembrandt Estate. A group of ecstatic people wave underneath the banner. If the residents are like their eighties counterparts, not a single one is in the photograph. Back then, only an idiot would have agreed to their image being on display. That way led to defacing with devil's horns, if you were lucky or engaging in a depiction of a sexual act, at worst. This sign is free of graffiti, proving even more how the estate has changed.

I park on Turner Road, deciding to use the walking time to summon courage. Dad must see I'm in charge, as if he could ever be a threat. If he wasn't deferring to Mum, he was apathetic to most things, except the pub. Hostility for his absences simmers. This anger is one I can use to get answers.

I become the child, taking the dare to walk past the scary house. My attempt to ignore the Roses' past home fails. There are no horrors, only a haunting of Johnny. I remember the boy, wondering if he's changed as a person. His Facebook profile picture holds no clues. Compared to my memories, it's flat and lifeless.

I can almost hear Rose shouting, accompanied by Rob's incessant swearing. Benny squeals as Johnny gives chase around the garden. I swallow against the lump in my throat. Benny lives only in the mind while he's still missing.

'Can I help you?'

I startle at the question, annoyed at my whimsy. This isn't the time to disappear into nostalgia. A harried woman is at the gate, gripping a wriggling toddler. I offer apologies and move along.

The estate has shrunk. Of course, it's not possible, unless half was bulldozed. The people of Troddington would love that. I'm Gulliver, treading on a land in which I don't fit. My presence as a stranger looms large.

The world was huge when I was a child. In a recent sentimental moment, I bought a Mars bar then checked the packaging, convinced I'd picked up something else. They've shrunk too. Eating a whole Mars was impossible when I was younger. I never made it beyond two-thirds. Johnny always finished the rest.

Forgetting the layout, I overshoot Renoir Road and linger on Munch Drive. I wonder which of the eighties residents stayed. The front door to their flat is now red rather than white. I turn away. I didn't ask Claire or Ellen about all the past residents still living here. Facing them, I wouldn't know what to say.

The park in between Renoir Road and Pollock Road was a space for igniting wild imaginations and strengthening friendships. It's diminished to a tiny patch of concrete, edged by a strip of grass and weeds. Two women cast their children sideways glances, offering disinterested praise for cartwheel displays. Both adults look like they'd rather be somewhere else. My presence disrupts their conversation. I am on their territory.

Visitors to the estate when I lived here were also interlopers. We knew enough of each other's business to recognise friends and relatives. Strangers raised our interest. For the kids, it was someone to interrogate and annoy. For the adults, their official-looking person antennae prickled. The customary response was to hide or make the person feel so unwelcome they left.

The women stare, expecting me to give a reason for being here. I assess the park, stripped of its playful soul, and ignore the assessing glares. Let them reap gossip about an unknown woman standing outside Mike Taylor's house. They won't know who I am but he will.

A curtain sways from a bedroom next door, of what was the Smiths' home. Felicity *must* have moved. She wouldn't have denied herself the opportunity to get one up on Mum. Whose is that shadow flitting through the nets? The spirit of nosey neighbour Felicity lives on.

Towering fencing panels fortress Dad's garden, hiding from the other houses in the terrace. I disrupt its introversion as I raise the gate latch and enter. Was Mum responsible for the fences? For someone who treated her home like a National Trust exhibit, it doesn't fit.

A jungle of lawn reaches knee height. Flowerbeds have turned to mud. A rotting patio set slumps upon mossy slabs. The garden has been punished. Is this Dad's way of retaliating against Mum's obsession with keeping it immaculate? It was the first impression of her residence, and therefore always nothing short of perfection. Dad must have put the fences up too. Someone got brave. I almost admire him.

I rap my knuckles hard on the patio door. It's gloomy inside. A veneer of water stains obscures my vision. I check the bedroom windows. The curtains are open. It's a weekday and early but Dad was never a late sleeper.

The net curtains next door move again. The sun reflects upon the window, shielding the snooper. I express my annoyance via the medium of my middle finger. It's immature but I don't care. I won't be returning.

I could have gone to the front of the house. It's partly habit directing me to the back. Mum only allowed us a key to the "tradesmen's entrance". The front was for guests only. The family's soiled shoes on the beige porch carpet wouldn't do. I want Dad to recognise me as he approaches the patio door. A swiftly opened door without the slow reveal of glass gives me less time to see who he is now.

An elderly man shuffles forwards. He wears a careworn face and an outfit too loose for his body. As he steps into the light, it displays a shell of my dad. His skin and clothes are grey. Dad has faded. Years of being Patricia Taylor's husband had done this.

I refuse to greet him, in response to the lack of discernible love on his face.

He grimaces as he slides open the door. 'What the hell are you doing here?'

I don't reply. *He* will provide the answers. I move alongside Dad and enter the house of my past.

10TH JANUARY 1981

M ike whistled as he parked the van in the driveway. Moving to the Rembrandt Estate was a new start. Patricia had delivered an ultimatum; if Mike didn't get them out of the two-bedroom house in Steadingham, she'd leave. He could keep their daughters and Liam would go with her. It was probably a bluff but he didn't want to take the risk.

Mike believed in the estate's ability to bring his family closer together. It was his last hope. He refused to allow Patricia's disinterest in Jen and Mandy to dampen his spirit. With the move, his wife might finally be content. He gave a prayer of thanks to the council housing gods who'd bumped them up the list after he'd begged. The Taylors got a perfect new house on the estate everyone talked about. His drinking companions at The Fox, in Steadingham, raised a glass to his fortune.

While pleased with their son's luck, his parents were also sad to hear the news. Having Mike live nearby for so long had been a gift. Steadingham to Troddington was seven miles, neither of his parents drove, and bus services out in "the sticks" were sporadic. Mike promised to visit often and did so until they moved to Spain after a windfall on the football pools. Patricia couldn't wait to leave her in-laws behind. She detested their "lowly" roots as a cleaner and dustbin man. No longer enduring them dropping by unannounced or her father-in-law farting after Sunday lunch was bliss.

Mike directed Liam to the rear of the van. His son lingered behind. Liam may have been only ten but already acted like an opinionated teenager. He also spent more time with Patricia than was healthy. Mike tried to engage him in fishing, snooker, and darts. Liam always looked horrified at the prospect of being with his dad. The Police commanded *Don't Stand So Close to Me*, on the radio. Mike refused to make the obvious connection.

'Turn off that drivel,' Liam said. 'Don't you have any taste, you simpleton?'

Mike tapped him on the head. Thinking parental authority had ended the rudeness, Mike lifted furniture. Liam held a box of his dad's treasured vinyl high. The precious cargo dropped to the pavement. Despite the agony of the shattering sound of his albums, Mike forced himself to accept it as an accident.

Jen bounded across the garden, excited at the prospect of living on an estate with other children. Before, they were stuck in a village where the only entertainment was a walk to the Post Office, set up in the front of Mrs King's house. Jen was hopeful of the friends she could make. The Rembrandt Estate would be her utopia.

Mike placed a chair on the pavement and sat, enjoying Jen's happiness. From the moment Patricia said she was pregnant again, he doted on Jen. Since her birth, his shame for not atoning for a cruel mum and an apathetic dad gnawed away at him.

With their first child, Patricia declared she would have an abortion. Mike pleaded to keep the baby and Patricia allowed him to think she'd relented. He should have known she had no intention of aborting the child. Patricia was always cunning. Mike passed the test and Patricia embraced the opportunity to cement a future as a wife and mother. At five months pregnant, they married. Patricia hid the bump under a carefully designed dress. Visibly pregnant brides screamed vulgarity, shotguns, and neediness.

When Liam was born, Patricia fell in love for the first time. She'd wanted a son to worship her, as her brothers had. From the moment she looked into Liam's eyes, Patricia hadn't relinquished ownership. Mike was pushed aside.

At Jen's birth, Patricia handed the child to Mike and stated it was his turn. He knew he disappointed Jen when he hid in the pub or at work, but dared not express the depth of his affection for her. If he showed indifference, Patricia would think he didn't care. She destroyed what others valued. His skewed logic proposed that, if she wasn't aware of his devotion to their daughter, she'd leave Jen alone.

Seven years later, he realised he'd made a mistake he couldn't rectify. Sometimes, he wished he could take his girls away. Liam was a lost cause. It was a foolish idea anyway. Patricia would never allow the family to splinter. Image was everything.

Mike considered how he shouldn't have slept with Patricia and allowed Mandy's conception. The moment of weakness resulted in another neglected child. Patricia needed a boy. Mandy signified another female disappointment.

Sensing his melancholy, Jen slipped her hand in his. He winced at her attempt to scavenge a crumb of love and avoided the inevitable confusion on her face. Amends had to be made. This estate could be their chance.

He dropped Jen's hand and continued unloading the van. Liam had disappeared.

Jen sat on the edge of the kerb. She often wondered if her dad was friend or foe.

PRESENT

'How dare you walk into this house as if you never left it?' Dad says. He moves to the side as I push past.

Sitting at the dining room table without an invitation, I refuse to be intimidated by anyone in the Taylor family again. Dad slumps against the wall. Before, witnessing his defeat would have seemed justifiable. Now, I realise his weakness doesn't give me strength. I will not be another woman who makes him feel worthless.

'I'm not here to fight. Please sit.' I pull out a chair as if I'm hosting. He takes a seat and focuses behind me, determined not to make eye contact.

The dining room and kitchen have changed beyond recognition. Gone are the robust oak units boasting a parade of china bird ornaments. No more are the cream and terracotta curtains with matching pelmets. The interior decorator wannabe that lived here is erased. Clinical white walls are covered with marks and stains. Scratches are gouged into the table. Mum's Eternal Beau collection no longer dominates the kitchen with its floral and ribbon pattern. Plates, cups, and even a butter dish were on display. The cardinal rule was never to use any of it.

Dad watches me assessing the rooms. 'It's not how your mum had it.'

'No.' I keep my reply short. I'm not here for small chat.

'I changed everything after she died. It needed to be different.'

I wonder if his annoyance is aimed at me or memories of Mum he's still fighting. The changes he's made are better. The house may not be beautiful but it's finally a lived-in home.

'You should have come to her funeral,' he says.

'I didn't know she was dead until recently. No one told me.'

He straightens his crumpled collar. 'No one knew where you were after you did a runner from Freddie and Liz's.'

I resolve to stay calm. This isn't the time to rake over old issues. I remind myself of the task. Can Dad help me find out what happened to Kelly? Maybe I'm being selfish and considering my needs first. I must face him and bury the past but Kelly deserves the focus to be on her for once.

'What was that?' I ask, in response to a sound in the hallway.

'Probably the cat.'

My finger traces a wooden ring on the table. 'I want to talk to you about Kelly Pratt.'

'Nice dive, Jen,' he says. 'You could never deal with being told off. Not coming to your mum's funeral was out of order.'

My nails dig into my palms. 'I spent years being mistreated by your wife, but you were oblivious. Easier to be in the pub and not see the abuse taking place under your own roof. I wouldn't have gone to her funeral if my life depended on it. Unlike you, I'm not a hypocrite.'

He opens his mouth to speak and then shuts it. If he'd defended Mum, I'm not sure what I would've done.

'I let you and Mandy down,' he says.

I won't offer forgiveness. Too much has happened. Words cannot instantly undo the long-lasting damage.

He continues. 'Mandy left and lived with the Normans for a while. History repeated itself.'

265

'Where is she now?' I contain the excitement at verging towards finding my little sister.

'In Bournemouth. She went to university in Southampton and then moved on. We occasionally speak on the phone.'

'Can I have her number?' I curse my quaking voice. Dad doesn't deserve to share my happiness.

He scans through the contacts list on his mobile and jots on a pad. I have the means to reunite with Mandy. This visit is worth the tension for that alone.

'Mandy's married to Will and they run a surf shop,' Dad says. 'She's got two girls. Emma's five and Isabel's three. Having two daughters keeps her on her toes.'

'I bet she's a great parent. Mandy would never ignore her children or make them feel unwanted.' I can't resist the swipe.

He bows his head. On the way here, I expected to take pleasure from his misery. I feel like I've kicked his puppy.

'Low blow,' I say. 'Sorry.'

He reaches towards me. Decades have passed since I've seen those calloused hands. I search for familiarity in a stranger's hand.

Awkwardness makes me launch into the reason for being here. 'I'm helping Doreen Pratt look into Kelly's death. Ellen Woods and her daughter Claire are assisting too.'

Despite the chilliness of the house, he sweats. Dad had little to do with the Pratt and Woods families. Why is he so nervous?

'We've been talking to people from the estate,' I say. 'I wondered if you have any useful information.'

He fiddles with his chevron moustache. Before, his face was always clean-shaven. Mum loved facial hair on men, considering it macho. As a small rebellion, Dad refused to grow one. The furry caterpillar on his lip is a comforter. He strokes it as you would a pet.

'Why do you think I can help?' he asks. 'Wasn't it suicide?'

'The coroner gave an open verdict. The leads we've followed so far suggest Kelly might've been killed.'

He sucks in a sharp breath. I consider asking what's bothering him but don't want to appear compassionate.

I continue. 'Claire and Constance Major saw Kelly that day. They both said she was injured, but not at death's door.'

'Head bleeds aren't always as bad as they look.' The realisation he's spoken something that should have remained a thought spreads across his face.

'How do you know Kelly had a head wound before she died?'

The defeated man sighs. 'You hurt her, didn't you. Her head cut open after you pushed her.'

I'm sweating too. 'How did you find out?'

'I've known for years. It wasn't a surprise you unleashed your frustration. Living with Patricia could do that to the best of us.'

'Who told you?'

For the first time since I arrived, he looks at me. 'You were seen. I'm sorry you've spent so long believing you killed Kelly. Can you forgive me?'

He reaches for me again. Afraid of what he is, I move away.

My dad killed Kelly.

PRESENT

Claire wishes she had gone with Jen to the Rembrandt Estate. Checking the old place out together would have been a blast and she'd have escaped listening to Doreen and Ellen's reminiscing. Claire enjoys a trip down memory lane but after hearing lengthy anecdotes involving unknown people, her resolve is diminishing. She reminds herself this activity serves a purpose. They are reading Kelly's diaries.

Yesterday, Doreen decided to write her will. Her loft was filled with tat but as a dedicated viewer of the *Antiques Roadshow*, she dreamed of unearthing valuables to leave to her friends.

Sitting on the landing, she listened to Tessa, one of the carers, sniping about the cobwebs in the loft. Tessa often vocalised the burdens of her job. Doreen sniggered at how giving the idle woman the task was probably subconscious revenge. As time ran out, Doreen cared less about other people's opinions. Tessa reported each item she discovered. Doreen prepared to bring the laborious task to an end when Tessa found some "manky old exercise books" with Kelly's name on them. Doreen forgot her daughter kept a diary.

Kelly guarded her secrets well. Doreen hadn't known of the

diaries until she'd aired her daughter's bed. A notebook laid under the mattress, upon it Kelly's scrawl ordered, "Keep Out". Doreen did. Discovering the diaries again, Doreen knew she must read them if it would help reveal the truth.

Kelly filled many books. After Tessa left, Doreen flicked through one. Kelly's writing skills were illuminating. She'd used phrases Doreen never realised were in her vocabulary. Kelly was an avid reader and often lugged a stack of novels back from the library. Her love of words transcended to the written. The realisation of an undiscovered talent made Doreen's heart hurt. Looking at the diaries became too much. She phoned Ellen and Claire for assistance.

The task hasn't been easy due to Kelly's lapses in adding the year to her entries. The three women piece the jigsaw puzzle order together. Kelly titled the first book, "My First Diary. 1985". Conversations based upon events help to place the other diaries in order. Ellen insists they read them all because reporters follow the trail as far back as it goes. An event in 1985 could have paved the way towards 16th October 1987.

Claire's eyes sting and her neck aches. At the beginning, the exercise was entertaining. As a child, reading her peers' diaries would have been hilarious. She recalls how a stolen diary resulted in an entry detailing an explicit dream, involving Prince, being spread across the school. For the rest of the year, the unfortunate girl was subjected to a lewd version of *Kiss*. Apparently, a Prince song *could* be made filthier.

Claire scolds her younger self for deciding Kelly was thick. She lacked common sense but her writing shows literary aptitude. Kelly appeared dumb because her imagination was buzzing and she disengaged with reality. Claire understands the habit of drifting away when immersed in creating. When she wrote, the world around her disappeared.

Claire relished delving into the first few diaries. Now she's on the eighth, the novelty wears off. The catalogue of bullying incidents makes for challenging reading. Kelly never detailed Graham's abuse, protecting him even in the privacy of her diaries. Claire is thankful Doreen won't relive it through reading, but sad Kelly didn't have an outlet.

'I think it's best we pick this up again tomorrow.' Ellen looks to Doreen for permission. Doreen murmurs agreement.

Claire is desperate to find something useful but the process of dating the entries is taxing. She's only just deduced the current diary is from 1987, due to its references to songs and films released that year.

Finally, Kelly wrote a date: 11th October 1987, five days before her death.

Claire's interest reignites and she reads the following pages with more attention. Teenage issues and tedious minutiae pave the way to striking gold.

'Oh, my giddy aunt.' Ellen and Doreen's heads pop up at Claire's outburst, awoken from scanning slumbers.

'What?' Ellen takes the diary.

From a recliner, Doreen tries to read over Ellen's shoulder. 'What? What is it?'

After reading the page, Ellen replies, 'There's an entry from the day before Kelly died. She names the father of her baby.' Ellen passes the book to Doreen.

Doreen fixes on one name. *Him?* It seems ludicrous, but her daughter wasn't a liar. Kelly wrote the truth and was ready to face the situation.

. . .

'She was scared of him,' Claire says, then startles. 'No! Jen's gone to the estate to speak to her dad. She's not safe.'

'Phone her,' Ellen says.

Claire tries Jen's number. The phone is switched off; Jen's habit for staying focused.

'Shall I call the police?' Doreen asks.

'I'll call them if I need to. I'm going to Mike's house.' Claire decides it's best dealt with quietly. They have little concrete evidence, the risk to Jen is unknown, and a reporter calls for reinforcements as a last resort. She hopes it's the right decision.

Ellen grabs the car keys, determined her daughter won't go alone. Neither argues. They must act fast to rescue Jen, if they're not already too late.

66

PRESENT

Everything is wrong. I'm on the Rembrandt Estate, back in the family house, and my dad murdered Kelly.

He cradles his head. 'I should've found you and told you.'

'*You* killed her? *You* were the father of Kelly's baby?'

He laughs. It gains momentum until he struggles for air. I rush to the sink and fill a glass from the draining board with water. Although he deserves to choke, I need him to be able to speak. As I pass the hallway, goosebumps form on my arms. "Just the cat," he said earlier. Being here with a murderer makes me jumpy.

Dad slugs the water and the coughing ends. 'You think I'd have sex with a girl the same age as my daughter?'

'It happens.' I shrug.

'I can't believe you'd consider me having a sexual relationship with a kid, let alone killing her. I really was a dreadful dad, wasn't I?'

I'm not attending his pity party. This needs to be over. 'Tell me what you know.'

'The day before Patricia died, she said you thought you'd killed Kelly.' He seeks a response. I remain composed. 'I'd finally decided to leave your mum.'

He blows out air as if purging himself of badness, to breathe strength in. I want to congratulate him for growing a set of balls but I daren't interrupt.

'She didn't take it well, as you'll understand. I retaliated by saying I wished I'd never married her. Then she gave that witchy cackle which wound me up a treat. I kept my cool though, offering to make the divorce easy and give her everything.'

In the past he would've had my sympathy. There's nothing left to offer.

He continues. 'At first it appeared she agreed to split. She stood aside as I went upstairs and packed.'

'What happened?'

He has the face of a prisoner denied bail. 'She barred the front door, said I couldn't leave, and then told me what you did to Kelly.'

She knew. Of course she did.

'Patricia missed nothing. If I left, she said she would tell everyone you murdered Kelly. She would rather have dragged your name through the mud than be made a divorcee. So I stayed.'

I'm not sure how to feel about him protecting me. It's unknown. I focus on getting answers. 'How did she know what happened between Kelly and me?'

He goes to the kitchen and switches on the kettle. 'Let's have a cup of tea. It'll take a while to explain. Can you stay a bit longer?'

I nod and he drops teabags into chipped mugs. A photograph of Mandy and me sits on the shelf above his head.

'That picture was taken not long before Kelly's death. Do you remember? I caught a snap of you in your uniforms, ready for the new school year, and kept it in my wallet. When Patricia died, I put it in a frame.' He stares at the photo and disappears somewhere else, probably contemplating what he's lost. 'I can't believe that a month after I took this picture, Kelly was killed.'

'So, she *was* murdered. Do you know who did it?'

'Yes. Your mum told me.'

67

13TH APRIL 2012

Patricia held the banister for support. Hysterics convulsed through her body. 'Did you honestly expect I'd let such a pathetic excuse for a man leave me?'

Mike glanced at the suitcases stacked at the foot of the stairs. Neither he nor they would ever make an exit. Patricia glided through the hall, beckoning him to come to heel. Her charm bracelet sounded a death knell.

He knew she didn't love him and that their marriage lasted for the sake of appearances. Patricia considered divorce vulgar. She criticised those who chose the option and detested the resulting single mothers. Mike's absence would force her to take up a membership.

He chastised himself for not going when she was at the nail salon. Ever the gentleman, he'd decided to do the decent thing and explain his reasons in person. Good manners trapped him.

Patricia took a seat, ready to interrogate. Mike shifted his feet onto the towel she insisted he use. The fluff from his black socks allegedly ruined the cream carpet. She scrutinised him for weaknesses and nodded, seemingly satisfied in noting many.

'You dare to leave me?' Patricia's measured tone clipped every word. '*No one* leaves me. Your daughters thought they had but they were wrong too.'

'But they *did* leave.' He tried not to sound smug.

'I could have Jennifer running back here in a heartbeat, begging me not to disclose what she did.'

'So what? Jen nicked some money from the Normans. She shouldn't have but they understood why. I sorted it.'

Patricia inspected her French manicure. 'This is more than theft. Jennifer is to blame for Kelly Pratt dying on the train track.'

Mike's open mouth provided a satisfying response. Patricia lived for hurting people with knowing their most damning secrets.

'Are you saying Jen killed her?' Mike asked. 'She was only a kid. That's an appalling accusation, even for you.'

'Will you call your child by the name I gave her?' Patricia's right nostril flared. The left behaved. 'Jennifer *thought* she'd killed Kelly.'

'She wasn't there.' Mike hoped this was the truth.

'Her doting little sister told me everything.' Patricia offered soundbites and took pleasure in making her husband work for information.

Mike bit. 'How did Mandy know?' He did a calculation. 'She was only eight.'

'Correct, Einstein. An eight-year-old can be most forthcoming when you grill them. Amanda saw it happen. She became subdued after Kelly died. Usually Amanda's noise went right through me.' She shivered at the memory. 'I wheedled it out of her. It didn't take much, especially as she knew I'd banned her from going on the railway track. My children weren't feral like the rest of the estate's children. Poor little Amanda needed to tell someone though. She certainly couldn't speak to her sister.'

'Why?' Mike dreaded the answer.

'Because she watched Jennifer shove Kelly so hard, the Pratt girl bled like a stuck pig. That's hilarious,' Patricia reflected. 'She resembled a pig too.'

'Jen hated confrontation.'

'Wake up, Michael. She was an aggressive madam and it was only a matter of time before she hurt someone. Kelly got it and she got it good.' Patricia rubbed her hands together.

'They weren't exactly friends but why would Jen do that to Kelly?' Mike asked.

'I neither know nor care. Amanda didn't hear the details of the argument. She was looking for Jennifer, saw them having a disagreement, and got so frightened she hid behind a bush. Amanda later told me what happened and I swore her to secrecy. I had my means of doing so.'

Mike feared what Patricia's method of silencing Mandy had been. He tried to recollect the events of 1987. The catalogue of abuse was a shameful haze.

'But did the head wound kill Kelly?' Mike hoped Jen remained his innocent girl. 'A train hit her. Maybe she killed herself?'

'Oh dear, Michael, you can't let go of Jennifer being your favourite, can you? I'll make it easier on you, seeing as I'm feeling charitable. No, she did not kill Kelly.'

He sagged with relief, then realising Patricia never made it easy, he straightened again. Patricia had already blindsided him. Preparation for her onslaughts had helped him survive their relationship up until then.

'Are you sure it wasn't Jen's fault?' Mike dared to ask. He had a feeling Patricia knew more. She *always* had more information than anyone else.

Patricia arranged coasters on the coffee table into a rigid square and moved the bowl of potpourri to the centre. The conversation became dull with Mike being more inquisitive than upset. She needed to reignite his distress.

'After Jennifer left Kelly bleeding, Amanda couldn't move.' Patricia fed on Mike's sorrow. 'Amanda believed Kelly was dead. She considered getting help when Claire Woods came along, later followed by that interfering bitch, Constance Major.'

'Mandy hid all that time?'

'Amanda listened to Claire and Constance talking to Kelly after the girl got up from the track. Your idiotic child worried they'd say she'd let Kelly down, so she stayed hidden. She moved in closer to hear. It's too boring to repeat. The general gist is Kelly was fine.'

Mike grabbed Patricia's shoulder. 'Did you tell Jen she wasn't responsible? Did she believe she'd killed Kelly?'

'Get your hands off me. Of course Jennifer did. Have you forgotten how she became even more unruly afterwards? Guilt will do that. I practically gift-wrapped her to the Normans. Out of sight was definitely out of mind.'

Mike didn't recognise the monster in front of him. He realised he never had. 'You never considered telling Jen she hadn't killed someone?'

'Why would I have done that?' Patricia brushed away a thin layer of dust on the coffee table. The new glass model showed up every speck, despite continual dusting.

Mike wrung his hands, trying not to wrap them around her throat. 'How could you? Why didn't you protect your daughter?'

Patricia sauntered over to the mantelpiece. 'Don't you dare call me a bad mother. I've given everything for my child.'

PRESENT

I interrupt Dad in his telling of what happened the day he tried to leave Mum. 'I haven't got all day. Say it.' I don't have the courage to voice my suspicions. Let him be the one to bear the shame.

'If I tell you, your life will never be the same. I don't want to hurt you.'

I grab his wrist. 'Who killed Kelly?'

'Mandy…' He stares at the floor, urging me to figure it out and share the burden.

Tea sloshes in my stomach, threatening to reappear. 'Don't be stupid. Mandy wouldn't hurt a fly. She was only a kid.' I let go of his wrist, aware of my tightening hold.

Dad hangs his head so low he's speaking to his chest. 'Mandy saw Kelly being killed and told Mum. Patricia took great pleasure in sharing with me what Mandy witnessed and the effect it had on her.'

My suppressed indignation erupts. 'How could she put a child through such torture? That creature wasn't human. I'm ashamed we're related and you're no better for keeping this quiet for so long.'

Dad grips the edge of the table as if his life depends on it. 'Please calm down. There's more to tell but I can't if you lose your temper.'

'Afraid I might kill you? Violence runs in the family, after all.'

One look from him and I am undone. *There* is the face of the dad I loved; open and honest.

'That was out of order.' I briefly touch his shoulder. 'Carry on.'

'Your mum had an inkling who killed Kelly. She watched and waited. Mandy confirmed what she already knew. No one ever duped Patricia.'

'Let me get this straight.' My voice is strangely controlled. 'My mother allowed me to think I'd killed someone when, at any moment, she could have saved me from living a life of guilt. She left Mandy to grow up, having seen a murder, and potentially being psychologically damaged. I can't believe this.' I shoot over a hostile look, daring him to interject. In response, he twists his fingers around each other.

'Don't make me say it, Jen. I'm trying to protect you. Please go home and leave this behind.'

I fold my arms to show I'm not going anywhere.

'Patricia knew I wouldn't leave when she told me who killed Kelly. She was prepared to turn the evidence towards you if I went. I'd never let that happen, no matter how much of a rubbish parent I was.'

I resolve to stay calm, knowing I must focus on the purpose for being here. With one word, one name, everything will change. Everything *has* changed. Dad stayed with Mum because he was looking out *for me*. He sacrificed his freedom *for me*.

'Where is that son of a bitch?' I ask.

A voice follows a shadow, emerging from the hallway. I should have trusted my earlier instincts. It wasn't the cat.

'I'm right here. So glad you could make it. Would you like to hear a story?'

16TH OCTOBER 1987

Liam Taylor always got his way. For seventeen years, everyone, except Patricia, bowed to his wants. That morning his mother had gone too far. When he announced he was enlisting for the Army, she wailed, begged, and blackmailed to keep him at home. He loathed her vulnerability. She wasn't supposed to be like other females. Her callousness had been her greatest asset. The snivelling wreck on the kitchen floor was repulsive.

How could you love and hate someone equally? When she draped herself over him, he deliberated whether to return the embrace or snap her neck. The overwhelming strength of the second choice made him keep a distance.

Satisfied he'd left Patricia in misery, he slammed the door. Mastering her was thrilling, almost seductive. He hardened as he prowled the estate, seeking to scratch the itch.

The railway track lay ahead. A tree had fallen near the gap many used as a shortcut. Throughout the night, Liam watched the wind's destruction. He revelled in cars swaying, debris flying, and the swings in the park tangling within the frame. The storm invigorated him. Liam left wreckages in his wake too.

Liam negotiated the slope, careful not to scuff his dress shoes.

He never wore trainers or casual clothing. Nothing less than a crisp shirt and trousers with a sharp front crease would do.

Two people were already on the track. He sped across and climbed up the opposite bank. The remaining trees provided cover. As he crept forwards, he recognised Jen and Kelly. Before he could consider the strangeness of them spending time together, they began to argue. Thrilled at the altercation, Liam moved in, mindful of the twigs underfoot.

Jen raged at Kelly mentioning Patricia. In his mind, Liam congratulated Kelly for hitting his sister's Achilles' heel. He swallowed a gasp as Jen attacked Kelly. The push was forceful and Kelly's clumsiness made it a sight to behold. Soon after, Jen's little boyfriend, Johnny, emerged from hiding and ran away in the opposite direction. Liam found it too marvellous for words. J&J would be no more after this.

The blood leeching from Kelly's head disrupted his thoughts. The pooling of the fluid that gave her life was hypnotic. Fascinated by the inner workings of the female, he inched closer to watch it flow. At no point did he feel a sense of duty to help. If Kelly died, it would be an advantage. Liam's earlier stirrings returned as he considered how much she wanted him. She claimed to be a virgin when he'd made the first move, and asked for gentleness. He shrugged off the perceived lie. Everyone knew her dad had been there already.

Liam wooed Kelly. He refused to view it as a perversion. They met in alleyways, secluded nooks, and even this railway track. He'd sat with her at the foot of the bridge and reeled lies of her special status, while concealing disgust at puppy fat that had forgotten to disappear and a grateful smile of wonky teeth. Kelly suited his purpose for a while. Older girls he'd hooked up with became wise. They wanted relationships, not an abnormal frenzied deviant act. When he first charmed her, Kelly was thirteen and compliant.

As she rose from the track, Liam's hope of her death plummeted. Kelly had become needy, often declaring plans for them to be together forever. He told her to be quiet. Sometimes he had to show her. She always behaved. He had Graham to thank for her subservience. Liam thought Kelly's father had prepared her sexually too. He soon realised his mistake. Their first time excited him. He knew something many didn't. Graham hadn't sexually abused Kelly. *Liam* defiled her, although he preferred to call it "an education".

Kelly held the back of her head, walked to her bags, and sat upon them. Liam felt assured her vulnerability would make her more appreciative of him being there. He needed to let off steam and Kelly was always good for that. Wearing her school uniform was practically a written invitation. She knew what he liked.

Before he could move, Claire Woods marched past. Liam considered, as he often did, how her cheerfulness should be erased. She carried a tape recorder, wittering away into it about fallen trees and using unsophisticated vocabulary. Her dream of being a reporter, like Ellen, was a joke. Working on the local rag was hardly hitting the journalistic big time.

Claire noticed Kelly. Liam listened to Claire's feigned concern, amused by the hypocrisy. Nearly all the estate kids hated Kelly, and most of the adults did too. Their shunning made her more receptive to Liam. She was desperate for someone's attention. Liam could be *most* attentive when he wanted to be.

Kelly saw Claire off. Her confidence surprised Liam. Maybe being with him had toughened her up. He decided to reward her when Constance appeared. The train track was more popular than Piccadilly Circus. The storm had ignited people's curiosity and nosiness led them to the track.

Liam scowled when he spotted Scruff. The scar on Liam's ankle, inflicted in retaliation for cruelty to the dog, flared. It was worth it. The memory of attacking the animal always brought him to the verge of ecstasy.

Liam enjoyed hearing others talk about Constance's misery at her dog's injuries. Unfortunately for him, Scruff made a good recovery and stared at his attacker, crouched behind the trees. Liam controlled his breathing, not daring to make a sound. Constance pulled the animal away and became interested in Kelly's business.

Liam listened as Constance checked Kelly over and suggested she see a doctor. As Scruff growled, Liam thought he'd be discovered. When Kelly insisted Constance take the dog home, Liam decided to thank Kelly in his own particular way. With Constance out of sight, Liam decided Kelly would see that, unlike the rest of the estate, he cared. At least she would think he did. He hadn't left her alone on the track. He knew how to make her feel special. Liam descended from the bank. Kelly was in his sights.

PRESENT

L iam narrates his part in Kelly's death with the emotion of reading out a shopping list.

'I can see you're somewhat shocked.' His roaring laugh is sickening.

He walked into the house as if he owned it, and forced us into the lounge. We knew not to resist. He never hit me when we were younger, but he had a threatening air I never messed with. The man sitting here is even more menacing. Assessing eyes reduce Dad and me to helpless spectators.

'How did you get in here?' I ask.

'He has a key,' Dad says. 'Patricia insisted he kept it. Liam lives next door.' It's the most Dad has said since Liam appeared.

'Thank you, Father. I can speak for myself.' Liam still hates others taking over. I store the information away, thinking it could be useful.

'Why aren't you at work?' Dad asks him.

'I'm working from home today. Not that it's any of your business. Glad I'm here. I couldn't miss this.'

'It was you at the window,' I say. 'I never had you down as a curtain twitcher. A bit nosey neighbour, isn't it? Still on the estate as well?' I give an exaggerated frown. 'Weren't you getting out and joining the Army?'

He leans over from the chair to the sofa where Dad and I huddle. A tree trunk arm extends a shovel hand that twists my wrist. After he lets go, finger marks pulsate on my skin. I don't react, remembering how frustrated he gets when denied pleasure.

Back in the spotlight, Liam continues. 'Where was I? Right. Kelly was injured because Jennifer went psycho. I finished the job. Then Mother found out. She didn't tell you, Jennifer, and you took the blame. Well, blamed yourself. I got off scot-free.'

He's in danger of bursting from his shirt if that chest is pushed out any further. Someone's become familiar with weights and probably steroids. Liam is certainly a lot angrier than he used to be. Back then he kept it hidden behind a cool exterior.

'Why did you dredge it up?' Liam asks me. 'You could've got away with pushing Kelly.'

'Some of us have a sense of decency.'

'Decency? So, you were an upstanding citizen in going straight to the police? Have you told them since then?' He scans my face for the answer. 'You're no better than me.'

'I'm nothing like you, you sick bastard.' I will not ally with this thing.

He raises his arm and my traitorous reflexes make me flinch. His hand advances upwards and then rakes through his hair.

'Did you think I was going to hurt you? Silly, Jennifer. Not yet.'

Dad whimpers.

'Scared, old man?' Liam says. 'You should be. I've had enough of living next door to you and playing happy families with my wife.'

Dad finally speaks. 'Mercedes is a good woman.'

'You married Mercedes?' I cannot hide my bewilderment. He taunted the "pretentious" Smiths. When the girls were in the garden, he pelted them with stones. Not only is he married to a Smith, he's living in their house.

'Snigger all you want, Jennifer. I had no choice. Mother said if I ever left the estate, she would tell the police everything. She forced me to marry Mercedes too. What a wonderful marriage it's been.' His tone conveys it's anything but.

'You've got three lovely daughters,' Dad interjects.

A vein protrudes at the side of Liam's forehead. Dad sinks against me. I hold on to him, confused by how I'm shielding my parent. Dad's arm is spindly. He's diminished. An unfamiliar sense of pity overwhelms me.

'Mercedes is obsessed with our offspring. She never wanted me, just the necessary juice to make it happen,' Liam says. 'All you lot ever want is to have babies. If Kelly hadn't told me she was pregnant and sorted it out herself, she might still be alive.'

71

16TH OCTOBER 1987

'I don't want to. My head is sore.' Kelly swiped Liam's hand away from her backside.

He'd considered an ear nibble, Kelly's favourite foreplay, but the blood staining her neck would taint his clothes. Instead, he pulled her towards the fallen trees.

'You'll soon be in the mood,' he said.

'I don't feel like it.' Kelly rooted her feet.

Affecting sympathy, he kissed the parts of her that weren't bloodied. The frown melted. She always gave in.

'I'll be gentle.' He trailed a finger along her mouth.

Kelly's frown returned. 'Will you? Last time hurt a lot.'

He had slammed her against the alley wall. She'd complained about the abrasive bricks. Immersed in pleasure, Liam ignored it. Her discomfort excited him.

'We can't have sex anyway.' Kelly further resisted. 'It might not be good for the baby.'

He ceased dragging her across the track. She stepped back and shielded her stomach.

'You what?' Liam kicked the gravel. Stones sprayed in Kelly's face.

Her look of maternal love gave way to confusion.

'How can you be pregnant?' he whispered. 'I use condoms.'

'One must have split.'

He wrenched her arm. 'Have you been with someone else?'

'I love you. You're the only one.' Kelly tried to loosen his hold.

'Get rid of it.'

'I couldn't ever kill my child. I'm keeping it.' She shrugged his hand away.

He despised how she loved the thing growing inside her more than him.

'Let's have this baby and maybe get married one day. We might be able to live in our own house on the estate.' Kelly never knew when to stop. She refused to acknowledge the dark cloud descending over Liam.

She didn't see him launch.

Another Taylor struck Kelly Pratt.

Her head slammed against the track.

Red rage smothered Liam. Kelly could ruin his life. He would be trapped on the Rembrandt Estate, in a miserable existence with Smelly Kelly and her brat.

He stood over her, deaf to the pleas.

Her extended hand was invisible.

He held the slab of concrete, crumbled from the boundary.

Her cries not to hurt their child went unheard.

He drifted into the darkness.

The boulder dropped.

A thud brought Liam back to reality. He wore a crimson fireworks display. Kelly had created another mess. Liam kicked the body to check the problem was resolved. Confirmation of Kelly's death revolted and invigorated him.

Crisis averted, Liam climbed the bank and made his way home.

72

PRESENT

Dad touches my knee. The gesture confirms I'm not alone with my murdering brother. Liam's excitement in relating how he killed Kelly is almost more terrifying than hearing how it happened. He tilts forwards in the armchair. Dad and I slink away. When Liam slaps his thigh, I refrain from commenting on the rubbish pantomime villain parody.

'Fortunately for me, a train came through not long after Kelly died,' Liam says. 'It eradicated the evidence and made it appear she took her own life.'

He awaits a response. Dad seems too stunned to speak. I know better than to feed a psychopath. Liam sleeks his razor sharp eyebrows; a graduate of the Patricia Taylor Academy of Preening.

'I'll confess I was amazed I killed her. I'm not an animal.' He looks over, daring us to contradict. 'I didn't plan Kelly's death, as such, although I had been considering how to get her out of my life. Maybe I wanted to kill her. Who cares? It's done. For a few moments after she hit the track, I thought someone would find her and the police would trace my fingerprints on the boulder. When the train came through, crushing Kelly and the evidence, I couldn't believe my luck.'

He kneels and takes hold of my hands. Their smooth clamminess is repulsive. Much to Dad's amusement, Liam went with Mum for manicures. From the look of his shaped nails, I expect he still has them. As I try to move away, Liam pulls me nearer. Throughout, I do not break eye contact.

'Do you recall when we were kids and I dropped a brick on a rat?' he asks. 'You came with me to the field because I said I'd found you a pet. So gullible. Remember the sound it made as the rock struck it? A human head makes a lot more noise and mess when a boulder drops on it.'

I wrench free to slap him. His punch blasts across my face. Pain zaps below my eyes and blood gushes from my nostrils. Dad rushes to help. Liam raises his leg, places a foot on Dad's chest, and kicks him backwards.

'Jennifer.' Liam takes a seat. 'If you attack me again, I'll do worse than that. Maybe your head will be smashed open like Kelly and Priscilla's were. Oops. Silly me. I wasn't supposed to mention her.'

He meant to tell us.

He killed Priscilla.

Liam enjoys killing females.

I have no doubt I'm next.

73

PRESENT

Claire scowls at her mobile. 'Jen's phone's still switched off. Are these cars ever going to shift?'

Since they left Doreen's house, Ellen has tried to put her foot down. The traffic on the outskirts of Aylesbury conspires against her.

'I always believed Liam was strange but I can't believe this.' Ellen's knuckles turn white on the steering wheel.

'I caught him doing something odd to Georgina once.' Claire surprises herself with the forgotten memory.

'Georgina Edney, from Picasso Way?'

'Yes.'

'Why didn't you tell me?'

'I guess I blotted it out. I originally kept quiet because he's Jen's brother and she was ashamed of her family. His threat to slash the throats of Georgina and her parents if we told, frightened me. I was only nine. She was a few years younger.'

Ellen clears her throat. 'Did he hurt either of you?'

'No. Not physically anyway. It was his birthday party. Jen begged Johnny and me to be there for solidarity. I snuck upstairs to have a snoop around. Patricia hardly ever let anyone into the house so I couldn't pass up the opportunity. I opened the door to Liam's bedroom. Georgina stood in front of him, naked and trembling. Since then, nothing I've encountered is as creepy as what he'd done and I've seen some freaky things.'

'What was it?'

Claire shakes her head, desperate to release the memory and never carry it again. 'He had a book open. I think it was one of Jen's. Did you know she collected medical textbooks?'

Ellen nods, while willing the stationary traffic to move.

'Georgina's body had the reproductive system drawn on it, labelling the bits and pieces. Liam trailed a knife over her, like a surgeon ready to operate.'

Ellen's mouth is dry. None of her past investigations come close to this. 'Had he cut her?'

'No. I reckon he would have if I hadn't appeared. I kept it together and said Georgina's mum was downstairs, waiting to collect her. It got us out of there.'

'You did the right thing. I wonder what her parents did about it.'

'Georgina scrubbed herself clean as soon as she got home and carried on as normal. She told me a few days later. After, she shut down and acted like it never happened. We didn't speak of it again. I should have told you. It might have prevented Liam escalating to killing.'

Ellen reaches over. 'You were young and scared. Don't blame yourself.'

'It gets worse. When I asked what he was doing, Liam said he was conducting research. He needed to understand how females work so he could master them. I didn't get what he meant at the time. I know now.'

'I remember you came back from the party saying you'd eaten too much and felt sick. I should've checked when you went to bed early.'

'I was fine, eventually. I wish I'd said something though. Kelly might still be alive.'

'No.' Ellen slaps the dashboard. 'Don't do that. Don't blame yourself for the actions of sickos. He will pay for all of this. We have evidence.' She looks at Kelly's diary, sitting in Claire's lap.

Realising they'll be stuck for a while longer, Claire opens the book. She turns to the damning page, written the day before Kelly died.

15th October

Dear Diary,

I am so confused. I love Liam with all my heart but he never says he loves me. So far, I've kept his name out of these diaries because I was worried someone might read them. Dad would kill us if he knew. I'm always protecting Liam by keeping our relationship hidden. There will be no more secrets. If I write the truth here, it will give me strength.

Liam Taylor is the father of my baby. I'm going to tell him tomorrow, after school. I tried to speak to him today when I was in town. When I called Liam's name, he looked through me as if I didn't exist.

I view him as my Heathcliff. Liam is mean and moody but irresistible. Our souls are connected. I shouldn't let him be so rough but he'll leave me if I don't. He said so, last time, when I complained about the marks. I'm used to being hit, but with someone you love, it's not right.

Liam scares me sometimes. When he looks at me, I wonder what he sees. Occasionally it seems like disgust, but how can that be? Those eyes once danced with joy when they cast themselves upon me. Recently, they are dark and almost hateful.

When he squeezed my neck, I thought I'd die. As I tried to free myself, he gripped tighter. When he finally let go, I told him our relationship was over if he did it again. He laughed and said I would never leave him. The shower of kisses confirmed I'm still his special girl. I hide the marks under polo necks. Mum would ask questions. Dad never strangles me. It's not his thing.

When Liam shows affection, I feel like I could fly. He doesn't give it much anymore. Maybe when I tell him I'm pregnant, he will cover me in kisses again. Maybe he'll be gentler when he knows I'm the mother of his child. We could be a family. Mum would be a brilliant grandma. All I've ever wanted is a family of my own, full of love, not hate.

Claire wishes she could reach into the page and grasp Kelly's writing hand, to rescue her. Reading over Claire's shoulder, Ellen leans against her daughter. They unite in grief for a girl murdered by a depraved young man. The grown-up version might also kill Jen if they don't get there in time.

The traffic moves.

74

PRESENT

Who is Liam? He's always been a mystery and we've never had a connection, but he's become a deranged stranger. My brother is a parody of evil. Instead of moustache twiddling, he smooths his groomed hair. Mum's tainted blood courses his veins. Even though he has many faults, I choose to have Dad's blood. That claret trickles from my busted nose. Dad's offered tissue staunches the flow.

'Didn't know Priscilla and I were well-acquainted?' Liam asks. 'You're not very good at this snooping business, Jennifer. I thought you'd worked it out when I saw she'd been on the phone to you. Shall I explain how she died?'

'No,' Dad replies.

'If you must,' I say at the same time.

Liam pushes Dad and me back into the sofa. 'Get comfortable, family. Too bad Amanda isn't here to complete the set.'

He notices the look I give Dad. 'No, I haven't killed her. Amanda is of no consequence to me.'

After Liam releases us, Dad and I remain pressed against the cushions. I edge my fingers to the rear pocket of my jeans, cursing the habit of turning off my mobile. It's wedged and I can't retrieve it without Liam noticing. Once he's finished narrating his murdering tales, I have no doubt we'll be next on the list. If we lived to tell it, he wouldn't confess to killing Kelly and Priscilla. Recounting his heinous deeds invigorates him. He needs recognition. The woman who bore us taught him everything. She also showed me how to play this scenario. Let him speak, for now.

'Priscilla was a good lay.' His tongue travels over his top lip. 'I saw her in town, which was fortunate as I don't bother with Troddington much. Small towns equal small minds. Mercedes demanded I get something for Charity's earache.' He walks to a photograph above the television and points. 'There are my girls: Faith, Hope, and Charity.'

This isn't the time to ask what he was on when naming his daughters. They are all blonde and blue-eyed. Mum lives within them. I hope it's the only similarity they share. Having Liam for a father is unfortunate enough. There's no fatherly love in his gaze upon the photo. I pity his offspring. Liam lays the picture face down.

'That first day, Priscilla invited me to her flat. She wanted it and I was willing to oblige.' He winks.

I can't understand why females pursue him. As a teenager he was arrogant and lean. Now he's an aggressive mound of muscle. The bottom half hasn't caught up. His reedy legs make the skinny trousers he's wearing baggy.

'Priscilla and I met occasionally,' he says. 'Mercedes doesn't care what I do anyway. After Charity was born, four years ago, I became surplus to requirements.'

The smile Dad lets slip makes me want to hug him. Throbbing in my nose makes it impossible, even if Liam allowed us to move.

'I thought Priscilla knew the score,' Liam says, 'but suddenly she wanted to get serious. Priscilla was useful until she tried to blackmail me into ending my marriage. She threatened to go to the police and tell them I was the father of Kelly's baby if I didn't commit to her.'

Priscilla had to send Claire and me down the wrong path. It's why she said Kelly was having a relationship with Rob. Priscilla protected a future she assumed Liam would offer. She's dead because of her need for love, just like Kelly.

'I gave Priscilla the routine of a grieving man who'd lost his girl-friend and baby. Boo hoo.' Liam mimics wiping away tears. 'She lapped it up, saying we were kindred spirits in caring about Kelly. Dumb whore never figured out I killed her friend too.'

I wince at his spite. Priscilla probably hardened under his influence. She was apologetic in her phone call and wanted to start over. Liam has seen to it we never will.

'Imagine my horror when Priscilla phoned to say she'd been divulging information to you and Claire.' The cracking of Liam's knuckles makes Dad flinch. 'She said she'd fed you bull about Rob being the father but that I should confess. We'd be free of the past and be together, apparently. I said I'd come by later to seal the deal. So, I did.'

'Why did you kill her?' I won't be quiet any longer. I came here for answers, not to be Liam's mute puppet.

'She needed silencing. I knew she'd be alone when locking up after work. As soon as I called out, I could've kicked myself when I saw her talking on the phone.' He focuses on me. 'Didn't you recognise my voice?'

'It was too faint and you sound deeper.'

'I'm a *real* man nowadays.' He flexes his biceps. In any other circumstance, I'd ridicule this pathetic performance.

Liam continues. 'I checked Priscilla's mobile afterwards and couldn't believe the lying minx had called you. I smashed the phone with the same brick that obliterated her skull. This time it's fair to label it as murder. With Kelly, it was seizing an opportunity. Priscilla had to die. When I saw the bricks for the café's extension, nostalgia took a hold. It was fitting to kill Priscilla similarly to Kelly.'

I feign apathy by looking at my feet. Dad tries his best not to wince at the sordid details. We're both aware Liam's ego inflates in response to others' terror and attention.

Sensing he's losing, Liam speech becomes louder and more urgent. 'A brick in the head requires a few bashes. It's not as complete as dropping a boulder. Priscilla took a while to die.'

'I don't understand how no one heard,' I say.

'I muffled her like I did with Constance's mutt, Scruff. Apt, really. Priscilla was an old dog too.' He snorts at his joke. 'She thought I was embracing her. I did what needed to be done and threw the body into the bins. Afterwards, I retrieved a spare set of clothes and shoes from my gym bag, cleaned up with wipes, and changed behind Mabel's Parlour. I'm always prepared. Mercedes was satisfied when I lit a bonfire at home. I got round to burning up the garden waste she'd been nagging about and the evidence with it. The only inconvenience was smashing the brick to dust first.'

Being near him makes me feel sick. I contemplate if Dad's wondering how he spawned such an abomination.

'The moral of this tale, boys and girls,' Liam adopts a childish voice, 'is to never blackmail or demand anything of Liam Taylor. Naughty females learn this lesson hard. Once upon a time there lived a girl called Kelly. Now she is no more, for trying to force Liam into a family situation. Priscilla met her demise because she tried to make Liam tell his secrets. And then there was…'

Dad finally speaks. 'Who?'

'Why, Daddy dearest, you've woken up. I'm pleased you've joined in because you're going to love this. Guess who else died because of me?'

'No, Liam. Not her.' Dad rises.

I haven't been part of their lives for a long time. What's passing between them is strange and unnerving.

Liam claps. 'Yes. I killed off Mother too.'

Dad lunges forward and connects with Liam's palm. Dad hits the floor. Liam pins him there with his foot. Satisfied with having a literally captive audience, Liam resumes his story.

75

14TH APRIL 2012

Liam resented the charade of Saturday afternoons with Patricia. From the moment she discovered he'd killed Kelly, Patricia imposed a list of rules upon him. If he disobeyed, she would turn him in to the police.

Liam despised his mother. After she related Mandy's confession, from witnessing Kelly's death, Patricia left him to agonise over it for a few weeks. With every knock on the door, Patricia quipped the police had arrived to take one of the Taylors away.

Now, he waited for Patricia to bring in the tea and cakes. She seated him in this very place, two weeks after Kelly's death, to share her knowledge that he'd fathered her child. Liam forgot nothing escaped his mother's notice.

The day after Kelly died, Patricia shook Liam from sleep, and said she knew he murdered Kelly Pratt. She exited the room and left Liam in torment. A fortnight later, Patricia mentioned the baby. Liam had been careless in not considering Mandy would have overheard. Patricia demanded no one must ever know. She was incensed he'd had sex with Kelly, let alone impregnated her. Patricia ended the rant with how Liam had done everyone a favour in removing Kelly and her bastard child. The list of conditions was then set.

He married Mercedes when she was eighteen and he was twenty. Resigned to obeying Patricia, Liam played the doting husband for a while. Then the affairs and slaps to keep his wife in order began. Hope was born. Like his mother, Liam wanted a boy. Two years later, Faith came along.

Patricia entered, carrying a tray holding a porcelain teapot, doilies, and a cake stand. 'Shall I be Mother?' She giggled at the lame joke as she poured tea.

Liam didn't respond. He would only offend. Instead he swallowed a mouthful of fruit cake before he began his speech. 'It's great we're doing this, Mother, because there's something I want to tell you.'

Patricia brushed a crumb from his lip. He imagined biting the tip off her finger and watching the blood spurt.

'I've been an obedient son. No one could love you more than I do.' Liam noted her joy and hammed it up some more. 'Having you steering my life has made me the man I am today.'

Patricia straightened. 'All you needed was discipline, direction, and a lot of affection.'

'You saved me from prison.' He instantly regretted the error. Any mention of 1987 was taboo.

'Darling, we don't talk about that.' Her shoulders rose. 'It's taken care of. I've even used it to my advantage recently.'

'You better not have told anyone.' The doting son act slipped.

'Only your father, but he'll keep quiet. I've made sure of it.'

Liam stood, knocking over a full cup of tea. Patricia raced to the kitchen and returned with a cloth.

'Look what you've done.' She scrubbed the spillage. 'I'll never get the stain out of this rug. It's cashmere.'

Liam stomped around the room. 'Stuff the rug. Why did you tell Father?'

Patricia continued to clean. 'Can you believe he was leaving me?'

Liam could.

'Yesterday, he had the audacity to detail my alleged faults and then demand a divorce,' Patricia said. 'I set him straight, relating how his precious Jennifer had hurt Kelly. It led to mentioning what you did.'

Liam stepped towards her. Still kneeling, she retreated from the stain. It wouldn't be the first time he'd tried to attack her. This time Liam looked set to kill.

Sweat trickled down Patricia's back and spiked across her forehead. Liam loomed over her. She crawled from the floor to the sofa.

'Please, lay off me. I don't feel well,' Patricia said.

'Couldn't you have made Father think Jennifer killed Kelly?' Liam shouted. 'Why did you tell him it was me?'

'He needed to understand I know everything. I have the control.' The effort of the outburst made Patricia pause. She brought a hand to her chest.

Liam reddened. 'I'm leaving Mercedes and getting out of this dump. I should have gone years ago, but you blackmailed me into staying. No more. I'm done with you too.'

'I only wanted the best for you.'

Liam's nose almost touched Patricia's. 'You've suffocated me by manipulating every move. You're too much. I detest you and never want to see you again.'

'You'll hate me a whole lot more when I tell the police what you did to Kelly.'

He dragged Patricia to her feet. Patricia grimaced.

Liam grasped her arms. 'Don't threaten me, woman. You'll regret it.'

'I'm really not well.'

He ignored the sweat running down Patricia's cheeks. 'Nice try, Mother. I'm not indulging your hypochondria.'

She wriggled from his grip. 'You will never leave me. I'll tell everyone what you did.'

...

Later, Liam couldn't say for certain that he'd recognised Patricia was having a heart attack. In that moment, her threat was the final blow. He let go of her.

Patricia crashed into the glass table. Cakes crushed beneath her. The teapot upended. Liam was mesmerised by his immaculate mother, made grubby. He stepped over her body. As he stood at the lounge door, he sought confirmation of death. Patricia lay lifeless on the floor, covered in buttercream and sponge, and bordered by shattered glass.

Liam returned home, deciding there was no longer any rush to leave. Patricia Taylor's rule had ended. The queen was dead. Long live her prince.

Liam Taylor was in charge.

76

PRESENT

Throughout Liam's telling of his role in Mum's death, Dad has blasted out a string of choice oaths. Liam laughed.

I may not have liked Mum, but letting her die wasn't right. Liam awaited a response when he explained what happened, expecting my allegiance. Lusts for control and killing blind him to the truth. I never rewarded her abuse with violence, no matter how close I came to it. I look at the floor where Mum died.

Liam bounces in his chair. My past experiences with drugs help to spot a user. Whatever he's taken, it's making him more unpredictable.

'It gets better,' Liam says. 'I stuck around after the witch died, believing it was over. No more wenches dictating what to do. Then my wife blackmails me too. You couldn't make this up.'

He awaits our engagement. Neither of us gives him the satisfaction. Liam ignores it, knowing we have no choice but to listen.

'I did the whole mourning Mummy business,' he says. 'Then Mercedes declared she knew I made Kelly pregnant and killed her. Mother got her revenge from the grave. She'd written a letter, a confessional, detailing my japes.'

I blanch at him likening killing a girl and her unborn child to an Enid Blyton adventure.

Liam addresses Dad. 'Do you remember asking Mercedes to sort through Mother's belongings because you couldn't bear it?'

Dad doesn't respond.

'If you'd done it yourself, my wife wouldn't have found the letter.'

Liam boots Dad in the leg. Dad howls. I try to help but Liam plants a hand on my face. Comets of agony blast through my nose.

'Mother thought I'd do away with her one day and wrote it out in case she died by questionable means,' Liam says. 'Mercedes used it to her advantage. You women are something else.'

I have a moment of clarity while riding out nausea. I'm Liam's enemy because I'm a female. He fears the opposite sex because they've controlled him or allegedly stolen his choices. It's true he's subdued them but maybe this time the woman wins.

Liam returns to his armchair throne. 'Mercedes was desperate for another child. I told her it wasn't happening. Then this letter emerges. Mercedes said if I didn't make her pregnant, she'd take it to the police. She hid the letter. To this day, I've never found it.'

Well done, Mercedes. You *did* win.

'Mercedes was desperate for the trilogy. Charity had to accompany Faith and Hope. I gave her what she wanted. No bother for me as she looks after the brats.'

'Those girls are wonderful,' Dad says. 'You drove them away.'

'You have the gall to label me a shoddy father? What do you reckon to that, Jennifer?'

I reply by squeezing Dad's hand. We must unite. It might be the only way we'll escape. Dad clutches in return. Liam flinches at the show of solidarity.

'Hope and Faith are living it up in Manchester,' he says. 'Charity won't come near me. Mercedes turned them against me. I gave her everything she desired. I even got a mortgage on the dump next door because she wanted the children to live next to their grand-parents. What a joke.'

'Is Mercedes alive?' I hope the question offends him.

'What a terrible impression you have of me, Jennifer. She's at work, probably telling her colleagues what a dreadful husband I am. She does her thing, I do mine. Mercedes knows if she leaves, I'll do something about it.'

I don't need to ask what. Just like Mum, appearances motivate Liam. He was leaving Mercedes before Mum died but he's devised a better plan since then.

'Wives are a nuisance, aren't they.' Liam speaks to Dad. 'A quick tap or allowing them to fall prey to a heart attack solves the prob-lem. Now, I need to deal with another errant woman. Right, sis?'

He closes in. I thought if someone tried to hurt me, I'd punch and scream. My limbs are lead and I've lost my voice. Liam's bulk darkens the room. He reaches for me. A movement flickers to my side.

Dad is on Liam's back, thumping and kicking. The feeble man trying to beat up The Hulk would be comical if it weren't deadly. Liam seizes Dad's throat. Liam drinks in Dad's fear as he brings him round to the front before hurling him across the room. Dad's head hitting the television makes a sickening sound. He lies, bleeding and motionless on the floor. I realise, maybe too late, what he means to me. If Dad's alive, I hope he'll forgive me for the choice I'm making.

Liam towers over Dad, admiring his handiwork.

I dart through the house and into the Rembrandt Estate.

77

PRESENT

The park whizzes by as I sprint. Dad might be dead and I'm fighting Liam alone. Should I stop and allow Liam to finish what he and Mum started? I'm tired of living with lies. My legs slow in response.

I remember how this estate was once a place where I belonged. A new surge of courage helps me continue.

The strikes of Liam's feet bear closer. I have an advantage from daily running. Liam isn't built for speed. A heavy torso makes his skinny legs work hard. Still, he's gaining ground. Fury at a woman outsmarting him spurs him on.

'I will kill you!' he shouts.

Faces appear in windows. Doors are cracked open. No one offers to help. Are they afraid or don't care? My faith in community is restored when an elderly man beckons me over. I won't make it. I hear a cry and see the man lying on the ground. He huddles inwards, braced for another kick. Liam stands over him.

The error in looking makes me fall. I land hard on the intersection between the estate's roads. My hip throbs but I cannot stop. Liam is running again.

The railway track is ahead. I halt. Not there. For Liam, it would be poetic justice to murder me where he took Kelly's life. Liam catches up, grunting with each footfall. I ignore my injuries and stand up. Where I am headed is nearby. Salvation has to be on Picasso Way.

A man and woman sit on a step, chatting and smoking. Their mouths open wide at the sight of a running woman, with blood staining her face and neck.

I cry, 'Help! He's going to kill me.'

They abandon their cigarettes and ready themselves for action. Blood flows into my mouth and I try to breathe through the coppery thickness. My destination is two doors away. Liam finds reserves of energy. His pace increases.

The man declares, 'That'll do it.'

My helpers pile on top of Liam. The woman lights another cigarette. I'm not sure how long they can hold Liam. He's already breaking loose.

My body slams against the potential refuge.

I bang on the door.

Liam is on his feet.

This isn't how it ends. I don't want to die here. My memories of the Rembrandt Estate should be about love and friendship. This is where I belong, not where I will exit.

I fall onto the doorstep and thump on the door.

A blurred profile appears behind the tempered glass.

Liam is close.

My rescuers dart indoors.

The door opens a fraction. A riot of curly grey hair emerges. I force my way in and fall onto her. She lands on the bottom step of the stairs, leading up to the flat. Spotting the threat behind, she kicks the door closed. Liam punches the glass. A crack spreads.

My source of hope takes us to the safety of upstairs. She barricades the flat's entrance with furniture. Energy leeches from my body and I collapse to the floor.

'Police please. A woman's in danger. A man's trying to hurt her.'

She lowers to the carpet and places my head upon her lap. Familiar arms hold me as she speaks to the call handler.

'Yes, of course. My name's Liz Norman.'

78

SEVEN MONTHS LATER

Dad refuses to acknowledge his former road as we drive through the Rembrandt Estate. Thankfully, his injuries from Liam's battering weren't serious. Dad has been living with me since he left hospital. Tomorrow he's flying to Spain to live in the villa he's always dreamed of. Although I'll miss him, I'm pleased. He needs to enjoy his freedom from Mum and Liam.

After catching up with me, Liam gave up bashing the Normans' door in and focused on escaping. He stopped for petrol before his getaway. Two policemen on a snack run noted Liam's crazed appearance and bloodied knuckles. The officers checked Liam's number plate. It matched a vehicle belonging to a raging psychopath. I may have made up the last part.

My grilling at the police station was an ordeal. Having a broken nose didn't help. They said my fight with Kelly was a scuffle between children. I should have checked she was okay but they understood my fear. There will be no charges, unlike Liam who's in prison, awaiting trial for killing Kelly and Priscilla.

I won't consider him any further. My mind is filled with the family I want. When we all sat in the hospital waiting room, scared Dad might die, I wanted to comfort Mandy. My little sister was grown up and still feisty. It was torture standing on the other side of our wall of hurt. I took a risk in approaching her, expecting rejection. As Mandy hugged me, I promised to never leave her again.

...

Rust has eroded the railway track and weeds sway in the breeze. It's become a prime fly-tipping hot spot. It's wrong this is where Kelly died. I try not to blame myself. Today is for Kelly and Doreen.

I watch Freddie and Liz place a white rose upon the place where Kelly was found. Liz tenderly pats the gravel then walks past with her arm around Freddie.

Dad shuffles along to pay his respects. He's frailer. Pondering on how one day he won't be around is upsetting. We've wasted too much time. There's been too much death.

Doreen died alone three weeks after Liam was arrested. At least she had some peace in knowing who her daughter's killer was. Doreen deserved so much more than life gave her.

Ellen places a rose on top of the others. She bows her head and then returns to the Normans' home.

Mandy reveals two sunflowers from behind her back. We agreed on roses. I consider questioning her as she ties them with a ribbon.

'Remember how we grew sunflowers when we were kids?' Mandy asks. 'This represents us as sisters and our connection. We'll always be together. We *were* always together. I never stopped thinking of you.'

A tear snakes down my cheek when she places the flowers. She blows me a kiss and leaves.

Claire coughs. 'Just us then, fart face.'

'Claire,' I groan. 'I didn't think even you could be such a tosspot at a memorial. You're even cockier with your swanky new job.'

Claire will soon be a journalist for a London newspaper. She wrote about Kelly's death on her website. The nationals caught on and soon it was everywhere. She played down my part. Claire's always been a good friend. I'll miss her when she moves to London – we'll always be in contact. She says she'll have me on speed dial for counselling sessions, now I'm qualified. Lucky me.

Claire lays a rose on the track. I'm sure I see her mouth, *Sorry*.

'I'll do mine and go back with you,' I say.

'Don't bother. You're going to be busy.'

A glorious and terrifying sound comes from the bank. 'Hello, Jenny Wren.'

I've dreamed of this moment. What if it's not real? What if it is? Claire reveals the answer as she swivels me around.

Johnny Rose, the man, grins with the kindness of the boy I knew.

'No need to thank me.' Claire gives Johnny a mischievous punch before leaving.

My mouth won't work. Here is Johnny, standing in the place where our friendship ended.

He steps forwards and takes my hands. 'I let you down. I wish I'd spoken to you rather than running away. You're not a killer. I was a stupid kid who jumped to conclusions.'

'That makes two of us. I thought you didn't care.'

'You were my world, Jen. Not a day has passed when I haven't thought of you.'

I assess if the real, adult, Johnny matches the one I've stored in my imagination. He's still amazingly tall. His hair remains short and thick but is speckled grey. I expected him to be wearing his treasured khaki jacket. The black jeans and a bomber jacket seem right too.

Johnny reaches into his jacket pocket, beckoning me to sit with him by the side of the track. 'How about we start creating new memories, mixed with the old, and see where we go from here?'

He places the lifeline for our renewed relationship on my lap. I haven't seen a Walkman since the eighties.

Johnny offers an ear bud. We place one each in our ears, connected by The Jam and the people we once were, hopefully still are.

He reaches over and removes the bud from my ear. A finger touches my cheek.

Johnny's voice replaces the music. 'Welcome home, Jen.'

ACKNOWLEDGMENTS

Firstly, thanks to you, the reader, for reading my book. Corny as it sounds, when I was writing I was thinking of you. I hope you enjoyed it.

Thank you, Bloodhound Books, for getting my novel out into the world. The support you've given is invaluable. I'm proud to be a pup.

Morgen, your editing skills have made this novel everything I wished for and more. Thank you!

I'm so grateful to my beta readers: Belinda, Ali, Sian, Simon, Paul, Chantelle, Sarah, Helen, and Bek. Your contributions and advice took this novel to a new level.

Thanks, Dad, for your enthusiasm and support for my writing career. It means so much.

Thank you, Dan, for the eighties silly dance and sharing some of the most difficult times of our lives. We've made it this far.

Belinda, you're a faithful friend and cheerleader. Thanks for being your beautiful kind self. You're an absolute gem. Are you crying yet?

Dave, no words could ever adequately express how amazing you are. From the moment you gave me a swish pen and notebook, the writing began. Without you, this book wouldn't exist. With you, I became a writer. You'll always be my favourite.

27429405R00192

Printed in Great Britain
by Amazon